Watch for More Stiletto Books Novels

by Don Tompkins

from Indigo Sea Press

indigoseapress.com

I Minus 72

By

Don Tompkins

Stiletto Books
Published by Indigo Sea Press
Winston-Salem

Stiletto Books
Indigo Sea Press
302 Ricks Drive
Winston-Salem, NC 27103

First Stiletto Books edition published
December, 2015
Stiletto Books, Moon Sailor and all production designs are trademarks of Indigo Sea Press, used under license.

For information regarding bulk purchases of this book, digital purchase and special discounts, please contact the publisher at indigoseapress.com

Cover design by Dianne Webb

Manufactured in the United States of America
ISBN 978-1-63066-259-2

To all the men and women who are serving or who have served
in the United States Armed Forces.
You do what you do so that we may be free to do what we do.
Thank you for your service and sacrifice.

To my wife, Kelly. You've read and edited the manuscript
dozens of times and still urged me on to completion.
Thanks for being there with me every step of the way.

Chapter 1

"Good morning, Mr. President. Congratulations on your election."

The President-elect greeted the DNI with a handshake, and said, "Good morning, Director. May I call you Bill?" Without waiting for an answer the President-elect continued. "Thanks for scheduling this briefing so early. These are busy times. What do you have for me? Oh, by the way, it's still Governor or President-elect until after the inauguration." He sat down in one of the briefing room's plush leather chairs.

"Yes, Sir," Barry began, still standing. "For this initial briefing, I have both information and intelligence,"

William C. Barry had been appointed Director of National Intelligence by the previous administration and Ted Mason, the new President-elect, didn't plan to replace him.

Mason motioned for Barry to sit down. They were in a small, but elegantly appointed briefing room, large enough for more, but today there were only the two of them. The room was in a secure area of the White House, but, even so had earlier been swept for electronic eavesdropping devices by the Secret Service. The room had no windows and was buried in one of the sub-floors.

Barry continued, "With your permission, Mr. President-elect, I'd like to start this briefing with an overview of what intelligence is and how we obtain it. Then we'll go on to current events you should be aware of."

Mason interrupted, "Look, Bill, can we skip the background today? Maybe we can cover it next week. I want to hear it, but my schedule is so tight that right now isn't the best time. Can we get straight to what's hot?"

"Of course, sir," Barry responded. He was used to Presidents changing the agenda. "We do have one major issue we need to deal with immediately."

"What's up?" Mason said, leaning back and crossing his legs. As was his habit, he put his elbows on the arms of the big chair and placed his hands together in his lap, intertwining his fingers.

"Sir, within the last two weeks, we've lost fourteen assets, all but one were foreign nationals. What makes this even more alarming is that they were all within the same intelligence network. We have to assume someone has targeted that particular network."

Mason immediately leaned forward and uncrossed his legs. "Did they take out the whole network?" he asked incredulously.

"No, sir, about twenty-five percent," Barry responded in his usual calm voice.

"We've lost a quarter of a spy network in two weeks? How many people were in it?" Mason leaned back in his chair, but his face still registered concern.

"We think there were about sixty informants in total." Barry continued, "But, there are probably people in the network we don't know about. Many of our foreign assets were allowed to recruit others and many of those wanted their identity kept completely secret. For some of those we just used code names. But there were usually others who were completely unidentified sources. Then, as now, as long as they fed us useful information," he shrugged, "we were generally willing to accept it. We're fairly certain we don't know about some of those people. The number for the entire network could be as high as eighty."

"Does the President know?" Mason was leaning forward again.

Barry replied in a controlled voice. "Yes sir. We briefed him thirty minutes ago." He'd been through a lot of intense briefings in his career, so he didn't get too excited when talking to high-ranking government officials, including Presidents.

Mason nodded. "If this has been going on for two weeks, why so long in notifying the President?"

Mason's voice was now calm, but Barry was worried where this might be going. "We didn't connect the deaths until a day ago. It's not unusual for assets, both ours and theirs, to miss contact times. But all of these disappearances were within the same network. That's what caught our attention. It means someone has turned, and Russia, or someone else, is taking these people out. It may be restricted to this one cluster or it may expand. We just don't know where this is going."

"Damn!" Mason said, leaning forward and putting both hands on the table. Then, after a slight pause during which the DNI said nothing, he leaned back again and continued, "Okay, what do you need from me?"

"Sir, we believe you are," the DNI paused, "on the list to ahh . . . eliminate."

At this, Mason stood up, leaned forward and slapped both hands down hard on the table. "Why the hell would I be on some intelligence network hit list?"

Barry briefly pressed his lips together, but answered calmly. "We don't really know for sure. One of our sources found a torn piece of paper in the hand of one of the dead informants. The paper had two names on it and a date." He paused, took a deep breath and continued, "Yours was one of the names and the date was your inauguration."

Mason's jaw dropped open. This was not what he expected to hear. He didn't know exactly what to say, so he said nothing.

The DNI quickly went on to explain, "We currently have no way to verify that this was a hit list, but because of all the other deaths, we have to take the threat seriously. We've put a number of actions in place to find out who's responsible and to tighten security throughout the whole inauguration process. We're calling the operation 'I minus 72'."

Getting no response other than a hard stare from the President-elect who was still leaning over the table, the DNI continued. "You see, we have 72 days until your inauguration."

Mason finally spoke, "I get it," he said dryly. He stared at Barry a moment, sat back down and said, "Look, I'm sure I don't have to tell you, but it would be very bad for a newly elected president to be 'ahh . . . eliminated' while taking the oath of office. Anyway, I can't think of a reason why I would ever make somebody's hit list, at least from an intelligence viewpoint. I was never in the field and didn't even understand how intelligence networks worked. Still don't, but this just can't be that tough to figure out, right?"

Barry grimaced a little, stood up and began to pace. "It's actually a lot more difficult than it looks Mr. President-elect. We believe you must have had access to some sort of information that might reveal why this is happening and who is targeting you. Since it was your only intel assignment, we assume it was right after you graduated from Annapolis, when you were with DIA. You can see why it's so vital that we quickly determine what you might have seen and why it resulted in your name being on the list. That may be the only shot we have at getting to the bottom of this in time."

"Who set this network up? Someone must have been in charge. Have you talked to him?" Mason leaned back in his chair and rubbed his temples while he watched the DNI pace.

"It's touchy because this network was set up by an Air Force officer who has since retired." Barry replied. "You see, in our world, information about who is providing what is closely guarded. At headquarters we don't necessarily have all the details of the network. The only person that normally has complete visibility is the person who sets it up and controls it."

"Okay, so, who was it?" Mason asked again, a little impatiently.

"Sir, the originator of this network is a man named Grant Thurmond. You may remember his name from your early days in the Navy. You were the administrative officer for his group in the Defense Intelligence Agency, the DIA."

"Hmm. I'm not sure. Tell me a little about him." Mason responded.

Barry sat back down, picked up and opened a folder. "Thurmond was early-selected for the Air Force Academy his junior year in high school. At the academy he majored in Astronautical Engineering, played football and still graduated near the top of his class. He went straight into intelligence training after graduation."

Mason nodded. "Yeah . . . maybe I do kinda remember him. If it's the guy I think it was, he's really sharp, nice enough, all military. But I only worked with him for a short while in an administrative role. I'm not sure I would even recognize him. Can you give me a little more background?."

Glancing down at a sheet in the folder Barry continued, "He's about 6'2" tall and at his exit physical when he left the service, he weighed about 200 pounds. His first assignment after graduating from the academy was with the NRO, the National Reconnaissance Office. Being in a headquarters role apparently didn't sit well with Thurmond, because shortly after he was assigned he called a few people and landed a field assignment with DIA. His first few missions were designed to test his ability to act in nebulous situations. He did great and was given increasingly important roles.

"He went on to establish extremely effective networks in Lebanon, Russia and Eastern Europe. The Eastern European and the associated Russia network are the ones we're discussing today."

Barry, leaned back in his chair, folded his hands on the table and continued, "I never knew him, but he clearly did a good job because the Air Force promoted him each time he was eligible, up through

O6, Colonel. Then about six years ago, the previous administration decided that human field assets were no longer needed. They believed we could obtain all the information we needed through satellites, drones and other electronic means. The President issued an order shutting down most field units, including the one Colonel Thurmond ran. Thurmond was offered a desk job at DIA headquarters. He promptly retired in protest."

"Where is he now?" the President-elect asked.

"The information we have says he bought a hundred acres or so in West Texas, put up a log cabin and has been living there ever since." Barry checked the paper again and said, "Says here he lives alone. He was married for a few years while he was in the Air Force, but he's been divorced for some time now."

This time it was Mason's turn to lean back in his chair. "Okay," he said, "My gut reaction is that we need to bring the Colonel out of retirement to solve this thing. Sounds like he's the only one with enough information to work on it. What's it gonna take?"

"Reactivate Colonel Thurmond? We'd need presidential authority. But, sir," Barry said leaning forward, "I'm not sure that's a good idea."

"Why not?" Mason shot him a penetrating look.

Barry paused and took a deep breath before answering, "Well, sir, to be honest, Colonel Thurmond is kind of a maverick. He's a field agent who never adjusted to the new electronic world of intelligence. We believe this should be an intellectual exercise and that our best chance of finding a solution is to look at the intelligence we have and think it through to a logical conclusion. Colonel Thurmond can provide us valuable background, but because of his age and the amount of time he's been out of it, I'm not sure about him going back into the field."

"An intellectual exercise?" Mason exclaimed, clearly frustrated. "Bill, people are dying, I'm targeted for assassination, and you want an intellectual exercise? Get me the paperwork to reactivate Colonel Thurmond and I want it within the hour. I'll personally take it to the President for signature."

Barry sighed. "I'll make it happen, sir," he said.

Mason got to his feet. Barry stood also. "By the way, who was the other name on that list?" Mason asked as he turned toward the door.

"Colonel Thurmond," Barry replied.

Chapter 2

I minus 58
West Texas

Damn, it was cold. November in west Texas could really be chilly, especially without central heating. The cabin was small and the wood stove did a good job, but usually died out by 3:00 a.m. and Thurmond hated to get up in the middle of the night to feed the fire. So it went out around three. He could live with that.

His house was situated on a bluff about a hundred feet high overlooking the plain below, giving him unobstructed views of his property. He didn't necessarily want a huge ranch. What he really wanted was privacy. And he had it. Hell, he could sit on his back porch naked and no one would notice. Probably a good thing too, since he'd put on a couple pounds since retiring. It wasn't the slight weight gain that bothered him. It was that he no longer worked out on a regular basis and he felt he'd gotten a little soft. He still looked pretty good in front of a mirror though, especially when he tightened up his gut.

At 6:00 a.m. Thurmond dragged his naked ass out of bed, grabbed a coffee mug, filled it up with two day old coffee that he heated for one minute in the microwave and walked outside. He was standing, as he did every morning, on his front porch, still naked and covered with goose bumps, sipping his stale, but hot, coffee.

Whup, whup, whup, whup—a helicopter, backlit by the sun, lifted up over the bluff and landed in his yard about sixty feet from the porch. Thurmond heard and felt it before he could see it and knew from the sound that it was military. Although he didn't know who they were or why they were here, he knew it wouldn't be good news.

Shaking his head, he turned and headed into the cabin to put on some clothes. By the time he reappeared on the porch, the rotors had stopped moving and a burly man was exiting the chopper.

As the man approached the porch, he said loudly, "Good morning, Colonel." It was a man Thurmond knew well—Lieutenant General Randall J. "Buck" Wheeler, his old boss at DIA. Although Thurmond hadn't seen him in several years, the General looked exactly the same. Wheeler was a stocky, gruff man with a short, military style haircut and even in his mid-fifties his hair was still dark with only a little gray mixed in. An Air Force ROTC student at Texas A&M, he'd been in intelligence his whole career and was now the senior military intelligence officer in the Army. Thurmond had reported to Wheeler the last two years before his retirement and admired his leadership style. Wonder if he's still with DIA, Thurmond thought.

"Mornin', General. What brings you this far west? Care for some coffee? It's not fresh but the mike makes it hot."

Wheeler waved him off. "No thanks, Colonel. I've been up a long time and I've had plenty. Mind if I sit down?" Wheeler said, matching Thurmond's casual tone. He then sat down in a comfortable rocker without waiting for Thurmond to respond.

"Not at all, help yourself." Thurmond chuckled

They both sat in silence on the porch. If anyone else had accompanied the General, they stayed out of sight on board the chopper.

Neither man spoke for a while, just rocked gently. Thurmond figured Wheeler would get to the point of the visit in his own time. Finally, after a couple of minutes, the General started with small talk, "Nice place you have here. After the hectic pace of Washington, the peace and quiet really feels good. I can see why you're out here. If I weren't here on such an urgent matter, I'd try to talk you into letting me stay for a few days. Maybe do some fishing." Both men continued to stare straight ahead, looking out over the plains rather than at each other.

Grant final broke the silence. "What's so urgent, General?" Grant asked, looking directly at Wheeler for the first time since they sat down.

Getting right to the point, Wheeler said, "Colonel, we have a situation we need your help with. It's highly classified and it would be better if I explained it to you in Washington. I need you ready to leave in ten minutes. Bring some clothes, both civilian and your uniform. Not sure you'll need it, but just in case...," his voice trailed off, not finishing the sentence.

Thurmond barked out a laugh. "General, with all due respect, I'm no longer on active duty. There is no one else around and even though the only sweeping I've done was with a broom, I assure you my porch is not bugged. Let's talk here. And by the way, I no longer have a uniform. Are you still with DIA?"

Wheeler chuckled. Thurmond hadn't changed at all, he thought. He was still as direct as ever. Wheeler turned serious and knowing Thurmond wasn't going anywhere without an explanation, he said, "Grant, we've lost fourteen assets within the past two weeks. Someone is systematically dismantling the network you spent over twenty years building and we have no reliable intelligence on who might be doing it. It could be the Russian government, could be an informant, or it could be a rogue agent—one of theirs or even one of ours who's gone off the reservation. Hell, we just don't know." Wheeler raised his hands in frustration.

"I assume, since I'm not already in chains, you don't think it was me, so how can I help?" Thurmond responded.

"In the hand of one of the dead informants, we found a torn piece of paper with two names on it. They weren't clear, but we're fairly certain that one was the new President-elect."

Thurmond whistled . . . a long low whistle. "Jesus, General," he said. "Anything else on the piece of paper? Any clue who dropped it?"

"Yes, there was a date—January 20th. And no, no clue who dropped it. We're assuming it was the killer. No fingerprints, so he must have been wearing gloves." The General shrugged his shoulders, indicating he didn't know any more than that.

Thurmond thought for a second. "Anything significant with that date?" he asked.

"Well, Yeah," Wheeler paused a moment. "It's Inauguration day. We believe they're targeting the President-elect's swearing-in ceremony. That means we only have fifty-eight days to solve this and we need you to lead the effort . . . starting today. I need you to come back to Washington with me. You're the only one who knows this network intimately. We're calling this 'Operation I Minus 72'. One other thing: you have to understand that the date may not be the actual date of the attempt. It may be a 'not later than' date. It's possible that the President-elect is vulnerable even today."

Thurmond frowned. "You say we only have fifty-eight days but the operation is called I minus 72? How long have we known about this?" Grant was dreading the answer.

"We found out and briefed both the President and the President-elect a little over two weeks ago. However, the DNI believes this should only be an analysis of data we already have and won't require any field work. An intellectual exercise, he calls it." The General looked down and wagged his head from side to side. He looked back up and continued, "And the President agrees with him. You know how he feels about human operations. Fortunately the President-elect wants you back leading the effort, doing whatever it takes to solve this. After all, it's his neck on the line so why wouldn't he? But, even though we know the threat is aimed directly at the President-elect, it's still taken a great deal of urging from him to get the President to agree to sign the order reactivating you."

Thurmond looked hard at the General, "So what have we been doing for the past two weeks, sitting on our thumbs?"

Wheeler turned in his chair to face Thurmond directly. He leaned forward, placing his hands on his knees. "Look Grant." He said, "We've been doing all we can without going into the field. We've had a group of analysts pouring through everything we have that might be relevant, but so far we're no closer to finding out who's doing this. Also, since then, we've lost two more assets. Guess that's why the President was finally convinced to sign the order." Wheeler took a deep breath. "As you can tell, I'm really frustrated it's taken this long to get you involved, and, you should know, the President-elect shares that frustration."

"And we haven't found anything that might help?" Thurmond asked.

"Nothing." The General pressed his lips tightly together.

Grant paused a moment. "General, you said there were two names on that scrap of paper. What was the other name?"

Wheeler let out a sigh. "Thurmond," he said.

Standing up, Thurmond paused only a second before he said, "Then we're way behind. Give me five to grab some clothes." Thurmond went inside to pack a bag and as he packed, he threw in his old .380 semi-automatic pistol he'd carried for over twenty years. He knew it to be accurate and reliable, at least at short distances. It didn't have a lot of stopping power, but it was small, light and easily concealable, no matter what he was wearing. And most likely he was going to need some fire power on this operation.

9

Chapter 3

I minus 57
Sam

After arriving in Washington, they settled him in temporary officer's quarters at Ft. Myer, the nearest military facility. The old Army post was adjacent to Arlington National Cemetery and, conveniently, just across from the Pentagon. They gave him an office in the DIA spaces deep inside the Pentagon, where he was now sitting at his desk, engrossed in the intelligence background report that had previously been supplied to the President. The small, internal, windowless office was nearly barren, having only a, beat-up gray metal desk, an empty gray metal bookcase, an armless gray desk chair on wheels and a black phone. The floor was gray linoleum tile. The walls were also painted light gray. Gray was still the military's favorite color.

"Good morning, Colonel," a woman's voice called out from the doorway. Before she spoke she'd spent a few minutes standing at the doorway checking out the man sitting at the ugly desk. Not bad. Tall, athletic looking, broad shoulders. He looked like the kind of guy who could take care of himself in just about any situation. He had a full head of short, cropped grayish hair and a strong jaw line, too. No, not bad at all.

The Colonel looked up through penetrating blue eyes. He saw that the woman who spoke wore an Army enlisted uniform. Her rank insignias showed her to be a Sergeant First Class. He couldn't help noticing how young she looked to be an E7. "Who are *you*?" he said without preamble.

"I'm your assistant, sir: Sergeant First Class Samantha Rogers." She moved into the room, standing just on the other side of his desk.

Thurmond shook his head, "Uh, uh. No, I didn't ask for an assistant and I don't need one. I don't even need a desk. I don't intend to spend much time here."

"Yes, sir, I understand what you mean, but I was assigned to provide you with whatever support you need." Rogers was tall, 5'10", lean, athletically built and, as Thurmond had also noticed, built. With dark, longish hair, pinned up to meet regs, and dark brown eyes, she was striking. A good student, she'd played volleyball all through high school and for two years at the local community college and she still kept herself fit. She also looked confident and poised in this first meeting with her new boss.

Thurmond looked at her. She had four rows of medals on her uniform blouse. He asked, "How long have you been in the Army?"

"Just under ten years, sir."

"Ten years and you have four rows of medals?"

"Yes, sir."

"I spent twenty-six years in and only have six medals, total. You must be some kind of hero or something," the Colonel paused. "What's your specialty? Admin?"

Deciding to answer his questions in order, she said, "Well, sir, in Iraq and Afghanistan they give medals out pretty freely. You don't have to be a hero. I'm in counterintelligence."

"Sit down." He said, gesturing to the metal guest chair. "You were in Iraq?" he asked.

She sat before answering. "Yes, sir. I've done two full combat tours. One in Iraq and another in Afghanistan."

Thurmond paused a moment, then reconsidered, "Counterintelligence, huh? Okay, maybe you *can* be useful. Do you know your way around this puzzle palace? Maybe find out where I can get a good cup of coffee?"

"Yes, sir, I'll get you a cup." She rose to her feet. "You take anything in it?"

"No, I don't want you to get it for me, just tell me where I can get one. Is there a Navy unit somewhere? They always have the best coffee—usually a couple of days old—what I'm used to. The stuff they have around here is like tea."

"Yes, sir, just two doors down is where the Naval Intelligence types hang out. I'm sure they'll have some."

"Okay, sit back down." He said. "I'll be right back. Wait here." He walked past her on his way out the door.

On his way to get the coffee he decided he wasn't sure what he was going to do with Rogers, but he'd give her a couple of days to work out.

When he returned with his coffee, he sat behind his battered desk and said, "Well, their coffee is fresh, but really strong. It's good. So what do I call you, Sergeant . . . Samantha?" Before she could answer, he said, "No, I'll just call you Sam. Okay, Sam, what do you know about this operation? Oh, by the way, I assume, being counterintelligence, that you're cleared for Top Secret with all the appropriate intelligence tickets?"

"Yes, sir, I'm cleared or I wouldn't be allowed in these spaces. But I received only a very sketchy briefing about the operation. Their assumption is that I'm just support and won't be active in the field. I've received no training for that stealth stuff anyway so I wouldn't really know what to do. I'd probably just get someone killed." She smiled at him.

"That's comforting," Thurmond responded without smiling back. Then he stared hard at her. After a full minute, during which she just looked calmly back at him, he said, "Okay, as I said, I don't need an admin. What I can use is someone I can count on to get me what I need, no matter what it takes. I'll need you to go around obstacles and over the head of bureaucratic desk jockeys who try to get in the way. That includes senior military officers. Are you up to it?"

"Sounds like fun, sir," she said, not smiling this time.

Thurmond nodded. "I don't think it'll be much fun, Sam. And, it might even jeopardize your career. I'm kind of like a bull in a china shop and the brass doesn't always like my approach. Mostly I don't really give a damn whether they like it or not, I just want results. As far as the methods used to get those results, well, whatever it takes."

"Colonel, I have about three months left on my current enlistment. I'm not at all sure I'm going to re-up, so there's not much to jeopardize. I'm willing to do whatever it takes."

The corners of Thurmond's mouth lifted slightly in his version of a smile. Sergeant First Class Samantha Rogers is gonna be ok, he thought. "Okay, then, let's get to it. What do you know about our mission?" He leaned forward with his forearms on his desk and his hands clasped together.

"A couple of days ago I was briefed that there was a threat to the President-elect and told it might happen on or before his inauguration. Other than that, I know only that you were involved earlier in a network that has lost several assets and it might be connected to the threat on the President-elect. I know none of the details about what you did or what the network was about." She shrugged.

"Okay, I'll fill you in on that part a little later. Now, the first thing we'll need is the complete list of names involved in my old network, from the top to the bottom. I'll have to reconstruct that myself—there's no written record. I destroyed the only printed list years ago and even it didn't include everyone. Once I put the high level list together, we'll highlight those who've been taken out. Then, we'll go . . . ." For the next three hours Thurmond talked, first giving Sam the background, then detailing the next steps for them both. Sam liked the confident way he spoke and acted. Not just good looking but really smart, too, she thought. This was going to be interesting. He may be a little old, but he sure didn't act like it.

Thurmond finished by outlining their first steps. "Okay, to put the full list together I need to get to Krakow, Poland. Some people there I need to talk to. Don't know how you want to set it up, but I need to get into the city center by Thursday morning. See what you can come up with. Feel free to talk to the CIA types to see if they have any current contacts I can call on if I need 'em while I'm there. Let's plan to get back together in a couple of hours. By the way, if you contact them, don't tell CIA what we're up to, just that I have to get into Krakow and need someone to contact if I want assistance." Grant nodded at her.

"Yes, sir, I'm on it." Sam left the room with an air of confidence.

This will be a good test, Thurmond thought. He wanted to see if Sam was resourceful enough to figure out a way for him to have people he could call in Poland in case he ran into trouble. In the past, he'd always had assets in-country to help him with the logistics, but those contacts were cold. He hoped Sam could find someone in DIA or CIA that could help. It was a short timeframe, but the whole operation would be working with short timeframes. She might as well get used to it from the beginning.

A half-hour later Sam walked into his office and said, "Okay, it's all set. You arrive in Krakow Thursday morning at 8:30 a.m."

Thurmond's jaw dropped slightly. "What? How did you set that up so quickly? Were you able to get me names of someone who could help once I'm there?" Who was this Sam anyway?

Fighting a grin she said. "I logged onto the Northwest Air Lines website and booked your flight—Business Class through Amsterdam. I assume your passport is up to date? If not, I can get it renewed tomorrow. Also, I've placed a call to our CIA counterparts who have responsibility for Eastern Europe. They said they'll get back to me with names later today."

Grant took a beat. "Okay," he said. "Thanks. My passport's current. I no longer have a government-issued passport, though. You might want to get that set up, just in case. If you can, make it black. You'll have to get General Wheeler to authorize that." Thinking ahead, Thurmond continued, "You know, depending upon what I find while in Poland, I may have to get into several other Eastern European countries. I'm sure they're also easy to enter, but I can't even remember which countries are which. I'm familiar with the old names, like Czechoslovakia and Yugoslavia, but not with the countries they became when the Soviet Union broke up." Suddenly he felt like an idiot.

"Well, you'll need a visa to get into some of them, but tourists go there all the time. It'll only take a couple of days, I think. I'll get right on it," Sam replied confidently.

"Go ahead and find out all the details, like which countries need visas, and stuff, but hold off on applying for them for a little while. I need to find out how compromised the network really is and how involved Russia is. I'd hate to fly into Russia and disappear. Speaking of which, I was told that I'm also on the elimination list."

Startled, Sam interrupted, "What? You're on the list?"

"Yeah. That means, depending on what you're exposed to, you might make the list, too. They're working on a safe house for me to live in while I'm here. We're gonna need for you to move in also. We have to make both of us tough to get to during this operation. Until this thing is over, you won't be able to tell anyone where you're living or where you're going. Will that be a problem?" He looked at her without blinking.

Sam took just a moment to reply, "No, sir. I can be ready to move tonight. I'll just tell my roommate that I'm going TDY for a while." She gave him a level gaze.

"Is this going to be okay with him?" Thurmond said, figuring he might as well know if she was living with some guy. It could make a difference during the mission.

"My roommate's a she and she's used to it. There is no he," Sam replied.

Thurmond nodded. "Then go find out the status of the safe house. Start with General Wheeler's office. He's the one setting it up. And don't tell anyone, including your roommate where you're going."

After Sam left, Thurmond started thinking about the old days, the people he'd recruited, the people who'd been taken out and what a devastating loss of intelligence the US would suffer with the disbanding of this network. Russia was still so unstable. The US had to know what they were planning to do. He wasn't just worried about the network falling apart. He also had a nagging uncertainty about his ability to solve this crisis before the inauguration. He had so little to work from and there just wasn't that much time. Right about now, he was also feeling a little rusty. He sat so deep in thought he didn't notice the man who stood leaning against his doorway, watching him for a few minutes.

"Well, if it isn't Colonel Grant Thurmond."

Startled, he answered, "Yeah, what can I do for you?" Looking up he immediately recognized the man standing there. "Garcia. What the hell are you doing here?" Thurmond wasn't particularly pleased to see him.

Marty Garcia was a career CIA operative that Thurmond had interacted with in the past. There had been a few joint operations when Garcia was just beginning his career in the intelligence community and Thurmond was nearing the end of his. The ops had been tentative outreaches by each agency to the other. From the beginning there'd been a natural competitiveness between them, as there was between their agencies. Thurmond thought of Garcia as young, daring and, in some cases, reckless. An agent with little respect for anyone else's abilities. But, in the time since Thurmond had retired, Garcia had risen in the hierarchy of the CIA. He was intelligent, quick, politically astute and driven to succeed. He had been recruited by the CIA in his senior year at Cornell and went from graduation to the Farm for training. He stood about six feet tall and weighed over two hundred pounds, with little fat. He had brown eyes and black hair. His grandparents had emigrated from Argentina eighty years ago and, although his parents were of South American heritage, both were born in the United States.

"Ah, it's great to see you, too, Thurmond." Garcia said with obvious sarcasm. "I'm your CIA liaison. You're supposed to work with me and I'm supposed to make sure you get all the CIA assistance you need to be successful. Including the request your assistant just phoned in." Thurmond started to reply, but Garcia, standing on both feet now, held his hand up and continued, "Look,

15

Thurmond. Before we get started, I've got something I need to get off my chest and I'm just going to lay it out on the table. I'm not deliberately trying to offend you, but I just don't see the merit in bringing an old fart like you out of retirement to tackle such a sensitive problem. I sure as hell wouldn't have done it, but it wasn't my call. Just wanted to say that." Garcia paused and looked at Thurmond.

Thurmond said nothing, just stared back at him.

Garcia continued, "Yeah, I know you were a hotshot when you were active, but it's been years since you've been involved. Just to let you know, I filed a brief suggesting this be a CIA operation, not led by DIA. I think DIA, and maybe you, caused the problem. Just wanted you to know where I stand." He leaned back into the door frame, his shoulders blocking the doorway. "Ahh, nice digs, by the way," he said grinning and looking around the small office.

"Well, at least you're frank, even if you are some kind of asshole. What do you know about what we're doing?" Thurmond was beyond annoyed. He had some respect for Garcia, but didn't personally like the man.

Without being invited, Garcia walked over and sat down in the guest chair. Crossing his arms and leaning back on the back two legs of the chair, the front legs raised about six inches off the ground, he said, "I've received a full briefing from General Wheeler. I know as much as you do. However, I know nothing about the network that's fallen apart. Unless they need help to save their ass, like now, DIA doesn't exactly keep us up to speed on their networks."

Thurmond thought for a moment. "Okay, you want to be involved? We're going to Krakow Wednesday night. See Sam in the next office to get the details. I'll expect you on that flight. And, by the way, this is my operation. You can tag along, but you're liaison, not lead. You'll take orders from me. Understood?" Thurmond's tone left little room for doubt. He'd handled cocky guys like Garcia before.

Garcia smirked. "Oh yeah, I understand. But if you screw up in any way, I'll be right there to take over." With that, Garcia brought the front legs of his chair down with a bang, stood and left the room.

Grant shook his head and went back to the list.

Garcia had been gone less than five minutes when a short, stocky man walked in unannounced.

16

"Good morning, Colonel."

"And you would be . . . ?" It's like Grand Central Station around here, Thurmond thought.

"I'm Bill Barry, the Director of National Intelligence. I'm your boss." The man replied wryly.

"Oh, good morning, sir. Sorry I didn't recognize you." Thurmond stood and walked around to the front of the desk to shake Barry's hand.

"Just wanted to start this thing out on the right foot. I don't want you gallivanting around the world digging up old bones. You'll just stir up more trouble for the Agency and we have all the problems we can handle right now. You're here to go through all the files, old intelligence reports, all the information we've received since you retired and offer suggestions on what's happening. I just talked with Garcia. Your trip to Poland is cancelled. Get comfortable here, 'cause this is where you'll be for the remainder of this operation. We have very little time to solve this puzzle and this is where all the information is. Your job is to comb through that information and identify a suspect or suspects and leave the field work to the guys who do it every day. You've been away for too long. So get to those files. And, I want a progress report from you daily. Clear?" Barry raised his eyebrows, waiting for an answer.

"Oh, yes, sir. Very clear." Grant stared at him.

With that, the DNI turned and left.

Within seconds Sam was in his office. "I didn't mean to eavesdrop, but I was just coming in before Director Barry got here." she said. Should I cancel the reservations?"

Thurmond let out a dry laugh. "Oh, hell no. I'm gonna do this my way. After all, I already retired once—what're they gonna do to me—send me back to my ranch? Screw 'em. Call Garcia and tell him he'd better be on that flight."

17

Chapter 4

I minus 53
Krakow

The flight arrived in Krakow right on schedule at 8:30 a.m. local time. Thurmond and Garcia boarded the Northwest flight the evening before and slept comfortably for five hours in the large Business Class seats, changing planes in Amsterdam. They were both carrying civilian passports with tourist visas. They had nothing on them or in their luggage that would identify them as representatives of the US Government.

After landing, they took a taxi to the Grand Hotel in downtown Krakow. Despite the name, it was not a five star hotel. It was average looking and had the advantage of having several other men in the lobby that looked like US business travelers. Thurmond thought they'd be indistinguishable from any of the other Americans. As they entered the lobby Thurmond looked around. There were lots of overstuffed sofas and chairs, but all of them looked a little on the shabby side. Same went for the thin, utilitarian carpeting. Holdovers from the Soviet days, he thought. Everything was in order when they checked in and afterwards each went to his separate room. As was the plan, they came back together in five minutes in Thurmond's room.

After letting Garcia in, Thurmond took a seat in one of the two worn armchairs and motioned for Garcia to sit in the other one.

Garcia spoke first. "Okay, I've been patient, but do you want to tell me why we're here?"

"I'm hoping to find and arrange a meeting with an old friend from back in the resistance days," said Thurmond. "I haven't talked with him in years, but my guess is that he still lives in the same area. I'll leave a mark at the usual place and then I'll wait."

Garcia raised his eyebrows. "A mark. Oh, that's rich, Thurmond. What if the guy doesn't show up? How long do we wait?"

"Our arrangement was for me to be at the meeting area for three consecutive days. I'm going to follow the old plan to see if he shows up." Thurmond explained, not so patiently.

"Leaving a mark, huh?" Garcia said sarcastically. "Damn, Thurmond, you're really an antique."

"Yeah, well, so are my contacts. They only know the old way," Thurmond said with a shrug.

"You know, if it rains, it'll wash the chalk off and you'll have no mark."

Thurmond sighed. "Garcia, it's November in Poland. It's not likely to rain. It may snow, but as cold as it is, it'll never rain, so don't worry about it. This is the way it's going down."

Garcia persisted. "And if he doesn't show up?"

Thurmond responded in a frustrated voice, "Then we'll go back home and start all over. Three days is all the time we have to spend on this part."

"How do you think he can help? Isn't his information really dated?"

"Yeah, Garcia it is," Thurmond explained, a growing edge in his voice. "That's what makes it valuable. I need him to reconstruct the old network. I need all the names and contact locations. It's the original members that are being eliminated and the newer guys may not even know all the old names."

"I was told you had the network name list," Garcia said.

"I only have part of it and that's just the part I can remember. The only written list was destroyed years ago and even it wasn't complete. I don't remember all the names or even how to make contact with all of the ones I do remember," Thurmond said.

"Why in the world didn't you, especially you who controlled the entire network, have a complete list? Why didn't you keep it secure in the DIA spaces?" Garcia asked incredulously.

Thurmond leaned back in his chair and responded. "In the old days we believed DIA headquarters might be infiltrated by Soviet moles. We had no hard evidence of that, but most of us in the field decided for our own safety and for the safety of the members of our network, to filter the information we fed Washington. We used what I call a star network, with the control officer in the middle. The next tier was the American agents and they each had a star cluster of informants that *they* used. Then each of the informants was allowed to develop their *own* cluster of informants."

Garcia leaned forward, put both hands up in front of him and asked. "I ask again, why didn't *you* have a list that you kept in *your* spaces in the Pentagon?"

Grant, too, leaned forward and said, "If you will let me finish without interrupting every few seconds, I'll explain it to you." He stopped talking for a second, and when Garcia didn't reply, said, "Headquarters usually only saw the first two tiers. Only the control officer saw the whole network and sometimes even he didn't have exposure to the last tier. Genoa Koslowski, the man we're looking for here, was the Eastern European cluster control. He was the only one who knew all the names. I didn't even know the last tier. It was a way of protecting sources. Surely you have something similar in the CIA."

"But, Koslowski knew all the names?" Garcia asked, ignoring the question.

"Just those for one part of the Eastern European cluster. Names I didn't even know. It's his cluster that's losing assets."

"And, we're here to get those names?"

"Yeah. If we don't get them we can still proceed, but our job gets a lot tougher. We'd better get a move on," Grant said.

They caught a taxi just outside the hotel and reached their destination within twenty minutes. They were in an older residential section of the city, populated by large, utilitarian apartment buildings with old, mostly Soviet-era cars lining the streets. They entered a small café on the corner and, after taking off and hanging up their overcoats, they sat down at a table by the window and ordered coffee. Garcia also ordered *paczki*, a favorite pastry in Poland. They sat quietly for about half an hour, rarely speaking. Thurmond used the time to observe the outside traffic, both auto and people. The café, though mostly empty today, looked pretty much the same as it used to, he thought. New menu, new tables, but otherwise, pretty much the same. Even after all this time, it felt very, very familiar sitting there. It didn't even look like they'd changed the art work on the dingy walls. He was sure he remembered some of the prints.

Thurmond, looking around one more time to make sure he couldn't be overheard, finally broke the silence. "It's hard to believe we can just fly in, take a taxi to a hotel, check in using our real names, and have open access around the city. Man how things have changed. You guys really have it easy these days."

Garcia remained quiet for a moment, then said in a serious tone, "We have different enemies these days, Thurmond."

"Look, the Soviet Union may have collapsed, but we still have Russia to worry about," Thurmond responded.

"Yeah, but we also have others . . . like the terrorists hiding in the mountains of Afghanistan and Pakistan, in the jungles of Malaysia and the Philippines and even in governments like Iran, North Korea, China, even Zimbabwe."

Thurmond replied, "I understand that, but why is it so different than before when our primary enemy was the Soviet Union? It's still just a matter of collecting information. You get people on the inside and they send us all matter of information, some of it useful. We use the useful information to protect the US."

Garcia shifted in his chair and took a sip of his coffee. "Our opponents now are incredibly secretive. They don't have a lot of recorded documents for us to tap into. It's mostly word of mouth. The terrorists have no headquarters buildings, no government bureaucracy, and, although they do have a command structure, getting into the inner circle is impossible without many years of trusted service and a proven background of terrorist activities. Our challenge today is different than yours was. And in many ways, more difficult." Garcia sounded frustrated.

Leaning back and crossing his legs, he continued, "Also, the actions of the last President didn't help. As you know, we were forced to pull hundreds of people off the street. We've lost so many of our eyes and ears that, even if the Presidential Directive is revoked, it'll take us years to get back to where we were before. These guys we face today are fanatics. To them, dying is an honor. Today, terrorism is our big threat, not communism."

"You're focused mainly on the Middle East?" Grant asked.

Garcia shrugged. "We're focused everywhere. There are terrorist training camps set up throughout the Middle East and also in many African countries. Even in Southern Asia. The people attending these camps are mostly young Muslims who are being fed a steady stream of hate propaganda about how evil the West is. They undergo physical exercise and are being trained in how to use weapons and explosives. Their goal is to bring down 'the infidels.' That's us. They are our real enemies and most of us are concerned that we can't get close enough to find out what they're going to do. Now you know what keeps *me* up at night." Garcia sat back and stared at Thurmond.

21

Thurmond stared back a moment then said, "Guess you're right. It really is a different world since 9/11." Then standing up he said, "We'd better get going."

Chapter 5

I minus 53
The Pentagon

Bill Barry, at the Pentagon for a DOD briefing, decided to check in and see how Thurmond was progressing. Seeing Thurmond's empty office, the DNI charged into Sam's adjoining office demanding to know where Thurmond was and telling her he'd better just be getting coffee.

"Sir, he just said he was going out. I haven't seen him since."

"Have him call me the minute he returns—and it'd better be soon!" Barry was almost shouting.

"Yes, sir," Sam said as Barry stormed out of her office.

Sam's first thought was oh shit! I have no way to contact the Colonel and I've got a cabinet member breathing down my neck. She figured it would be better if she weren't around the next time the DNI came by, so she decided to go home early. Although she had no way to reach him, the Colonel had her cell number if he needed her. Maybe he'd call and she could tell him about the DNI's visit. Then she thought about General Wheeler. I should call him, she thought, he'll know what to do.

"General, this is Sergeant First Class Rogers. I'm Colonel Thurmond's assistant. We have a slight problem you should know about." She explained the situation and asked what she should do next.

"Okay, just sit tight, Rogers." Said the General, "I'll call the DNI and settle him down. I'll tell him I ordered the Colonel to complete the trip so he was just following my orders. The DNI's really a pretty good guy, so that should buy us a couple of days. But if you hear from the Colonel, call me. I want to know what's going on, so keep me in the loop."

***

After he left the Thurmond's office, Bill Barry headed straight to the President-elect's offices. As his driver pulled into the turning circle outside the building, he got the general's call. Although he wasn't happy with the conversation, he at least owed the General time to get the Colonel under control. He'd ordered a briefing for Monday morning. Thurmond had better, by God, be back by then.

Leaning forward, Barry raised his voice. "Driver, this meeting won't take long. Wait close by. When I finish here I'll need you to take me to my office at the White House."

"Yes, sir," the driver said. "I'll be right out front."

Chapter 6

I minus 53
Krakow

As they were walking down the street, Garcia asked, "How do you propose to contact Koslowski?"

"Well, this might sound old fashioned, but as I said earlier, I'm going to use the same mark at the same place I did in the old days. If he still lives close by and still walks to market every day, he'll see it. Hopefully, he'll show up at the meeting place. My fear is that after all this time, he'll think it's a trap and we'll never see him. So, I intend to get to the spot early and stay late. You won't be able to be with me on this part—he'd get too suspicious. I want him to walk by and clearly see it's me. Only me. Got it?"

"Yeah, I got it." Garcia let out a small laugh. "Actually, even though I joked about it earlier, it's not that old fashioned," Garcia assented. "I was just giving you a hard time. In some parts of the world, we use pretty much the same system today."

Grant stopped walking, turned to face Garcia and said, "Okay, here we are. See if you can sorta shield me while I bend down and mark the curb with white chalk. It'll only take a sec."

"I know the drill," Garcia said.

While Garcia looked around, Thurmond made a quick inverted V mark on the curb, quickly rose and said, "Let's get outta here."

They walked back to the café, caught a cab to the hotel and then, later, met at the restaurant for a late lunch. After stuffing themselves on *Kotlet schabowy, Kłopsiki,* and *Placki kartoflane,* they finished up with *Makowiec,* a sweet, cake-like poppy-seed roll most popular around Christmastime, for dessert. After splitting the check, they went to their rooms to catch up on sleep.

The next morning, after an American-style breakfast of pancakes, sausages and eggs, Thurmond left for the meeting place. His station was the corner table nearest the street in the outside dining area of the same café he and Garcia had visited the day before. A place where any passerby on the street could easily see him. It was the classic 'hide in plain sight' plan. The more obvious he was, the less likely it was that anyone would give him a second look.

Man, it was a lot easier these days, he thought. In the past, the waiting time grated on his nerves; always worrying about being stopped by a Soviet officer to check his papers. Today, with nothing really to fear, he enjoyed the time outside. Cold enough for a warm coat, but not too bad for November. At least there was no snow.

He ordered coffee, which he sipped slowly as he watched the steam rise from the glass. The Poles make their coffee very strong. First, they place a large spoonful of grounds in a flat bottomed glass. Then boiling water is poured over the coffee and, depending on personal taste, sugar is added. This coffee is affectionately called "spit-coffee" by drinkers because of the reaction of anyone who unwisely gets to the sludge at the bottom.

After his second cup, enough time had passed that Thurmond decided Koslowski wasn't going to show, so he went back to his hotel to meet with Garcia.

"How'd it go?" Garcia asked as he approached Thurmond.

"Nada. A no show," shrugged Thurmond.

"So what now?"

"We wait 'til tomorrow and do it again."

Grant repeated the process the next day, still with no success.

The third morning, as Thurmond sat at the cafe, he watched as an older gentleman approached and leaned over the low metal fence. The man asked Thurmond if he had a match. Koslowski.

After lighting his cigarette with shaky fingers, the old man handed the matches back to Thurmond, said "thank you" and strolled on down the street. Thurmond watched him walk away for a few seconds, and then laid some bills on the table. Unhurriedly he left the café, but when he rounded the corner he walked quickly down the street in the same direction as Koslowski. He caught up with him by the end of the block.

As they stood facing each other on the curb, Thurmond said with a broad smile, *"Graba,* my old friend."

Koslowski, also smiling, replied *"Graba!"* They shook hands.

"It's been a long time. I heard you retired," said Koslowski, putting his hands back into his coat pockets to shield them from the cold.

"Yes, it has been a long time and yes, I did retire. However, some urgent business came up and I'm back for a while." Grant answered, also putting his hands in his pockets.

Koslowski nodded. "Well, whatever the reason you're here, it's good to see you."

"And, you. You're looking well." Thurmond said with genuine affection.

"Oh, I have some aches and pains . . . but, all in all, I do well. But, what do you want with me? I can't believe you came all this way just to inquire into an old man's health. And . . ." he shrugged, "we don't have the Soviets to spy on anymore." Koslowski smiled.

"So I've discovered. I would like to say it's a social visit, but, unfortunately, we have a serious matter to discuss." To make sure no one could overhear, Thurmond looked around them and found the sidewalks empty. He quickly explained the situation.

Koslowski was quiet until Grant finished, then said, "My, my. Yes, that is a serious problem. Of course, I know the names of all of the people who were in my network. After all, I worked with most of them for over twenty years. They were all loyal to the cause and the information they provided was always correct and extremely valuable. I can give you those names, but," he paused. "you must guard it with your life. If the Russians found out who they were, I'm afraid they wouldn't last a month. Many of them remain in sensitive positions, some even in Russia." Koslowski stared at him with his serious pale blue eyes.

"I'll be extremely guarded with the list. I realize how important it is that these brave people not be compromised," Thurmond said seriously.

"I do not have the list written down. I would ask that of you also. You must memorize the names and meeting locations, as I have done. We will walk now while I tell you about each person." Koslowski turned and starting walking slowly.

It was over an hour later when Thurmond finally had it all committed to memory.

As Thurmond turned to leave, he said "Thank you for your help. This information is extremely valuable and will help save other lives. I will protect it with my life. I also want to thank you for your work with us in the past. You gave us valuable information which allowed us to counter Soviet activities in many parts of the world. These counter thrusts, I fully believe, contributed significantly to the collapse of the USSR. You and your people are true patriots. *Do widzenia.*" Thurmond clasped the right hand of the old man with both of his.

"*Do widzenia*," replied Koslowski, who turned and walked away without looking back.

***

Thurmond had to walk about ten blocks before he came to a main street and could find a taxi. He arrived back at his hotel less than four hours after he left. Garcia was waiting in the lobby.

"Come on, let's get lunch and a beer," Garcia said, getting to his feet. "I need a complete update. I contacted CIA headquarters while you were gone and gave them an update on our activities. They were very interested in whether or not you found Koslowski and, if so, whether you had gotten the list."

"You did what? Garcia, you dumb shit. You told them about Koslowski and the list? On an unsecure phone? What were you thinking, man? You know we have to keep this extremely close. The person killing all these people will take out Koslowski if he learns his name. There are moles everywhere, especially in CIA headquarters!"

"Well, buddy, I'm afraid you have no choice. If you don't give the list to me, the DDI will simply go over your head to the DNI and get it."

Thurmond frowned,"First of all, I am not your 'buddy'. You don't mean shit to me and neither does the CIA. I don't report up that chain of command and I owe you nothing. And, secondly, there is no list."

"What? You didn't find Koslowski?" Garcia exclaimed. He couldn't believe it.

"Oh, I found him all right. He's a blabbering old man with no memory of the past. He didn't even know me or what I was talking about. He passed right by me without a trace of recognition. I had to run down the street to catch him. Even after reminding him that we used to work together, he had no memory of it. He never even saw the mark I left. He was simply on his way to the market when he passed by the café. Just dumb luck that I saw him at all. He's a dead end." Thurmond really sounded discouraged.

Showing his frustration by holding his hands up, Garcia said,

28

"Damn, all this for nothing? What do we do now?"

"We go home and start over." Thurmond said with a shrug and a flip of his hands.

There was no flight out that evening, so they left for home late the next morning. They arrived back in Washington around ten that night and both went straight home. Thurmond got to his apartment by eleven and immediately went to bed. He couldn't get his mind to quiet down, so as he lay there he thought over and over about Koslowski and the list of names. He finally fell asleep a little after two. When he got up the next morning it was nearly nine. Sam's door was open and her room was empty. He figured, correctly, that she had already gone to the office. He knew he had to update General Wheeler immediately, so he got dressed and headed down the road to the Pentagon.

Chapter 7

I minus 52
Washington

Sitting at his desk Bill Barry picked up the secure phone and called the head of the Secret Service detail covering the President-elect.

"Carlisle."

Barry got right to the point. "David, I need to alert you to a potential problem. We have indications that the President-elect may be facing a threat on Inauguration day. No action is required now, but for planning purposes, I thought you should know."

"Sir, may I ask the nature of the threat?" asked David Carlisle. Carlisle, age 47, was a career Secret Service agent who had been on Presidential Detail for several years. He was the overwhelming choice when selected to lead the detail protecting the President-elect. After the oath of office, he would be heading the elite and prestigious Presidential Secret Service Unit, a promotion earned by years of outstanding service as a member of the detail protecting the past two Presidents.

"I can only tell you that we've received unsubstantiated information that someone may be trying to assassinate the President-elect and we think the attempt will be made sometime on or before inauguration day. I'm sorry, but the details of our intelligence investigation must remain tightly held for now. Any kind of leak would lead to deaths throughout the intelligence community and potentially to your new boss. I promise to keep you up to date on anything we find that would be of value to you in protecting the President-elect."

"You're taking this threat very seriously, then?" Carlisle asked.

Barry leaned back in his chair, "Yes we are. However, I don't believe there's any immediate danger. Just in case though, stay vigilant and advise your detail to be especially alert."

"Yes, sir. Please let me know if the threat level either increases or decreases."

"You got it." He put his feet on his desk and thought about next steps for a full half hour.

It had been a long day, so the DNI then headed home, oblivious to the large truck with furniture store markings on the side which followed his Town Car at a discreet distance. His driver didn't notice anything either, so he delivered Barry to his residence in McLean and headed back to drop off the car at the government garage in the District. At the garage, the car would be cleaned and filled with fuel for the next day. The driver would pick up the car early the next morning, drive to the DNI's house, pick him up and drive him wherever he wanted to go. Because of the extremely sensitive nature of the DNI's job, it was assumed that he could become a kidnapping or assassination target. Therefore, all routine routes were varied each day, even if it was just to and from his office. Also, Because of the secrecy surrounding the DNI's schedule, no one would know where he was going until his driver picked him up.

As the driver drove in the dark down the Washington Parkway, he paid little attention to the large truck speeding behind him. As the truck moved alongside and overtook the Town Car, it swerved suddenly to the right, pushing the Town Car off the side of the road into an embankment, crashing violently into a tree. It was late and there was no one around. The truck stopped quickly, the driver got out, went back to check the condition of the Town Car driver and, satisfied that he was dead, he gave a quick jerk on the badge the driver had pinned to his shirt and put the badge in his pocket.

Another quick look around confirmed he was still alone, so he reached into his jacket pocket, pulled out a small bottle of gasoline, poured it into the engine compartment of the car and threw in a match. The Town Car exploded into flame. With the flames destroying both the exterior and the interior of the car, no one would notice the missing badge. He knew that any investigation would indicate the fire had originated in the engine compartment and was most likely initiated by a gasoline leak caused by the wreck. The ruling would be accidental death.

The man got back into his truck and drove away. Early next morning, another man arrived at the government garage in the District, notified the guard that the previous driver for the DNI had died the night before in a crash and asked that a new Town Car be assigned. He said that early this morning, he had gotten a call and was told that he would be the new driver. The guard confirmed that the man had a valid badge with the appropriate picture and everything else was in order. Lacking any other authority on site, the guard logged him in, swiped his badge, which came back valid, and gave him the keys to the DNI's new Town Car. The man signed the log and drove off. The guard went on to other things.

Chapter 8

I minus 49
The Pentagon

"Hey, good morning. Welcome back, Colonel." Sam smiled as Thurmond came through the door to her office.

"Good morning, Sam." Thurmond returned her smile and sat down in her guest chair.

Sam started right in. "Well, sir, you've created quite a stir your first week back. The DNI was here looking for you. I tried to cover; I called General Wheeler for support and he called the DNI and told him he had ordered you to go. The DNI is waiting for your report. You might want to touch base with General Wheeler first, though. Another thing, I called—"

"Whoa. Slow down. I'm having trouble keeping up. Jet lag, I guess." Thurmond laughed.

Sam, realizing she had been a little intense, said, "Oh, sorry. Guess I'm relieved you're back safely. I couldn't imagine what you were doing and what trouble you might have gotten into. We have to get you a phone that will be active wherever you are. I'll work on that today. Did you find the guy you were looking for?"

"Koslowski. Yes, I found him." Thurmond paused and looked around. "Has this room been swept since it was assigned to us?"

"I don't know, sir. I haven't ordered a sweep. If you didn't, then I'm sure it hasn't."

"Get it swept this morning and stay right next to the team. If they find anything—anything at all—I want to know. Okay?" Thurmond wasn't smiling now.

"Yes, Sir. I'll get on it right away." Sam said, matching Grant's serious tone.

Thurmond went down to the Navy guys to get more coffee. Boy, they really knew how to do it. The other coffee messes in the DIA spaces had coffee that was weak, almost like tea. It had no character. But the Navy coffee was great. He went from there to his office. He could hear Sam talking, but couldn't make out what she was saying. Must be on the phone, he thought.

33

Later that morning a team showed up to sweep Thurmond's office for bugs. He wasn't terribly surprised when they found two. He was told they were the latest and greatest technology. Even the sweepers were surprised that they were so current. They told Thurmond that these bugs were created for the CIA and, as far as the sweepers knew, no other agency, except maybe NSA, had access to them yet. Thurmond didn't know exactly who wanted to listen in on his conversations, but he could guess. Sometimes, in this business, your colleagues were the ones you could trust the least.

Very few people had access to offices within the DIA spaces. Buried deeply inside the Pentagon, there was only one way to get in. That entrance was guarded by two armed marines, twenty-four-seven. You didn't get in unless you were recognized with a valid badge or were on the guest list. Even with the guest list, you didn't get further than the reception area. Each guest, no matter who they were or what their rank or clearance level, had to be picked up, signed in, and escorted at all times by the DIA officer they were visiting. That meant that the bugs had to have been planted by someone who had free access to all the spaces. Although he didn't know for sure who did it, the only CIA person who had full access and would have any interest in what he was doing was Garcia.

He told the sweepers to leave the bugs in place. No use letting whoever planted them know they'd been discovered. Maybe he could use them to his advantage.

***

That afternoon in his office, armed with the knowledge of the bugs, Thurmond told Sam exactly what he had told Garcia about Koslowski. He'd set Sam straight later, but it would be good for Garcia, or anyone else who was listening in, to hear a consistent story. For now, he wanted everyone to think that Koslowski was a dead end.

Chapter 9

I minus 49
The DNI

The new driver picked up the DNI in McLean at 0730. As the driver stood there holding the rear passenger side door open, Barry realized this wasn't his regular guy.

"Where's Bradley? He sick?" Barry asked, pausing before entering the car.

The driver responded in a serious voice. "Good morning, sir. I'm afraid I have some bad news. Bradley died in a traffic accident last night on the Washington Parkway. I've been temporarily assigned as his replacement."

"My God. He's been my driver for several years now." Barry exclaimed. "I hardly knew him, but I'm really sorry he died. Geez, I don't even remember his last name."

"Parker, sir. His name was Bradley Parker."

"Parker, huh? Well thank you. While we're at it, what's your name? Will you be my regular driver from now on?" Barry asked as he got into the car.

"My name is Matt, sir, Matt Riley. I would really like to be your regular driver, but you need to call the garage and tell the supervisor that you want me as your driver. Right now, as I said, I'm just temporary."

"I'll do that as soon as I get to the office, Matt. By the way, I assume you're cleared?" Barry asked.

"Oh, yes, sir, all your drivers have to have Top Secret clearance. Here's my badge."

"Great," the DNI said, after satisfying himself that the driver's face matched the one on the badge. Also, the badge contained a small yellow dot under the plastic coating indicating he was cleared for access to classified information. Barry knew he should verify the access level by swiping the magnetic strip located on the back of the badge, but he didn't have a reader in the car so he figured he'd have his admin do it later back at the office. He'd had other substitute drivers in the past and it had always worked out okay.

After the driver got into the car, Barry began his daily routine. He generally started the day in his Town Car, making calls on the secure phone all cabinet level officers had in their cars. His first call was to Garcia at CIA headquarters. He knew Garcia was scheduled to be back in the office this morning, so he put his call on speakerphone, leaned back in his comfortable leather seat, and dialed.

Garcia answered on the second ring. "Garcia."

"Garcia, Barry. I got the full details of your call while you were in Krakow. Did you find this guy Koslowski, the old cluster leader? Did he give up the list?" Barry asked impatiently.

"Yes, sir, we did. However, as you point out he was old and was completely incoherent so we learned nothing helpful. Thurmond should have verified this before we left, but, obviously, he didn't. So, we wasted four days for nothing." Garcia sounded disgusted.

"There was no way to get information out of this guy?"

"Well, sir, I really didn't get a chance to talk with him. Thurmond insisted on meeting with him alone and came back with nothing." Garcia leaned back and smiled. This was going well. With any luck the DNI will assign him to partner with Thurmond.

"Damn. So where are we?" Barry responded, gruffly, crossing his legs in the roomy back seat.

"We're nowhere, sir. Back to square one. Are you sure Thurmond's the one to be heading this up?" Garcia hoped he wasn't overdoing it.

"I'll call Thurmond, get his take." With that the DNI hung up, not waiting for Garcia to reply. The driver couldn't help but smile slightly at how easy this was.

After dropping the DNI off at his office, Riley remained in the parking area with the other White House staff drivers. Generally they would talk together, read books, or listen to music while waiting for a call to take their respective bosses to the next destination. Today was no exception and the new driver fitted right in with the others.

Chapter 10

I minus 49
The Safe House

"Well, it isn't exactly a palace, but it's not too bad. And it's safe and functional." Thurmond and Sam had been assigned an eighth floor, two bedroom, two bath apartment in a high rise close to Key Bridge.

"Not exactly a beautiful place," Sam said quietly, running her hand over the back of a worn green sofa.

"Well, I guess it. . ." Thurmond started to reply.

"Better than a tent in Iraq, though," she said, smiling at him.

Although the furnishings weren't plush, they were adequate. Looked to Thurmond like they were standard rental stuff. The apartment was located just down the road from the Pentagon, but that's not why Thurmond liked it. DIA had some secure offices in the same building that Thurmond could use.

Thurmond still didn't know for sure who had bugged his office in the Pentagon, but it was a sure bet he wouldn't trust it in the future. Their new office space was on the unmarked seventh floor of the same apartment building within a Sensitive Compartmented Information Facility, or SCIF, maintained by DIA. Because the space housed computers and communications equipment that handled the most highly sensitive intelligence information, it was one of the most secure spaces outside of the Pentagon itself. No elevator stopped on that floor and, in fact, there were no markings in the elevator that would even indicate there was a floor there. To gain entrance, one had to go to either the 6th or the 8th floor (marked 7 in the elevator) and take the stairway either up or down to the floor in between.

The gray steel door on that floor was unmarked and always locked. There was absolutely no indication of what was behind the door. To get inside, you had to pass your badge through a reader, then press your palm to the scanner, and finally, enter a code on the cipher lock. If the magnetic strip allowed access, the reader pulled the badge into the interior for the guards to view. You then had to stand in front of a one-way mirror situated at face level in the center of the door for positive ID. Just knocking on the steel door did no good—no one answered. If the badge didn't pass the scan, or was suspect in some other way, or the picture didn't match the person standing there, it was retained on the inside by the guard and you were denied entrance. And you could count on having company very shortly.

"Oh, I think this place will work out fine," Sam said, looking around with her hands on her hips. "We even have a TV and a DVD player. I also saw a blender in the kitchen. Margaritas anyone?" she asked with a smile. "Oh, by the way, I had this place thoroughly swept this morning . . . no bugs."

"Great, but don't get too comfortable—we won't be spending much time here. I just need a couple of days to think about our next steps." Grant said, impatient to get started.

"As you requested, I managed to get us entrance authorization to the SCIF spaces. Here's your new badge. I used the photo you had taken for your Pentagon badge. The cipher lock code is 6392 and it's changed weekly. We have a fairly large office with plenty of file space. I also arranged for the paper files we need to be transferred from the Pentagon to the SCIF. The first time in, you'll have to go through some administrative procedures, like registering your palm print and things like that," Sam explained, sitting down on the living room sofa.

Grant sat in one of the two easy chairs. "You've been busy. Good work. Who knows we're using these spaces?"

"Only General Wheeler, sir."

"Not Garcia or the DNI?"

"No, sir. Thought I'd leave that up to you. The General assured me he won't tell anyone about it." Sam responded.

"Well, the DNI will probably have a fit when he finds out. Wheeler's on our side, but he'll have to tell him when asked. We'll just keep Garcia guessing for awhile. He's probably okay, but he'll end up being a pain in the ass. He can't help it, he's CIA. Sam, there's another thing I need to talk with you about." Thurmond paused.

"Sure, sir. Go ahead, ask anything. You have my full attention."

Grant leaned forward in his chair with the outer sides of his hands on his knees. "I'm going to need help. I can't count on the CIA, and my own agency might have been the one to bug my offices.

I don't know who I can trust . . . except you. I trust you. And, *because* I trust you, you're the only one I can turn to for help. What do you think? Are you ready to jump into the middle of this?" He stared directly into Sam's eyes.

Sam recognized how serious Grant was. "I don't know exactly what it means to jump into the middle of this, but I do know that I am fully committed to doing what I can to help."

"It might be dangerous and you might end up traveling all over Eastern Europe, maybe even Russia. Are you sure you can handle it?" Grant said, still leaning forward.

Sam paused a moment, not exactly sure how to answer. She decided to just spit it out. "Sir, when I was assigned to a combat unit in Iraq and was issued an M16 rifle and a Berretta 9MM sidearm, I was scared. Yeah, I knew how to shoot—I qualified for the sharpshooter medal in basic. But, I had never shot at human targets. I didn't know how I would react when that happened. When it eventually did, I found out that I was well trained, and the first time I confronted an enemy, it was he who went down, not me. I'm ready," She finished confidently.

Leaning back, Thurmond nodded, pleased with her enthusiasm. "Great. The first thing we need to do is to establish a new working relationship. I am retired and my name is Grant, not sir or Colonel. I have a tendency to walk around inappropriately dressed at home, but I'll try to spare you the embarrassment of seeing me in my underwear or, worse, naked. If I slip up and you see me, you're gonna have to overlook that. Sometimes I like to have a drink—usually every day. I never get drunk—don't like the feeling of being out of control. I curse. Does that offend you?"

"No, sir, that doesn't offend me. So do I."

"Good answer, but I'm Grant, not sir."

"Yes, sir . . . . I mean Grant. That part's gonna be tough. I'm not used to calling a senior officer by their first name. Or any officer for that matter." Sam said with a nervous smile.

With their new working relationship somewhat established, Grant suggested lunch. Sam enthusiastically agreed. They drove across Key Bridge into Georgetown and had lunch in a trendy café with outside seating. It was the best cheeseburger Grant had tasted since he started cooking for himself. Since he was on full expenses, he resolved to eat out the whole time he was on this assignment—an assignment he increasingly felt was an impossible task. Somehow, though, he felt good that Sam had signed up to help. But then that thought made him feel uncomfortable again.

Chapter 11

I minus 49
CIA Headquarters

Garcia sat at his desk, wondering why Thurmond had not returned any of his calls today. Guess he'd have to go to the Pentagon and talk to him. Ever since their confrontation in Poland, they'd had little to say, and on the flight back they hardly talked. It was odd, though. He knew the bugs in Thurmond's office were working because he had picked up Thurmond's conversation with Sam confirming what Thurmond had told him about Koslowski. But he hadn't heard a word since. Due to his position at the CIA, Garcia had unlimited access to all DIA spaces, and it had been ridiculously easy to plant the bugs. Before he went over to talk to Thurmond, though, he needed to talk with his boss and bring her up to speed. She was okay, but she wasn't a real field agent.

Nora Ames, Garcia's immediate superior, was a longtime CIA employee. She had never been in the field, instead spending most of her career as an analyst at headquarters in Langley. Over the years, she had many times shown brilliance when matching seemingly unrelated bits of information to derive true intelligence, intelligence with meaning for America. That's how she thought of it— to keep America safe. For her continued loyalty and excellent work, she was rewarded with fairly rapid promotions. Now she led a unit of agents who had spent their careers in the field. Many of them resented reporting to someone with no field experience. Garcia was one of them.

Garcia called Ames on the secure internal line. "Nora, you got a minute? I need to bring you up to date on this inauguration thing."

"Sure, Marty. Give me fifteen minutes then come on up."

Garcia walked into Nora's office spaces and her admin told him to go right in, she was expecting him.

Director Ames was still quite young, maybe 38, Garcia thought. She was about 5'6", slender, and had dark hair, pulled severely back into a low pony tail. She was wearing a navy suit with a skirt and matching low, navy heels. A simple, but expensive probably silk, blouse was underneath the jacket. Garcia had never seen her outside her office and there were times he wondered if she ever let her hair down. She was unmarried, he knew.

Nora's office was what one would expect a senior CIA executive's office to look like. Located in a corner of the 5th floor, the office was large, containing a dark wood desk with a tall, plush leather swivel chair and two comfortable side chairs across the desk from hers. The office also had a conference table with six chairs, and a comfortable sitting area in one corner had a sofa and two leather easy chairs. There were potted plants throughout the space which were diligently maintained by Nora's administrative assistant. Another nice feature which Garcia especially liked was that she had tinted windows on two walls, affording her a nice view of the back side of the CIA campus. Garcia was always impressed when he entered. Someday, he thought, someday.

He joined Nora at the conference table, sitting across from her.

"Hi, Nora. Just wanted to bring you up to date. I went with Thurmond to Krakow and it was a dead end," He said.

"What do mean 'a dead end?'" she replied, leaning forward with her elbows on the table and hands crossed under her chin.

"The old guy he went to see was a basket case with no memory. Didn't even know Thurmond. By the way, I already told this to the DNI. Sorry,, but he called me for an update and I had no choice but to tell him."

"I'm sure you didn't, Marty. But next time, I would appreciate it if you would tell me first," Nora complained, sitting back and crossing her arms.

"Oh, sure. I meant to this time, but, well, he called me and, well, you know." Garcia looked at her and shrugged.

She held his gaze for a moment and then said, "Okay, what's the next step?"

"Well, I don't really know. There were a lot of people around, so Thurmond and I didn't talk much on the way home. I've called and left messages several times, but he hasn't called back. Thought I'd head over to the Pentagon today and talk with him personally." Garcia deliberately didn't tell her about the bugs. If they were discovered before he could retrieve them, well . . . easier to get forgiveness than permission.

Nora looked a little peeved, but responded calmly. "Okay. Look, you guys are supposed to be a team. If he doesn't want to cooperate, you have to convince him you can help. This is sensitive enough that I can't do anything to help you. Thurmond is running the show. He has the authority all the way up to the President-elect and that's way above my pay grade."

"Okay, Nora, I'll work with him. I'll get back to you in the next couple of days with an update."

"Don't keep me in the dark, Marty. If the DNI calls the Director, the Director will call me. I want to be able to answer his questions." She stood, indicating the meeting had ended.

Garcia stood and said, "I'll keep you up to speed."

Garcia left Langley heading towards the Pentagon. When he got there, he went straight to Thurmond's office. Nothing was different except Thurmond wasn't there. Sam wasn't in her office either. Not knowing exactly what to do next, he went into the Pentagon's five-acre center plaza to grab some lunch and listen to the band that was playing. After eating and sitting in the sun for a while, Garcia went back to Thurmond's office and found it the same—empty. At that point, he triggered the transceiver in his pocket which sent a signal to the two bugs to transmit back any noise they had picked up. He would listen to it once he was back in his office in Langley. This had been his routine since planting the bugs the day before Thurmond arrived.

He exited the building and, thankful it wasn't raining, took the long walk through the massive parking lot to his car. On his way back to his office, he used his cell phone to call Thurmond's number and, getting no answer, left another urgent message. This sure was strange. He was beginning to think Thurmond went off on his own, deliberately not telling Garcia where he was going. He couldn't understand why Sam wasn't there, though. She certainly wasn't a field agent and surely Thurmond wouldn't risk the whole operation by involving someone with no experience. But, who knows, he thought, Thurmond was a real cowboy. He might do anything.

Chapter 12

I minus 49
Krakow

Riley called the number he had been given to report his status and was surprised when a man's voice said, "Yes?" He expected to reach voice mail as he usually did. After a brief pause, Riley said, "I'm in place. Barry called the garage just as I asked and I'm now his permanent driver. What do you want me to do next?"

"Do your job. Be his driver. Keep your eyes and ears open and relay everything you hear."

"Everything? How do I know if it's important?" Riley asked.

"You don't have to know. Just tell me everything. I'll determine what may be of value to me," the voice replied.

"Yes, sir. It's your money." Riley then related the DNI's telephone conversation about Koslowski and the man said "Is that all?" When Riley said, "Yes," the man hung up without saying another word.

The man on the phone spoke English with a slight accent. Eastern European, Riley thought, maybe even Russian. Riley didn't have a clue where the man was located and knew nothing about him, just that he paid well . . . and that was enough.

A single shingle PI with no real training, Riley was pretty sleazy. For several years now, he'd barely eked out a living taking jobs that no reputable PI would take . . . and not all of them were above board. Nothing terribly illegal, but he was not against breaking laws to make a few bucks. He was in his early fifties, though looked slightly younger because he kept his weight down. Thick blond hair added to the illusion. He'd been looking for a bigger score recently. Something he could use to buy a condo down in Florida, maybe. So when he was contacted by phone about two months ago, with the caller telling him he needed him for some work to be done in the near future, he'd jumped at the chance. He was put on a fat weekly retainer and told to get a job as a driver for the US Government and await further instructions.

He'd managed to do that fairly quickly; seems they were always looking for part-time drivers. Since then he'd been on call, driving for a variety of people. He had a clean record, so the LAC/NAC went quickly and he was granted a SECRET clearance. This was indicated by a small red dot under the plastic coating of his badge and, along with his demographic information like height, weight, eye and hair color, was also recorded on the magnetic strip on the back of the card. His picture was on the front.

However, he now had a new badge that he'd found this morning in an envelope stuffed under his door. While it looked identical to the other one, under the plastic coating it had a little yellow dot instead of the red one. He thought that might indicate a different access level. Riley didn't know what security level the dot indicated, but, since the badge had his picture on it, he'd worn it all day. He'd never met the guy with the accent, but the deposit showed up every week at his bank right on schedule. And to boot, he was getting good pay as a government driver. Good thing, too, because he didn't have any other cases right now and the old bank account was getting mighty low. Also, this was a good diversion from his usual boring casework.

***

The man with the accent walked quickly through the residential streets of Krakow. He'd arrived early this morning, catching a late night flight from Dulles two hours after shoving the badge under Riley's door. It had taken him less than two days to determine that the Koslowski mentioned in the call was Genoa Koslowski, a past Soviet middle manager in the old Polish Ministry of Defense. He must have been cooperating with the Americans for a long time. The man needed to know if Koslowski had mentioned his name to the Americans and, if so, to whom. Either way, Koslowski had to be eliminated. Today. When this was over, there could be no one left alive who had seen or heard his name in conjunction with any American spy operation.

"Yes, I'm coming," came the response in Polish from the other side of the door. As Koslowski opened the door a crack, the man standing there pushed sharply, knocking Koslowski backwards into the apartment. The man quickly entered, closing the door behind him.

Within thirty minutes he had all the information he had come for.

Even more, for Koslowski had revealed that he had actually run a fairly large network, and now the man had all the names. Any one of the people on this list could have heard his name, so all would have to be eliminated. Too bad the old man died before answering all his questions. Well, he had all the names and knew generally in which city they lived, but just didn't know how to contact all of them. That's more than he'd hoped for. Adding these names to the list he had obtained earlier gave him a good picture of the network. Too bad the paper was torn in the earlier case, but he was sure it went unnoticed. All in all, a good day's work. He would have vodka tonight.

Chapter 13

I minus 49
Washington

After lunch, Grant and Sam returned to their new apartment to begin the task of matching names with Grant's memory and the reams of specific intelligence requests made over a twenty-year period.

Looking at the pile of paperwork, Sam said, "What are specific intelligence requests about? What were we trying to find out?"

Grant thought she sounded a little frustrated, so, leaning back in his chair he explained. "These were requests for information that could be about any one of many things." Before continuing, he paused and crossed his legs, thinking for a moment how to put this. "For this network, all requests were about information that could be provided through the Soviet Ministry of Defense. That was the information DIA wanted, anything regarding the Soviet military—troop movements, ship movements, munitions shipments, especially missiles, nuclear warheads, truck mounted or other portable launchers . . . that kind of stuff. DIA had only passing interest in anything political. Certainly not enough interest to request a special operation to discover it. All the political stuff was left to the CIA—that's their charter. At DIA we wanted any information that would help us if we were to ever get into a shooting war with the Soviets. Or, better yet, help us prevent it. Even any information that would help our allies."

Sam interrupted. "But what about this case?" She was leaning forward now, with her elbows on the table. Obviously interested in details.

Grant continued. "That was where Koslowski came in. His job at the Ministry of Defense's Office of Logistics gave him visibility to a lot of the Soviet's Eastern European military information. As he spent more time in place, he brought in people in other departments and other locations who were willing to provide information. Some would provide anything interesting they came across; others were occasionally tasked for specific information. Over time, Koslowski controlled dozens of people employed in the Soviet dominated Ministry of Defense. The list."

"Okay, I can see why that list is so secret. The name of the person killing all the others might be on it and if that's true, that person could be trying to kill everyone on Koslowski's list," Sam said.

Grant nodded, impressed with how intuitive Sam was. "Or, I suppose, since many of those people might still be in sensitive jobs, the current Russian intelligence group could be systematically eliminating what they still consider a threat. It could even be someone from the old Soviet intelligence operation who is out for revenge. There are way too many possibilities, and we have only a short time to solve it."

Grant continued, "What I can't figure out, though, is why the President-elect is on the list. He was never part of the network. And another thing complicating this is that Koslowski has been retired a few years now. They tell me that the guy he turned the network over to is one of the people who've been killed. In fact, as far as we can tell, he was the first. Much of the rest of the network is still providing information, so someone else obviously picked up the reins. We don't know his name or the names of any people the new person may have recruited . . . or even how many," Grant sounded frustrated as he stood up and started pacing around the room.

"Was the President-elect involved in any of the operations? Would he have known Koslowski?" Sam followed Grant with her eyes.

"No," Thurmond replied. "He was an administrative officer, supervising the files and other paperwork in the DIA spaces in the Pentagon. I hardly knew him. I recall him being bright and ambitious and asking a lot of questions, most of which, for security reasons, I didn't answer. But he was strictly an eight-to-five guy. I just don't get it."

"Well, it seems to me we might find a way to get started by going through all these files, looking for clues," Sam suggested.

Grant snorted. "Yeah, and in about half an hour I would be going stark raving mad. Look, I gotta get outta the office. How about this as a start? You stay here and go through all the files and I'll try to see the President-elect to find out what he knows."

"Thanks," Sam said with a slight frown. "What'll I be looking for?"

"Anything that might show who was involved. Any mention of other names or reports that mention people who might be growing suspicious of any of the submitters, and so on. You'll know it when you see it. If you have any doubt, set it aside and I'll look at it when I get back."

"What if I miss something important?" Sam sounded worried.

Grant chuckled. "Don't worry about it. I just can't believe the solution will be in one single piece of information, anyway. My guess is that it'll be several little clues that we put together or follow down a path. If you miss one at this early research stage, we'll have time to come back around to it. Now get your nose into those files. And start with those cases that involved Koslowski. I'm convinced this whole thing revolves around his network somehow."

"Yes, sir . . . I mean, Grant." Sam sighed as she picked up the first of the many, many file folders on the table. And there were so many more in boxes stacked in a corner. She wondered if this might be an impossible task. And, no matter what Grant said, she was worried that she'd miss the one important clue in the files.

Grant picked up his new flip-open cell phone and headed outside the apartment building to call the number he was given for General Wheeler. After Wheeler answered, Grant reminded him that he was on an open phone and then brought him up to speed without mentioning details.

"Sir, the subject was located and the information obtained. But, you're the only person besides me who knows that. I'd like to keep it to just the two of us for a while."

Then he asked if the General could get him an appointment today with the President-elect.

Wheeler responded with, "Good work. I'll tell the President-elect's office it's urgent. How much time do you need? And, yeah, I'll cover your ass for a while on the other issue. But, I can't keep it just to the two of us very long." Wheeler actually chuckled as he said the last part. "Not a good business to lie to the DNI."

Thurmond smiled, "Well, I could use as much time with the President-elect as I can get, but I can cover most of what I need in twenty minutes, half an hour at the most."

Ten minutes later Grant's phone rang—it was General Wheeler.

"You got fifteen minutes at noon—sharp, while he's eating lunch. I'd get there ten minutes early in case his other meeting ends a little early. Don't count on it, though. They usually run late. Good luck."

"Thanks, General. Uh, have you heard anything from the DNI or Garcia at CIA?"

"Not a word."

"Good. I'll talk with you soon," Grant said as he closed his phone.

Grant arrived half an hour early and as he sat in the outer office waiting for his time with the President-elect, his cell phone rang. It was Sam.

"Grant, I think I may have stumbled onto something. I'm on the secure line."

Grant replied, "Don't say anything more. My cell phone isn't secure. They must have a secure phone here. I'll see if I can use it and call you right back."

Grant asked the assistant sitting outside the office if they had a secure phone he could use and was led inside to a red phone on the President-elect's desk.

"Keep it short, though," she said. "He'll be back momentarily."

Grant called Sam. Without preamble he said, "Okay, what do you have?"

"Well, I was reading through the tenth or eleventh file and I saw a notation that a list of names for a network in Eastern Europe had been permanently removed. That must have been the list you destroyed. It was a Koslowski file. You were right—the clue was in the Koslowski files. This has to have something to do with him." She sounded excited.

Grant was quiet for a moment as he thought about what Sam had said. "Damn. I remember something about that. It was nearly twenty years ago. That list was inadvertently left in a file folder that one of our guys reviewed. He was looking for matches between the list and people filing intelligence reports. I was back in town for a review and had the list in my office safe. He borrowed the list from me and when he didn't return it within the hour, I asked him where it was. He said something about probably leaving it in the file folder he had returned to admin. Wasn't really a big deal because everyone in admin was cleared, but I didn't want any list of people I controlled lying around, even if was only a partial list. I went to pick it up and the admin officer pulled it out and gave it to me. He must have inserted the note about it being removed. Is there a name on the note?"

Sam was so excited she almost shouted. "Grant, it's signed, LTJG T.R. Mason."

"Bingo! Okay, thanks. Great work. Gotta go . . . I'll call you on the way back." Sam was working out great, he thought, a big help.

Even though he sat in the President-elect's office while using the secure phone, he was startled when a voice behind him said: "Colonel, it's good to see you again. You haven't changed too much; hair a little grayer, less of it." Mason chuckled.

Thurmond stood up and moved from behind the President-elect's desk. "It's good to see you, too, sir. Thanks for making time for me." They both smiled as they shook hands.

"I assume this is about the subject that brought you back on active duty?" Mason asked.

"Yes, sir. I just need a few minutes of your time."

The President-elect sat down and motioned for Grant to do the same. "Time is something I have very little of these days. I'm really sorry, but I can only spare you fifteen minutes, one of which we've already used up. By the way, hope you don't mind my eating a sandwich while we talk. The only time I have to eat during the day is to squeeze meals in between meetings. Wonder if it will get any better when I'm President?"

Grant, not wanting to waste any more time, leaned forward, placed his hands on his knees and got right to it. "Sir, I just received some information that may help us keep this short. During the time when you were admin officer for the DIA department, I picked up a list of names from you that had inadvertently been left in a file folder. The person in my group who reviewed the list used it as a bookmark and forgot to remove it when he returned the folder to admin. After I picked it up, you made a notation in the file folder saying the list had been permanently removed."

"Yeah, it makes sense that I would. It was standard procedure. I can't say that I remember the actual incident, though. Hmmm. Wait a minute, I do remember something about that. It was highly unusual for anyone to permanently remove anything from the file folders. Our process was to count every page both when a folder was checked out and when it was returned. Any differences would be noted on the inside front of the file folder. I can't recall if there was any notation of the folder containing an extra page when it was returned. Do you remember who checked the folder back in? Was it me? Each folder should have a list of the names of both the person who checked it out and in and the admin duty officer who gave it to them and then received it back from them."

"Sir, I don't have a clue who checked it in. I have the file now, though, so I can look to see if anything was noted. I'll do that as soon as I get back."

"Colonel, you should know that, uh, there were times when the files were merely looked through to see if we could spot any pages out of order and every page wasn't always counted. That was strictly against policy, but, in the rush of things, it happened sometimes. That may have happened in this case. Damn, I sure hope I wasn't the one who checked it back in," Mason said shaking his head slightly.

"Sir, the important thing now is that we may know why your name was on that piece of paper they found near one of the bodies. We have to assume that someone on that list knew you saw his name. Did you ever tell anyone about the list?" Grant asked.

"Oh, possibly. Since it was an unusual occurrence I may have talked about it at a staff meeting. If so, probably fifteen people, both civilian and military, heard about it. I don't know. They were all cleared, though, and they were just administrative types. I think I used it as an example of what can happen if we didn't follow procedures."

"Sir, I may ask you later to help us put together the list of people who were at that staff meeting. Right now I'll see if I can get the minutes of all the staff meetings during your tour. I'll let you know if I need anything further. I'm going to attempt to compile a list of all the people who might have heard or seen that list. We'll have to check on the current whereabouts of each of them. It's possible that we might have had a mole who fed the list of names back to the Soviets. If that's the case, your name would probably have been mentioned. Thanks for your time today and if you think of anything that might help, *anything*, no matter how insignificant you think it is, please call me."

"I will, Colonel, you can count on it." the President-elect said earnestly, then returned to eating his sandwich.

Grant took that as a signal the meeting was over, so he stood up, said goodbye and left.

Chapter 14

I minus 48
Moscow

Drugs, the Eastern European thought. That's the key. Not like the old days when you had to torture information out of people. He didn't mind the killing, but torture was distasteful to him. All the screaming and blood and then having to dispose of the bodies to keep others from knowing they were tortured before they died. And it took too long, sometimes days. Today you just gave 'em a shot and seconds later they're blabbering, answering everything you ask. You can even add a substance that keeps them from remembering anything about the incident. He was so accurate at mixing drugs now that they wouldn't even miss the time. But Koslowski had to die anyway. No one who had seen his name could live. Now he had six new people he hadn't known about before his visit to Krakow. They might have seen his name and would also have to die over the next few weeks. It surprised him to find that some of them now lived in Russia and all but one of those in Moscow, his home for now.

He thought about all the years he had fed disinformation through Koslowski, throwing in just enough real stuff to keep the Americans believing all the lies. Now he had been secretly indicted by the Russian government for throwing in too much real information, supposedly giving the Americans an uneven edge and costing Russia valuable leverage. His one trusted contact remaining in the new intelligence services had sent him a message to disappear. If they could find him, they were going to arrest him and he knew he'd never be found. There would never be a trial. The KGB hadn't gone away, it was just renamed and they were as ruthless and lethal as ever. He was sure, though, that he had kept his new identity secret enough so that no one could track him down. His code name was the only link between his old identity and his new identity. Of course they knew the code name and his old identity. That's how they provided him with the disinformation and how he told them what information the people in Koslowski's network were giving to the Americans. He didn't see everything all the people gave, but enough

53

to give the Soviet Union and later Russia a little edge. Knowing both what lies he was feeding the Americans and what real information the others gave, allowed his government to control America's reaction in certain situations. And yes, sometimes he had to throw in more real information than he probably should have, but he wanted the Americans to trust him enough to believe the misinformation he supplied.

Also, he wasn't naïve enough to believe he was the only double agent the Soviets used. There could have been dozens. In addition, the Soviet Union had deep cover moles everywhere in the United States military organizations back then, even in administrative roles. But always in sensitive organizations where their people had access to highly classified information, especially anything that identified the source of that information or how they had obtained it. That's how he'd learned that someone deep inside one of America's intelligence organizations had seen his code name on a list of known informants. And now, when his own government had turned against him, he needed to make sure that when he left Russia permanently for the US, no one was left alive who could tell either the Americans or the Russians that he was the one who had been a double agent for over twenty years. They all had to die, including the key Americans who had seen the list. One in particular, was going to be a difficult target—Mason, the new American President. But he had a plan.

Chapter 15

I minus 45
Washington

"The clock's ticking, Sam. We've connected the President-elect to the list, but we're no closer to finding out who's doing this." Grant and Sam were having an early evening glass of wine before dinner and recapping what they'd discovered during the day. The secure phone rang and Sam answered.

"SFC Rogers. How may I help you?"

Grant looked at her, pointed to himself and shook his head, meaning "I'm not here".

"This is the DNI, put Thurmond on."

"Oh, I'm sorry sir; he's not in the office at the moment. May I take a message?"

"Tell him he damn well better call my secure number at home within half an hour."

"Sir, I'm not sure I can reach him within half an hour."

"You'd better." And with that, Barry hung up.

"Grant, it looks like you have a call to make. That was the DNI and he wants to hear from you within half an hour."

"Oh, let him stew for a while. I'll call him back in a little while from my cell phone and tell him I have no access to a secure line until tomorrow. He'll have no choice but to accept it."

"You really think it's a good idea to antagonize the DNI?" Sam asked.

Grant smiled, thinking of what General Wheeler had said about lying to the DNI. "I'm probably the only one who can get away with it, so sure. I'll calm him down later."

Meanwhile, Barry had immediately called Garcia at CIA to learn that he hadn't heard from Thurmond, either. His next call was to General Wheeler, who brought him up to speed with all the information he had received from Grant earlier in the day, leaving out the part about Grant getting the list. The General knew it was risky holding out information from the DNI, but this was obviously important to Thurmond and he had to trust him. As was his custom, the Barry used the secure phone in his car and had the speakerphone on for the entire conversation.

After dropping the DNI at his home, Riley drove away and called his contact number from his cell phone. With the speakerphone, he had been able to hear both sides of the conversation, so he could repeat everything he had heard to the voice mail service the line was connected to. He had only spoken to a real person a couple of times, mostly just the robot voice that told him to leave a message at the tone. He couldn't help thinking . . . easy money.

***

After finishing his glass of wine, Grant used his cell phone to call the DNI at his home.

When Barry answered, he said, "Sir, I understand you called. I'm out of the facility right now and am calling on a non-secure phone. I hope it will be okay for me to call you in the morning and give you a complete update."

"I talked to General Wheeler a few minutes ago. Do you have anything that he doesn't know about?" Barry responded.

"Not really, sir. We're still going through the files trying to match names to incidents. We've not discovered anything that would point to the killer." He couldn't mention their discovery about the list being seen by the President-elect until he could talk with the DNI on a secure line.

"Okay, thanks. I don't have to tell you, Colonel, that we're running outta time. A lot of people have complete confidence in you, believe that you're the right person for this job . . . and I'm one of them by the way. Keep me in the loop and let me know how I can help. If you run into any roadblocks or bureaucratic bullshit or stalling let me know. I promise you I'll clear the way immediately. Any blocks I can't clear, the President-elect can. We're both at your disposal. And, by the way, I'm keeping the current President briefed every day. You can count on him, also."

"Well, thank you sir. That's more than I could hope for."

After he hung up he turned to Sam and with his shoulders up and his hands spread out in front of him said, "I may be forming a new opinion of the DNI. He may turn out to be a good guy after all. If he's serious about helping, he certainly could be useful. I just don't want him to get in the way. Thoughts?"

Sam looked puzzled for a moment, then said, "Geez, Grant, I just don't know where to turn. I'm way out of my league here and feeling a bit overwhelmed at the moment. Do we have time to take a break? Maybe go get dinner, talk about something else for a while?"

This rather abrupt shift in topic left Grant puzzled, but he decided to put a good face on it and in a positive tone said, "Sure. Sounds good. Let's go."

Dinner was uneventful. They talked about each other, sharing things about their pasts. It was easy banter. For Grant, it was much easier being with Sam than it had been being with any other woman in a long time. Usually he was tight lipped, having little to say, allowing his companion to do most of the talking. Tonight, however, with Sam, it seemed comfortable and he talked freely. She was the same, smiling as she recalled her life. She talked about high school, how she didn't care much for the high drama of the social scene, how volleyball was her life. She said she didn't date much, although, looking the way she did, Grant couldn't figure out why. Maybe the guys were too intimidated—she *was* a force.

Grant talked about his time in high school, the girlfriend he'd had all four years who'd dumped him in his first year at the academy. He smiled, recalling the football, the camaraderie, and the few classmates he'd kept in touch with. Two hours flew by and the waiter hovered close to their table, clearly hoping they'd finish up and settle the bill.

Finally, Sam said, "Suppose we oughta pay. Looks like he's trying to clean everything up and go home."

Grant insisted on paying. After all he was on full expenses; he could afford to be generous.

They continued talking as they walked back to the apartment, arriving a little after 10:00 p.m.

"How about one more glass of wine?" Sam asked when they were inside.

Grant hesitated a moment and then said, "Sure—red or white?"

"I think I'll continue with red, thanks," she smiled . . . something she seemed to be doing a lot when she was around Grant.

While Grant opened the wine, Sam lit the three candles that were on the coffee table in front of the sofa. As he brought her the wine, Grant couldn't help noticing how attractive she was, sitting on the sofa in the candlelight with her hair down. It was longer than he thought. She should wear it down more often . . . screw regs. They continued to talk, getting more and more into personal things they normally wouldn't share. Although neither would admit it, the attraction was obvious to both.

It was after midnight when they went to bed in their separate bedrooms. Grant lay in bed thinking about the evening and his growing attraction to Sam. He pictured them together in easier times, smiling, holding hands, kissing . . . .Wait. He was close to twenty years older than Sam. What was he thinking? She probably looked at him as a father figure. What a schmuck he was. Grant turned over and closed his eyes to go to sleep, but lay awake a while longer. He just couldn't get Sam out of his mind. He didn't need this right now. He had a job to do and this distraction could get someone killed. He finally drifted off to sleep, but Sam was in his dreams.

Chapter 16

I minus 44
Koslowski

"Hey, Thurmond, this is Garcia. Call me back. One of our guys who reviews the news found something important. You'll wanna know." Garcia left a secure number where Thurmond could reach him, hung up and turned to another case file.

Grant called back within fifteen minutes: "Garcia, I got your message. What's up?"

"Where the hell you been? I've been trying to reach you since we got back."

"Around. Fill me in." Grant responded, determined not to reveal anything to Garcia.

"You on a secure line?"

"Yes," Grant answered.

"Well, I put the word out to the Eastern European desk to look for anything that mentioned Koslowski. They got a hit this morning. The Krakow paper carried a small item about a long-term government employee dying. It went into his past about how he secretly aided the underground right after WWII during the Soviet occupation. Nothing about him and us. Thought you'd like to know the old guy croaked."

"Did it say how he died?" Grant asked.

"Yeah, said of natural causes. Looks like he just stopped breathing."

"Okay, Garcia, thanks for the info. Gotta go." Grant said.

"Hey, wait a minute! What are you up to—we're supposed to be partners, remember?" Garcia stood up and leaned over with one hand on his desk.

"Probably same as you. Just going through files, trying to see anything that stands out. A needle in the haystack, but it's the only thing we can do right now. Want to help? We have hundreds."

"Help go through files? No thanks, but keep me in the loop. I'm under a lot of pressure from the DDI to keep her up to speed." Garcia sat back down behind his desk.

"You got it. You get any brainy ideas, let me know. See ya," Grant said, hanging up without saying anything further. He smiled.

After Grant hung up, Garcia sat for a while, then slammed his open palms down on his desk. "He's up to something!" he exclaimed out loud.

At the same time, Grant turned to Sam and said, "Okay, let's go. We have to get to the source—that means going back to Poland and probably Moscow. Get visas and tickets for us both. We'll pose as an American couple traveling together to see the world. It'll work. And, while we're waiting for the visas, I need a history lesson. I know there've been a lot of changes after the Soviet Union split up, but I really haven't kept track of them. Would you see if we can get someone from the Eastern Europe desk to bring me up to speed?"

"I'll get right on it. I assume, since we're going as tourists, we won't be using our government passports?" Sam asked as she started towards the door.

"Not this time. Remember, we're just two people traveling together to see the sights." Grant said, thinking, I wish.

Chapter 17

I Minus 43

"Okay, so a united Germany I get. Poland is the same and so are Romania, Hungary, and Bulgaria. Czechoslovakia has been split up and part of it is the Czech Republic and the other part is Slovakia. There is no Yugoslavia?" Grant asked, raising his eyebrows.

"No, sir," the young analyst from the Eastern European Desk said. "Yugoslavia is now six independent states: Serbia is the largest and contains the old capital Belgrade. Then, in alphabetical order, there's Albania, Bosnia, Croatia, Macedonia and Slovenia. Also, in addition to the Eastern European states, there are a lot of other former Soviet Union republics that have declared their independence: Estonia, Latvia, Lithuania, Belarus, Ukraine, Moldova, Armenia, Azerbaijan, Georgia, Kazakhstan, Kyrgyzstan, Tajikistan, Turkmenistan, and Uzbekistan. For travel purposes, all of these now must be dealt with as independent states."

"Holy shit. I'll never remember all this." At that point Grant yelled out, "Sam! Get in here!"

"Yes, sir?" Sam asked from the doorway.

"You'd better study these maps. I'm going to rely on you to keep all this straight." Sam thought Grant looked really frustrated and knew she'd better make sure she was up to speed. It was obvious that Grant wasn't going to remember all the names.

"Yes, sir. Most of it I think I already know, but I'll study them." She responded, smiling slightly.

Grant liked that slight smile she had. He'd noticed it before. "Okay, thanks. I also need maps the way it used to be so I can plan our travel. If I have to use the modern maps, I'll never find where I want ta go. I'll figure out the plan using the old maps and you'll have to show me how that relates to the new ones." He then turned to the briefer and said, "Thanks, John. Appreciate your time and patience."

"No sweat, sir." The briefer left.

Sam, bending over a desktop PC said, "Grant, I'm bringing up the pre-Soviet collapse maps now. You can just scroll through them to get at each country."

"What ever happened to the pull down maps we used to have?" Grant asked, his eyebrows knotted together. "They were big and easy to read and worked like window shades." Then, looking down at the personal computer on Sam's desk, he said, "I'll never be able to find anything on that small screen."

Sam chuckled, "I haven't seen one of those pull down maps since I was in sixth grade. We had some tactical maps in combat, but even there we used PCs for planning. We even had touch screen panels in the field. Today *everything's* computerized. But, for you, we might have better luck projecting the PC images on a large screen. Why don't I see if I can set that up?"

Grant felt like an idiot. An old idiot. "Sure, let's give it a try. Where'd you find those maps online?"

"They were produced by the CIA," Sam said matter-of-factly.

"You have access to the CIA computer system?" Grant exclaimed in a surprised voice, his eyebrows tightly knotted again.

"In a way, sir. The CIA has an internal intelligence file-sharing protocol that we have access to via ARPANET."

"ARPANET? What's that?" Grant asked.

"DARPA is the Defense Advanced Research Projects Agency. They developed a backbone network allowing computer users to access other's files. Part of that technology has been commercialized and is being used by civilian companies and individuals. That part is the Internet. But part remains only within Department of Defense and a subset of that is for the intelligence community. It provides a secure way to access other computer systems. Every user has to be registered and has a user profile allowing them to access certain systems and certain files within that system. It's all based on clearance level and need to know."

"And you can just log on and get to their files, right?"

"Not *all* their files, just those that fit my profile. As part of DIA, I do have access to nearly all background files, just not anything that deals directly with sources, agents or operations. A lot of what the CIA has in their files is demographic data on countries. It's not really classified, but provides background info for mission planners. I was briefed and got a profile established when they first decided to bring you back. They thought it would provide another useful resource for us to use."

"That's great. I never knew that even existed. Sure glad to have you on board. How're you coming on the visas?" Grant asked.

Sam looked at his and shook her head. "Can't do them until you tell me where we're going. We'd better start planning the trip. I presume you want me to make sure we're not overheard or interrupted while we talk?"

"Yeah. I don't want anyone to know where we're really going. Get visas for everywhere. That way they won't be entirely sure where we are at any one point in time. Okay, let's get what equipment we need and go back to the SCIF."

"Should take me no more than ten minutes to check out a projector. Be right back, then we can leave."

Grant said seriously, "Good. I expect Garcia or Barry to pop their head in at any minute and I don't want to be here to explain what we're doing." He then went down the hall to get some of that Navy coffee while Sam went looking for a projector.

Sam was able to quickly find a projector and within fifteen minutes they were leaving the Pentagon parking lot heading towards Key Bridge.

***

They hooked the projector up to a PC in the outer offices of the SCIF and displayed the maps on a blank wall. This area was less secure than the actual lead-lined SCIF and they were able to obtain access to the internet. After spending several hours pouring over maps and mentally comparing the list of names and locations he had gotten from Koslowski, Grant had the trip planned. They left the SCIF and went upstairs to the apartment. Sam went into her bedroom to freshen up.

Sam had been gone for less than fifteen minutes when Grant spread out a pile of papers on the dining room table and called, "Sam, can you come in here, please?"

"Yes?" She said, coming into the dining area.

Without looking up, Grant said, "Okay, here's where we're going." With that he laid out the trip.

After explaining where they would be going, he said, "I don't know how long this is going to take, so only book the first flight over, leaving the return open. We'll rent a car and drive to most places and just book flights at the last minute where we have greater distances. That leaves fewer records of where we've been and it'll be nearly impossible to predict where we'll be."

With raised eyebrows and her hands on her hips, she asked, "What'll we tell the DNI?"

Grant smiled. "Just the overview. I'll tell him that most of the places we'll have to go will come from the information received from each person I'm able to contact. So, at this time, I just don't know where all we'll be. He'll understand that. Did you apply for visas for all the countries?"

"I did, but haven't gotten the passports back, yet. Takes a little while to get them to all the embassies. But, citing needs of the government, I asked to expedite the process, so they're messengering them between each of the facilities. I expect them back to us tomorrow or the next day."

Grant looked surprised. "Great work. But, I'd really like to get going, so if we don't get 'em tomorrow, see if someone can shake 'em loose. In the meantime, I'll call General Wheeler and the DNI and fill them in on the overview."

Grant sat down on the living room sofa in front of the secure phone on the coffee table and dialed General Wheeler. When the General was on the line Grant leaned back comfortably and said, "General, just wanted to let you know that I'm heading back to Poland to follow up on the information I've gotten by going through the files. There are a number of people I need to see in person and I expect them to lead me to others. So I'll be leaving within the next couple of days and will be back in about a week."

"Okay Colonel. Thanks for letting me know. I'll run interference from this end, but you need to fill in the DNI before you go."

"Thanks, General. I'm calling him next." Grant said, hanging up.

Grant leaned forward again and dialed the DNI's secure line, knowing it would transfer to his car line if he wasn't in the office. Barry, in his car heading to a luncheon with the President-elect and the soon-to-be First Lady, punched the speakerphone button on the second ring. "Barry."

"Sir, this is Grant Thurmond. I'm calling to update you on where we are. I am . . ."

The DNI interrupted. "Thurmond, I hope you're making progress. We're well into the plans for the inauguration and I need to know that the President-elect is going to be safe. We're taking extreme precautions, but I don't need to tell you what a disaster it would be if an attempt were made on his life. Even if it were unsuccessful it would be embarrassing." The DNI sounded deadly serious.

Grant matched his tone, "I know, sir. As I was saying, I'm heading to Europe to follow up on some leads I've uncovered in the files. I'll be gone about a week and will call you immediately upon my return."

"Keep it to a week unless you're really on to something. If you do uncover something we need to know, get to a US Embassy or Attaché office and use their secure communications line to brief me. Don't wait 'til you get back. Understand? Oh, by the way, where're you flying into?"

"Yes sir. Got it. I'll let you know immediately if I find something vital. I'm flying into Warsaw. I'll stay there for a couple of days. I have a room at the Hilton downtown."

"Okay. And if you need anything on this end, I'll make it happen. Just let me know. And don't forget to call me *immediately* if you find anything," the DNI said adamantly and hung up.

"Yes, sir. See you when I get back." Grant said to a dead phone. But he was satisfied he'd put the DNI on hold, at least for now.

He sat for a while with his arms crossed over his chest thinking about what he needed to do in the next couple of days to prepare for the trip. Wonder if I could get a gun into Poland, he thought. He knew that if he declared it, the airlines would carry it in the baggage compartment and let him claim it when he arrived. He decided it would be too revealing picking it up and then going through customs. He'd never be able to explain why he had it. Why would a tourist traveling with his female friend need a handgun? The only thing that would work was for him to prove he was on official US business and show his government passport. Even if they bought that, it would call too much attention to himself. Better leave it at home. Probably have to review those damn maps again, though.

***

Later that night, Riley called his contact number and left a voice mail message: "Hey, it looks like this guy Thurmond is heading to Europe. He's gonna fly into Warsaw in the next couple of days and stay at the Hilton. If I hear more, I'll let you know. Oh, and he said something about something happening to the President-elect at his inauguration. He didn't say what exactly, but it sounded to me like someone was going to try to kill him. He also said security was going to be really tight. Not sure you care about that information, but you said tell you everything." Yes, it certainly was easy money. Just listen and leave a message.

**

When Vladimir picked up the message he couldn't believe what he heard. How could they possibly know about the inauguration? Well, it didn't bother him much about how tight security was going to be. He had a foolproof plan. But, this guy Thurmond had to be the next person eliminated. He knew way too much and was getting too close. He was already on the list to die, but he had planned it for later, when it was more convenient. Well, at least now he wouldn't have to go all the way to the US to kill him.

He'd head to Warsaw this afternoon and get there before Thurmond did. He had some business to attend to there anyway. Then he made a plan for finding Thurmond. Starting tomorrow, he'd just sit in the lobby of the Hilton, close enough to the registration desk to overhear everyone checking in. When he heard the right name, he'd casually glance over to see what he looked like. That way he could follow him and take him out when the time was right. It would be great if he could meet up with him late at night in a dark alley, but, well, that only happened in movies. The man code named Vladimir chuckled at the thought.

Chapter 18

I Minus 42
Warsaw

"Wow, the air quality here is worse than D.C.," Sam coughed, wrinkling her nose. "Smells like coal smoke." They stood just outside the hotel entrance while the bellman was retrieving their luggage from the trunk of the taxi.

"Yeah," Thurmond replied, "but it's a lot better than it used to be. Last time I was here you could barely see the sun—not that I had a chance to see it very often. The whole sky was a vast gray cloud of pollutants, so many factories spewing out tons of junk into the atmosphere. Looks like they're trying to clean up their act a little bit. Still using coal-fired furnaces, though. Let's go check in." Thurmond lowered his voice to just above a whisper and leaned closer to Sam, "Uh, I'm not exactly sure how to work this. We're supposed to be traveling as a couple and it'll seem really odd for us to get two rooms."

To Sam, he seemed embarrassed so she said, "Don't worry about sharing a room. Just make sure we get two beds. And, I hope you brought pajamas," Sam replied with a smile.

And I hope you forgot yours, Grant thought and then smiled, hoping she couldn't read his thoughts.

As they entered, he saw there were a lot of people sitting in the chairs and sofas scattered about the crowded lobby. So many, in fact, that as they approached the registration counter, he didn't notice one man sitting nearby who glanced up while pretending to read a newspaper. When Thurmond told the desk clerk his name, the man looked again; this time giving him a more thorough review, committing his appearance to memory. The man noticed the girl, too. Good looking. He didn't know who she was, but she was obviously with Thurmond. She'd be easy to remember. His mind went through his usual thought sequence . . . another operative? . . . someone he should worry about?

Once Grant and Sam were in their room and the bellman delivered their luggage, Grant suggested they go down to the hotel restaurant for lunch.

"Okay, that sounds great. First I have to unpack, hang up some things and freshen up a bit. I don't want to have to iron anything. You go ahead and I'll join you in a few minutes."

"I'll meet you there," Grant replied and went into the hall towards the elevators. It wasn't wrinkled clothes he was worried about.

Grant took the elevator to the first floor, wandered around the lobby until he found the restaurant and took a seat in a booth near the door. The man, still sitting reading his paper, noticed him as he entered the lobby and watched him go into the restaurant. From his vantage point, he couldn't see where Thurmond sat, but there was only one way in and one out. He knew Thurmond wouldn't be going out another door. The man waited for about three minutes, didn't want to seem too obvious, and entered the restaurant. Without waiting to be seated, he took a table in a place in the darkest corner he could find.

Grant casually looked around and noticed that the seats were covered with a red plastic-like material and, at least in his booth, there were several punctures in the plastic where the stuffing showed through. He continued to look around, checking out everyone in the restaurant. Since no one knew they were in Poland, Grant was sure they weren't being watched, but, well, you couldn't be too careful. After a few minutes, a waitress approached his booth and asked, in Polish, what he wanted. He asked if she spoke English, to which she replied, "Yes, some."

"Enough that I can order in English?"

"Yes," she said. "We have all learned English because we have so many foreign visitors to serve. English is the standard language for travelers, you know, no matter where they are from."

"Great. I'm expecting my companion to arrive shortly and we'll be having lunch."

"Would you like anything while you wait?" the waitress asked.

"I think I'll have a beer." Grant responded.

"What beer you will have?"

"Do you have Tyskie?" He asked. It was the only beer name he could remember.

"Yes, of course," she responded with a smile.

"Then that's what I'll have," he said.

The waitress soon returned with a full pilsner glass of beer, topped by a generous head. Grant took a sip, wiped off the foam mustache and thought, Man, that's great. Better than I remembered. Wonder if they've changed the formula since the Soviets left?

He finished one glass and, breaking his usual routine of only having one drink when on a mission, started on the second by the time Sam arrived.

"What're you drinking?" she asked as she sat down across the booth from him.

"Tyskie, a local beer. I'll order one for you."

"Thanks," she smiled.

As this was happening, in the dark corner of the restaurant Vladimir watched both of them as they talked. He had not been informed that Thurmond would be traveling with a companion. Again he thought, was she an agent? A girlfriend? No, he'd never risk a girlfriend on a mission. Whatever, she was certainly an added complication, but not an insurmountable one. In handling her, though, he had to assume that she was trained and could be dangerous.

After a very pleasant, local-style lunch of sausages and potatoes, Grant suggested to Sam that they walk around Warsaw's downtown area, both to familiarize themselves with the layout and to see the sights. Although he didn't want to alarm Sam, what he really wanted was to see if they were being followed. After strolling along the main street for about half an hour, Grant paused a moment to look into a store front window.

"You seem awfully interested in women's clothing," Sam joked with a smile.

Grant replied in a low voice, "Just checking on something." He then bent over to retie his right shoe, taking a good look around as he did so.

His tone got Sam's attention. "What? Did you see something?"

"I thought I saw someone following us, but I don't see him now. Wish I'd gotten a better look at him. Didn't see the face at all. It may be a coincidence, although I'm not really a big believer in coincidences. We'd better stay alert. Let me know immediately if you see *anything* out of the ordinary, no matter how unimportant you think it is."

"Will do. Now you've got me a little nervous." Sam was no longer smiling.

"Good. You'll be more observant if you're expecting something to happen. Just don't be obvious about it." Grant replied, then suggested they continue walking.

Grant didn't notice anything suspicious for the rest of their walk and when they arrived back at the hotel a couple of hours later he told Sam he needed time to go over the list and study the detailed map of Warsaw. He knew the markings, the mark points and the meeting time and place for each of the three people remaining in this area. He explained to Sam that his plan was to try the marks this afternoon. He had no knowledge of whether the contacts were still alive and, if so, if any of them were still in the area. Nor did he know if they would follow up on the marks even if they saw them. But, it was all he had.

Koslowski told him that although several of the people in the network had moved, some back to Russia, he thought these three were still in place. Grant felt he had no choice but to go for it. Since the old scheduled meeting times were hours apart, he could do all three in one day. Hopefully he could wrap up the three interviews within two or three days and get onto the next leg of the trip, wherever that might be. Who knows, maybe he would get enough information to even identify the killer while he's here. He wasn't counting on it, however. These things usually didn't work out that well.

Chapter 19

I Minus 42
Vladimir

Vladimir watched as Thurmond and his lady friend passed through the lobby on the way to their room. He'd followed Thurmond and the girl when they left the hotel and when Thurmond stopped to tie his shoe he was certain he'd been noticed. That's when he split off onto one of the side streets and returned to the hotel. Better to lose contact than to be identified. He'd been sitting in the lobby ever since.

He was sure that at some point Thurmond was going to try to make contact with the three informants in Warsaw. Koslowski, under the influence of a powerful truth serum, gave Vladimir those names and with a little research he'd discovered the address of one of the three on the list. A quick visit late last night and that informant, who fortunately lived alone, was dead. Of the remaining two, one was a more common name and there were multiple choices of addresses listed in the phone book, so he couldn't pin down which one belonged to the target. With his limited time on this trip, he knew he wouldn't be able to try all the addresses. Anyway, asking the kind of questions he needed answers to would make some of them suspicious. He wouldn't want any of them left alive to alert the police and he couldn't afford to take out all the people at all the addresses. So, he needed another plan for that one.

The third person had just one name, so it was probably a code name, just like his. He didn't have any idea how to contact that person, so he'd decided to follow Thurmond to the first meeting and identify the contact. His plan was to follow the contact back home and, if possible, kill him there. If the timing wasn't right, he'd come back another time. At least he'd know where the contact lived. He knew Thurmond would return to the hotel so it would be easy enough to pick up the tail later. He would then try to take out Thurmond and the third contact when they met. If the woman was with Thurmond throughout this, he'd have to find a way to eliminate her too.

71

He figured he'd have two or three days to make the hits . . . plenty of time. He was also staying at the Hilton. It was really expensive for him, but a great way to cover the true reason for his loitering in the hotel lobby. He decided to go upstairs to his room and check his US voice mail. All in all this was turning out just fine. Maybe he'd have a vodka from the mini bar in his room. Just one, though, he needed to stay sharp and they were really expensive.

Chapter 20

I Minus 42
Warsaw

Grant, with Sam in tow, headed out to the first marking location. Just to be on the safe side, they exited the hotel through a side entrance, rather than the lobby. He didn't have any hard evidence they were being watched, but it was always good to mix things up a bit. He wanted to make sure he didn't unnecessarily endanger Sam, but she would be good cover as he made marks at the three separate locations. Then, if all went well, the first meeting would be tomorrow at 9:00 a.m. The other two were at 12:00 noon and 3:00 p.m. respectively. They had plenty of time between meets to get answers to the questions he had for each of the informants. If they didn't show, the arrangement was that he'd be at the meeting place at the same time for the following two days. He'd have to assume something might have come up and they didn't see the mark the first day or couldn't leave work at the appointed time. A lot of things could happen, that's why they were allowed three days to make contact. If they never showed, Grant would have to decide whether to try again, or just assume the contact was no longer available and try something else. He wasn't sure what that something else would be.

When they got to the first location, Grant said, "Okay Sam, you look casually around while I bend down to tie my shoe. If all's clear, just say 'okay.' Got it? Then I'll make the mark on the curb."

"Let's do it," Sam replied.

Grant bent down with a piece of white chalk concealed in his hand. Tying his shoe with the chalk in his hand was a bit clumsy, but as he finished Sam gave the okay. He quickly wrote 'V/' on the curb and stood up. They then walked away. So far, so good. This was easier with someone watching for you. In the past, he'd had to do most things by himself. For having no experience in the field, Sam was working out just fine.

The next two marks, one on the corner of a brick building and the other on a telephone pole, went well and Grant and Sam returned to the hotel. Now came the part he hated most—waiting. Not his best thing, especially since he didn't know the faces of the people he was trying to meet. They could walk right past him and he wouldn't know. They were supposed to approach him with a code phrase. If he gave the right response, they would nod and he would catch up with them as they walked away. Same routine he used with Koslowski. Grant sure hoped this wasn't a wild goose chase that would waste three or four precious days.

The next morning, Grant and Sam were having breakfast and exchanging pleasantries in the hotel restaurant when Sam suddenly stopped smiling and became serious.

"This is going to be safe, isn't it? I mean, you're not in any danger meeting these people?"

"No, this is a piece of cake. These are brave people, but are low to mid-level bureaucrats in government service. They're not dangerous at all," Grant said confidently.

Sam looked concerned and chewed on her lower lip a bit before answering. "Grant, what if one of them is the killer? Have you thought about that?"

"I have and I'd like to think that with a little questioning, I could pick him out." Grant replied.

Sam didn't think Grant sounded one hundred percent confident and she wasn't reassured. "Well, you sure you don't want me along as lookout?" Sam asked.

"No, I'm afraid they might get spooked seeing two people, and I'm not going to let you out of my sight except here at the hotel."

"I don't feel like I'm helping much," Sam said. "And I'm worried about you getting into trouble and not having a backup."

Grant smiled slightly, reached across the table to touch her arm and said, "Don't worry about it. There'll be plenty of opportunity later for you to help. Let's just see how it goes with the first one."

After breakfast, Grant set out for his first meet. He left Sam at the hotel, promising to return immediately after the meeting. The meeting place was a certain marker deep inside the Mausoleum Kaukaski. It was an easy trek from the apartments just across Mlynarska Street where he made his first mark but quite a distance from the Hilton. Grant flagged down a taxi and, with all the traffic around him, didn't notice when a non-descript car pulled out from the curb a few cars behind him on the busy thoroughfare. Not that he was on high alert. No one knew they were here, so he was pretty certain no one would be following him. He was still cautious, just not as intense as he would be if others knew he was here. He certainly didn't see how the killer would know.

Grant waited at the marker for over two hours, but no one approached him. He returned to the hotel and briefed Sam. He had the same lack of success for the next two meetings that were scheduled that day. He was a little discouraged, but was used to this activity taking more than one day. Tomorrow he'd start all over. That was the way this job was . . . mostly boring.

Meanwhile, Vladimir was elated. He had successfully followed Thurmond to three locations, waiting at each in one spot for more than an hour. No one paid Thurmond any attention and no one talked with him. They must have been no shows, but there were clearly three separate meetings planned. That made sense since there were three names on Koslowski's Warsaw list. But, he was disappointed that he didn't know how Thurmond set up the meetings. Obviously Thurmond had slipped out without him noticing. He'd have to be more diligent. His days were going to get a little longer. He had to get up earlier and go to his room later, and he needed a better vantage point in the hotel lobby—one where he could see the elevator. The hotel was kind enough to have the elevator ding when it arrived on the lobby floor. That would help him. He would only have to look at the elevator when it dinged.

***

The next day was equally unsuccessful, with no one showing up at any of the three meeting places. That night at dinner, Sam observed that Grant was noticeably quieter. He would answer her questions, but if she stopped talking the conversation lagged. Finally, she had to ask.

"This getting to you?" she asked.

Grant shrugged, "Yeah, a little. I was sure at least one of them would show up. I'm out of practice, I guess. This used to be a fairly common occurrence and I just took it in stride. But now, with the President-elect's life hanging in the balance, it seems like we're just wasting time. But, you know, there just isn't any choice but to continue."

"Well, we've got another day tomorrow. Maybe someone will

come." Sam replied, trying to cheer him up a bit. He just shrugged again.

The next day, the first meet was once again a no show. Grant waited over two hours before he gave up. At the second, closer to downtown at the intersection of two busy streets, Grant was approached by a middle-aged woman who looked to be in her 50's. In broken English, she first asked him the time, then directions to a tobacco shop. Bingo! The right questions. Grant gave the prepared responses; the lady nodded, crossed the busy street, and began walking along the curb on a side street.

Grant waited until she was half a block down the side street before going after her. As he caught up to her, he noticed that the sidewalk was partially blocked off for repairs. Since his contact was forced to walk along the curb, he had no choice but to walk on the street surface. Even though she was walking on a surface five inches higher than the street, Grant still towered over her. She was small and walked slowly. There was no parking on this side of the street, so nothing got in Grant's way as they walked. Cars were zooming around them, but having cars pass close by didn't bother Grant. This was Eastern Europe and many drivers left little room for error when passing by pedestrians. Grant was so intent on looking into the woman's eye's while telling her why he was making contact that he didn't notice one of the cars coming down the street heading right for him. Grant, hearing an engine roar, looked up just in time to see the car bearing down on him only ten feet away. He immediately leapt to the left with the idea of pushing the woman out of the way, but too late. The car, which had to be traveling at least 70 kilometers an hour, hit both of them head on.

When Grant awoke, he was lying on his back, but not in the street, and was confused because he was surrounded by people dressed in white. Then it came back to him—he was hit by a car. His first thought was his contact.

"Excuse me, does anyone speak English?" Grant croaked to the crowd of people bending over him.

One of the men answered in English: "Yes, we do. But we want you to remain quiet while we finish. I will answer your questions at that time."

"What about the woman who was next to me? Is she all right?" His voice was a little closer to normal this time.

"There was a woman who was also hit, but unfortunately, she is dead. Please, lie still while we finish."

"Do you know who hit us? It looked like they were coming straight for us."

"I can see that you are going to be a difficult patient. If I allow the policeman to answer your immediate questions now, will you allow us to finish up while you are talking?"

"Sure." With that, Grant tried to sit up but was immediately gripped with severe pain.

"Ooooh, that hurts. How bad is it?" he asked, lying back down.

"It could have been worse. You have a couple fractured ribs, and though painful, none of the fractures are serious. You also have four cuts that have so far required a total of twenty-two stitches and you may have internal injuries. We will not know about that until we can schedule you for an MRI and the results come back. That could take up to two days. Okay, what are your questions?"

Grant turned his head towards the policeman. "The car, has anyone talked to the driver?"

"The car has not been located. Witnesses only described it as small and dark. It looked just like every other car on the road and had nothing to make it stand out. They could not see who was inside."

"So you have no idea who did this?" Grant asked.

"No. But we will continue our investigation. He was probably drunk. We have many drunk drivers in Warsaw. Now that I have answered your questions, I need you to answer some questions from me."

"Okay, but I don't know much." Grant replied.

"Who was the woman that was killed?" the policeman asked.

"I don't know. She was just someone on the street I was asking directions from. I've never seen her before. I don't know her name or anything about her," Grant lied.

"What are you doing in Warsaw?"

"I'm here with a female companion on holiday," Grant replied.

"Where is she?" the policeman continued.

"She's back at the hotel, the Hilton. Would someone please call her and tell her where I am?"

"Yes" answered the policeman, "I'll do it myself. How long are you planning to stay in Warsaw?"

This guy was all business. Grant responded, "Well, we had

planned to stay another couple of days, but I need to hear from the doctors when I can be released from the hospital. How about it Doc?" he said, turning his head to look at the doctor who had been talking before.

"We want you to stay for a few days so we can observe you. As I said, we want to do an MRI and, if you have internal injuries, we might not know for a day or two," the doctor answered.

"What is your companion's name and what is her room number at the Hilton?" asked the policeman.

"Her name is Sam and she's in room 817. Please ask her to come here right away." Grant replied.

Without another word, the policeman turned and left the room. At the same time, the doctor said, "Okay, we are finished with you for now. Please do not try to sit up or move around. We need you to rest. I will go see about scheduling the MRI."

"How long will that take?" Grant asked.

The Doctor replied, "There are only two in Warsaw and they are very busy." Then he left.

Finally alone, Grant's first thought was how this would interfere with his mission. He couldn't remember the last time he'd been banged up this badly. He wasn't sure he could even get up, much less walk, but he knew he'd have to try. Further, this contact was dead and Grant was in the emergency room at the time of the third contact meeting so he didn't know if that contact showed or not. He was fairly certain he wouldn't make tomorrow's meetings either. Damn! His next thought was about the car that hit him. Was it an accident? Could it have been deliberate? If so, it had to be the same person or group that was killing the other contacts. He was still trying to sort it all out a few minutes later when he drifted off, the pain meds finally taking control.

Grant slept for a couple of hours and when he opened his eyes, he looked straight into Sam's face. Seeing his eyes blink open, she asked, "How are you feeling?"

I'm a little groggy, but I'll make it," Grant replied in a scratchy voice. "How much do you know?"

"The policeman that called filled me in on what happened and the doctors told me your condition. Grant, it isn't good. They're still trying to schedule an MRI, but it looks like it will be two or three days before they can get you in. I hope they have good food in here, 'cause it looks you're going to be here awhile." Sam said, fighting to hold back the tears that were flooding her eyes.

"I can't stay here. Too much to do," Grant said, his voice almost a whisper.

Wiping away the tears with the back of her hand, Sam said, "Look Grant, I know you're a tough guy and all, but you're still mortal. These injuries are serious. You could have major internal damage that could be life threatening if you don't stay put." She continued leaning over him, wiping her eyes with the back of her hands.

"Sorry, Sam, but I've got to get back on the street before we lose any more contacts. After this accident, though, I'm gonna need you more than ever."

His voice was obviously weakening, but Sam persisted, "Do you really think this was an accident, just a coincidence?" She asked incredulously.

Grant sighed and whispered, "I've told you before how I feel about coincidences. I shouldn't have used the word 'accident.' I don't know that it was deliberate, but I have to assume it was. I tried to push the contact out of the way, but the car veered towards us. It all happened so fast I can't be sure he was trying to hit us, though. Now sit back in your chair. I can barely keep my eyes open." Grant managed to eke out a small smile.

***

Vladimir, meanwhile, was sitting in his room having another vodka from his mini-bar. To hell with the cost. This was a great occasion. He had hit both of them so solidly they had to be dead. Hurling towards them in his car he had a last second thought that by killing Thurmond now, he might not be able to find out where all the contacts lived. That's why he swerved towards the woman. Unfortunately, when Thurmond leaned towards the woman, probably trying to push her out of the way, he'd hit him harder than he wanted. Oh well, at least now Thurmond wouldn't be able to track him down. He didn't know how much Thurmond's woman knew. Just in case, he'd have to take care of her. No one who knew about him could stay alive. He would have to find another way to find the other informants, but he was confident he could do it. He'd found all the others hadn't he? There were only a few more who might know who he was. After that, he could go to the United States and take care of the last one. Then, the good life. American women were the best. Russian women were so bossy and so many of them slept with anyone they met. He didn't want a Russian whore. He wanted the pristine, petite American women who were true to their man and took care of the home. And of the man.

Chapter 21

I minus 39

The DNI, growing more anxious with each passing day finally had to know more, so he called General Wheeler. "General, we're down to just over a month before the inauguration. What do I tell the President-elect? Do I push harder on moving the swearing-in ceremony to a more secure location? We could do it in private in the White House, I suppose. My gut tells me the President-elect isn't going to go along with moving it, though." The DNI sighed and then continued. "Where the hell *is* Thurmond, anyway?"

"He's still in Warsaw, according to his schedule. We agreed that he'd call in when he had anything significant to report. He's probably still trying to connect with the contacts. I'm sure he'll let us know the minute anything important comes up." General Wheeler explained, then continued, "Look, Director, Thurmond's a good guy and..."

Barry cut him off, "He'd better be. We're running out of time to make this decision. By the way, is Garcia with him?"

"No, sir, he's not. Thurmond thought it would be best for fewer people to be involved in the search for contacts. Too many strange faces might spook them," Wheeler said.

"I told him to keep Garcia in the loop!" The DNI was almost shouting.

The General took a deep breath and let it out slowly, hoping the DNI wouldn't hear. He said, "I know, sir, but in this case I had to agree with Thurmond. I'm sorry I didn't consult with you before I made the decision to let Thurmond go alone, but I didn't know it would be an issue. I'll make sure Garcia is briefed each time I hear from Thurmond."

"Good. Sorry, General, guess I'm a little tense right now." Barry said in a gentler tone.

"No sweat, sir. I understand. I'll call you tomorrow with an update."

"Thanks." With that the DNI hung up.

At almost the same time, the General's secure phone rang. "Wheeler!" he barked.

"General, this is Sergeant First Class Rogers," said Sam.

Relieved to be hearing from her, he softened his tone when he continued, "Rogers, good. I just got off the phone with the DNI and he's hopping mad. What the hell's going on and why haven't you guys kept me up to speed?"

"Well, sir, there's been an accident. Or, what looks like an accident." Over the next ten minutes, Sam filled him in on the details.

"You say he's injured pretty badly, but he's staying? Yeah, that sounds like the Thurmond I know. Look, Rogers, trying to talk him into coming back home is useless. You're going to have to take care of him and help him through the rest of this mission. If you need anything, anything at all, just call. I'll make it happen. Ask him if he wants me to send Garcia over." Wheeler leaned back in his leather chair.

Sam sighed, "Alright, sir, I'll ask. But, I don't think he'll want that. He wants to do this his way."

"Yeah, I'm sure he does. Okay, I won't send Garcia unless I hear from you that I should. Put the Colonel on." Wheeler said.

"Sir, I thought it would be best to have this conversation on the secure phone, so I'm at the embassy in Warsaw. The Colonel is still in the hospital, although he swears he's going to check himself out by this evening. I'm going to try to convince him to stay put overnight and reevaluate the situation tomorrow morning." Sam explained.

Wheeler paused a moment before continuing, "Okay. Keep me informed. Thanks for calling me with this update."

"You're welcome, sir. I'll give you another update tomorrow," sam said, relieved to have the conversation over with.

"Thanks." Wheeler said, then hung up and frowned. Thurmond injured? Not the first time, but this is the worst time for him to be laid up. Well, we'll see what Sam's made of. He really thought he should send Garcia for back up, but he'd give it another twenty-four hours to see if Thurmond was up and about. No longer than that though.

Wheeler thought for a few minutes more about what happened and then decided he'd better call the DNI back and give him the news. As usual, the DNI was mobile and used the secure speakerphone in his car. When he had finished the call with General

Wheeler, the DNI called Garcia.

"Garcia."

"Garcia, this is Barry," the DNI said. "Look, I've heard some bad news about Thurmond you ought to know." Barry spent the next few minutes updating Garcia.

Garcia smiled to himself, but said, "Whew. Too bad about Thurmond. I should have been there watching his back. I'm glad he thinks he'll be okay, but he's going to need lots of help. I'll plan to leave immediately. I can be there by tomorrow morning."

"No, don't go just yet. I'm waiting on word from Thurmond that he wants help."

Garcia responded immediately, "Sir, you and I both know Thurmond is never going to say he needs help from me. I think I just ought to show up. Maybe I can just watch him without him knowing I'm there. That way, he feels free to do what he wants and I can provide cover."

"Hmmm. You know, that sounds like a good idea. You think you can do it without him seeing you?" Barry said.

"That's what I'm trained to do," Garcia responded confidently.

"Okay, then. He's staying at the Hilton in Warsaw. His assistant says he's threatening to check himself out of the hospital today, but she's trying to talk him into staying overnight. If she can, that should give you time to get there before he does. But, you'd better be prepared for him to already be there. I'll call your cell when I know more," Barry said.

"I'm on it. My cell works in Europe, so you should be able to reach me at any time. Same number."

"Good. You know if Thurmond does see you, all hell's will break loose. You'll have to come up with something. And don't tell anyone you're going—I don't want Thurmond hearing about this from someone else. That means the DDI as well. If there's any fallout, I'll take the heat."

"Yes, Sir, I'll take care of it. No one will know."

Garcia, smiling broadly, couldn't believe his luck. Not only would he be able to keep tabs on Thurmond, but he'd also be able to quietly photograph every person Thurmond met with and he could learn what the contact process was, which was just as important. With a little more luck, he might even get a shot at the guy who was killing all the contacts. That guy needed to die before anyone, especially Thurmond, could question him. Garcia nodded to himself. He had his orders.

After dropping off the DNI at his office, Riley placed a call. "Looks like you're going to have more company. Somebody named Garcia is on his way to Warsaw to quietly track Thurmond. Also, this guy Thurmond got hit by a car and is in the hospital, but is expected to be out by tomorrow. Garcia's supposed to cover his ass from now on without him knowing about it." Ka-ching! Riley was already spending the money.

Chapter 22

I minus 39

The President-elect was busy from early in the morning to late at night with cabinet selections, meeting with select congressional leaders from both houses, and all those political appointments. There were hundreds. Most of the high level positions, like ambassadors and undersecretaries of departments, were going to major financial supporters of his campaign and there were even some for his most loyal campaign workers. His campaign manager, who would become his White House Chief of Staff, was leading the candidate selection. Mason would make the final decision on all major appointments, however. The cabinet members would be selected from industry. He felt strongly about surrounding himself with people who knew what he didn't. He hated the idea of "yes men", or "yes women" and wanted someone in each department who could think and act independently with only broad guidance from him.

With all this activity, he'd had little time to think about the threat to his life. But just now, with a brief break from meetings, he sat leaning back with his feet on his desk and his hands clasped behind his head and wondered how the investigation was going. He hadn't had a briefing from the DNI in several days, so he assumed nothing significant had been discovered. He hoped Thurmond was up to the task. Although he wouldn't admit it to anyone else, he was getting a little nervous. An attack could come from anywhere and regardless what date was written on the piece of paper, anytime. No one had a clue who might have him in their sights. Maybe he'd delay the start of his next meeting long enough to get in a quick call with Barry. With that, he put his feet on the floor, leaned forward and picked up the wad of message slips his secretary had left on his desk.

***

At nearly the same time, Vladamir was picking up his messages. As he listened to the report about Thurmond, he was shocked to find he had somehow survived the attack . . . and when he heard the news about someone new, Garcia, he grew concerned. He didn't know that name and was concerned that, since he didn't know what this Garcia looked like, he might expose himself while trying to track Thurmond. This would require him to re-plan his tactics to find all the names on the list. He'd have to be a lot more careful. Maybe, though, if he watched Thurmond from a greater distance, he might be able to spot Garcia, too. If so, maybe he could set a trap and eliminate him. Things had become very complicated, though and if he wasn't careful, this could be really bad.

***

Back in Washington, the DNI sitting at his desk reading the latest intelligence estimates on the Middle East, answered the chirp from his secure phone. "Barry, this is Mason," the President-elect said. "Where are we with finding that creep who wants to kill me? I've only got a minute, so keep it really short."

The DNI filled the President-elect in on what happened to Thurmond, deliberately not mentioning that he'd sent Garcia to shadow him. He had intended to tell him, but just at the last second he thought maybe it would be a good idea to keep the secret close for now. He could always mention it in the next update.

Mason concluded with, "Thanks for the update. Please keep me in the loop. If anything significant happens, call me immediately. My assistant will always know where I am and will be able to patch your call through."

"You can count on it, sir"

Chapter 23

I minus 39

Grant awoke; slowly opening his eyes he saw Sam sitting in the chair next to him staring at his face. As soon as she saw his eyes open, she started right in. "Grant, I briefed General Wheeler on the secure phone at the embassy. He agrees with me. You have to stay until the test results are in, at least overnight."

Grant sighed. He stretched slowly, locating the sore spots. "Only one way I'll do that, Sam. If I can stand up and walk, I'm out of here tonight. If I can't, then I'll stay until tomorrow morning."

Sam gave a big sigh. "Okay, tough guy, but I think you're crazy. By the way, while you were sleeping I talked with the doctor; he'll be back in to see you before he goes home. Maybe *he* can convince you the injuries are severe enough to keep you here for a while."

Grant smiled weakly. "Yeah, good luck with that. Have the police had any luck finding the person who hit us?"

"Haven't heard a word from them. I'll call that police detective in a little bit—see what he knows. He gave me his card before he left."

"Okay." Grant said, "Now we have to plan out the rest of this trip. We have two possibilities about the hit and run driver: Either it was a complete accident and the driver didn't want to be implicated in a major personal injury accident, so he took off. Or, someone is out to stop me. If that's it, then my guess is it's the same guy who's killing all the others and this is just the first attempt."

Sam asked, "Which do you think it is? By the way, the policeman told me it's not unusual for a driver involved in an accident to leave the scene. Happens all the time. Especially a drunk driver. Seems like they want to avoid the police just as they did during the Soviet era."

"All I remember is that when I moved to push the contact out of the car's path, it swerved in the same direction, obviously to get both of us."

"Really? So you do think it was deliberate?" She was sitting forward now.

"Sam, think about it. If this guy is trying to kill all the contacts and I'm in the way, you know he's going after me too. And remember, I'm already on his hit list. So, although I don't have any hard evidence, my bet is that it was a deliberate hit. That means this guy knows what I look like and will keep trying until he gets me . . . or I get him. Looks like it's personal now. That means danger for you, too, you know."

Both were silent for just a moment, then Grant looked directly into her eyes and said, "I think it's time for you to go home and coordinate from there."

Sam crossed her arms and said firmly, "No way. I'm not going to leave you here in this shape, knowing some madman is out to kill you. How stupid do you think I am?"

"I know you're not stupid, Sam. That's why it should make sense to you to get your ass out of the danger zone," Grant countered with a slightly irritated voice.

"Forget it, Grant. It's not going to happen. I'm here and I'm staying," she said, with finality in her voice.

Grant was silent for a moment and Sam could tell he was steaming. Then, "You know, you can be pretty hard-headed sometimes," he said, "but I'm in no position to force you to go home. We'd better think through how to proceed. If he's been tailing me, he's probably seen you with me, so you have to assume you're now a target too. You may not be, but we can't take any chances. Damn. I wish we know what this guy looked like. When I get out of the hospital, we're going to spend a couple of hours with me teaching you basic surveillance techniques. It will . . ."

Sam interrupted, "You really think I need to know all that?"

"Sam, please, just listen for a minute. It's too dangerous now for us to be together all the time, but I need someone to cover me while I'm trying to meet with the contacts. I'll teach you how to recognize when you're being followed . . . and for you to tell if I'm being followed. Also, we need a way to stay in close touch when we're not together. Maybe the Defense Attaché at the embassy can provide us with a couple of walkie-talkies, or something like that. Or, the CIA guys will probably have something more sophisticated. Somehow, though, we have to make sure they don't contact Langley because if Garcia finds out we're over here without including him, he'll be really pissed. Any ideas of what we can use as a cover?" Grant groaned quietly as he tried to turn over on his side to face her.

"Why don't we keep you out of it?" Sam replied. "I could get General Wheeler to call the Intelligence Attaché and tell him that he's got a combat sergeant who'll be on special assignment in the area for a week or so and needs communication devices. If he puts it like that, they'll never question me about the mission. They'll assume it's for DIA and I'm sure they won't mention it to anyone for fear of compromising me. Think that'll work?"

Grant brightened a bit. "That's brilliant. Do it this afternoon. Also, see if you can check out a handgun—a .380 would be okay, potent enough at close range and easy to conceal. In addition to that, we also now have to make sure our room is secure. I can work on that when I get out of here. We're going clandestine. That son-of-a-bitch won't have such an easy time getting to us from now on. Here's the way it's going to work . . . ." Grant spent the next hour, interrupted often by Sam asking questions, and talking about techniques they would use to be less visible to anyone who might be watching. After finishing, Grant yawned and said to Sam, "Okay, now get out of here so I can rest. If I'm able, I still want to leave here after dark this evening. Go call General Wheeler and pick up those communicators." He managed a weak smile.

Heading towards the door, Sam replied, "Yes, sir, I'm on my way. But, don't you try to move from that bed until I get back here. Understand?" Her voice was stern, but Grant could see a small smile.

"Go, just go."

As Sam walked out the door of his hospital room, Grant smiled. She was getting so bossy and, to his surprise, he liked it. He was getting really close to Sam and felt a very strong urge to protect her. But, he'd have to be at the top of his game if he wanted to keep her safe, and, unfortunately, he wasn't. Not only was he a little rusty, he was injured. Maybe he was pushing too hard to get out of the hospital that night. Maybe tomorrow morning he'd feel stronger. Well, she'd just have to sleep here tonight. He wasn't going to have her alone all night way back at the hotel. In fact, he didn't even know what part of the city the hospital was in and how far it was from the hospital. I'll have to ask, he thought as he drifted off.

When Grant awoke early that evening, Sam was back, communicators in hand. As she showed him how they worked he was amazed at how small they were.

"What's the range on these? They're pretty small."

"The guy at the attaché's office said up to a mile. They're small so they can be easily hidden in your ear. If anyone notices it, they'll just think it's a hearing aid. It has an integrated microphone that is voice activated, so you can just talk and not have to push any buttons. The battery is rechargeable and goes about three days between charges. And, I was able to check out a very small 9MM. About the same size as a .380, but with a lot more stopping power. It's also untraceable. They gave me a box of fifty jacketed hollow points to go with it."

Grant raised his eyebrows. She was one impressive lady . . . er, young lady. That part still discouraged him. "Nice work, Sam. The gun just might come in handy. I'll carry it. And these communicators are nice. Much better than we had when I was in the field. Oh, by the way, just in case I *am* a target, you'd better call the hotel, check out of the room we had in my name, book a room in your own name and ask the hotel to transfer all personal items to the new room. Tell them also that if anyone asks for me, just say that I've checked out and tell them not to mention that we've swapped rooms. Do you have a credit card?"

"Yes, I do. I never leave home without it." She laughed at her own corny joke. She used her mobile phone to call the hotel. They said they would be most happy to do as she asked and the rooms would be switched within the hour. Anyone who inquired would simply be told that Mr. Thurmond has checked out with no forwarding address.

Grant then told Sam he'd decided it would be safer if they both stayed at the hospital that night. They could go back to the hotel before dawn the next day. They spent the rest of the evening talking about a variety of things, then Sam bid Grant a good night and arranged herself in the easy chair in his room. At least she had a blanket. Grant's last thought before drifting off was how nice it would be if she were lying next to him instead of in that chair. Sam's last thought was how nice it would be if she were lying next to him instead of in that chair.

That night he dreamed. Vivid dreams of his time in Lebanon. Dreams he hadn't had for a while. He had been sent in by DIA to set up intelligence gathering networks that might help identify terrorists. At that time, the terrorists in Lebanon were bombing US' and other western interests and kidnapping both civilian and military personnel. The goal was to determine who was supplying the various terrorist cells with weapons and explosives. Were they also supplying armor and other vehicles? Were other countries, such as Syria or Iran, supplying not just weapons but training? They had identified AK47s taken off dead terrorists in Beirut as originating in the Soviet Union, so how involved were they? His job was to find out.

Many of his missions were hazardous but many were also routine, and a major challenge was not becoming complacent. He traveled with just an Israeli Army translator and would be away from his operational base in Israel for up to a week at a time. To provide some level of protection, they didn't use a car. The roads weren't safe. So, a chopper would drop him and his interpreter off at a location away from people and would meet him a few days later in another designated location. Although he knew that a few of the towns in the area were terrorist strongholds, he felt reasonably safe asking the local town leaders to give him information about whom they saw passing through. His goal was to set up a clandestine network of villagers who would keep track of who they saw and feed that information back to him. He had photographs of uniforms of the different armies in the region, including Russia, and would show these to people living both in the countryside and in towns. Sometimes the people would respond and sometimes, out of fear, they would keep silent. The terrorists were brutal to informers.

The mission he dreamed of while sleeping in the hospital had ended in disaster. As usual, the town he approached had only one main road. He guessed there were about two hundred residents. He had been there a few times before and had been greeted warmly, been fed and offered a bed at night. He had never stayed, fearing the terrorists would come in the night. Given this history, he felt he had nothing to fear as one morning he and his interpreter walked straight into the middle of the town with their sidearms concealed. The village was normally very quiet, but as he approached he realized there were absolutely no people around. Almost as if the village was deserted. Before he could draw his weapon and take cover, more than fifty armed men in all sorts of dress came out of the buildings and surrounded them, shouting for them to lie down on their stomachs. They were quickly disarmed, hands and legs tied, then beaten, kicked and dragged around the dusty streets of the village for what seemed like hours. There was lots of cheering and celebrating, with men firing their rifles into the air. For three nights they were kept in a barn, with the beating and taunting continuing during the day.

On the fourth day, someone completely dressed in black and with only his eyes showing began to question them. Thurmond was accused of being a CIA spy because he was American and in civilian clothes. His interpreter was accused of being an Israeli spy. He was informed that he would continue to be beaten until he admitted he was a CIA spy and confessed to war crimes of aiding Israel in killing innocent Muslims. Of course, Thurmond couldn't admit that he was part of an American military intelligence organization without confirming he was a spy and he would die rather than betray his country's trust in him.

Early one morning two days after they had been questioned by the man in black, he and the Israeli soldier were brought into the center of town and told they were to be executed for spying. They were both bound, stood side by side and the man who questioned them, brandishing a semi-automatic pistol, walked up behind them. He first stood behind the interpreter, pulled back the hammer and fired one shot into the back of his head. The man fell forward, face down into the dirt. The officer then walked up behind Thurmond, cocked the gun and . . . .

At that moment, Grant was startled awake by someone shaking him violently. He came up quickly with a wild look on his face, hands up in a defensive posture.

"Grant, it's me, Sam," she said, putting her hand on his arm. "You were really out. You must have been having a nightmare."

"Uh, sorry. Yeah, a bad dream about a bad mission. Sort of a recurring nightmare. Don't usually sleep that hard. Did they give me something in the IV?"

"They did pump something into you, but I don't know what. Probably IV morphine. That stuff really works. Had it once in Iraq when I was hit by shrapnel from an IED. A really pleasant feeling and I slept like a baby."

"You were wounded in Iraq?" Grant was still groggy, but was coming around.

"Yeah, painful, but as it turned out, not serious. I declined medevac to the States. Thought I ought to finish my combat tour. I was assigned to you as soon as I returned. They called this 'light duty'. Looks like I'm even getting a Purple Heart out of it."

"Another medal? Seems like I find out something new about you every day. You're quite a woman." Grant just looked at her for a moment and then finally said, "Okay, let's get out of here. I want to be in our hotel room before dawn. Now where're my clothes?"

"I suppose there's no way I can talk you out of this? What about just one more day in here to make sure there are no complications?" Sam asked, biting her lower lip again.

"Where are my clothes?" Grant repeated a little slowly and more forcefully.

Grant found movement a little painful, but tolerable, and as they walked out of the hospital and headed back to the Hilton, Sam asked about his dream. Grant told her the highlights and that he had spent over a month in captivity before being traded to Israel for an imprisoned terrorist leader. After nearly two months in captivity, Grant, at 6'2" tall had lost nearly thirty pounds. They shipped him back to Bethesda Naval Hospital for treatment and recuperation.

When he finally got home almost nine months after he'd initially left, he found the note from his wife telling him she couldn't take it anymore. He only saw her once since, that was at the divorce hearing.

When Grant finished, Sam was quiet. "I'm sorry I didn't know you then," she said softly.

Twenty minutes later as they approached the hotel, Grant said, "At this hour, it's not likely that anyone will be watching, but I think we should take precautions. You go in through the front door and pick up the keycards for our new room. Examine the lobby very closely to see if anyone's there. If you see someone, memorize the face. I'll go to the side door and wait for you to open it. They usually lock the side doors at night, but they're rarely alarmed. Keep your voice low at the desk. Don't want anyone to overhear your name. No use making this any easier for our tail than we have to." Grant, out of breath from the walk, sat down on a low rock fence in front of an old house.

Sam saw no one other than the registration desk clerk in the lobby, and she and Grant were in their new room in five minutes. It was hard to believe anyone spotted them going in. True to their word, the hotel had transferred all their personal belongings to the new room and, since it was identical to the other one, all the items were in the same place.

Chapter 24

I minus 39

Later that night, after checking and finding he had no new messages, Vladimir sat back, opened yet another vodka from the mini-bar and thought about his next steps. There were too many hospitals in Warsaw to track down the one where Thurmond was, so he would just have to wait him out. That meant a lot of lobby time, but it would be worth it. Wonder if Thurmond knew he was targeted? Probably not. Probably just thinks it was a hit and run. Maybe some drunk. So he most likely won't be on guard any more than usual. If things got too dicey with him, Vladimir figured he could always snatch the girl and use her to force Thurmond to meet. Then he would take them both out.

Deciding to see if he could worm Thurmond's room number out of the clerk, he placed a call to the desk asking to be connected to his room. The clerk told him Thurmond had checked out and left no forwarding address. This was not good news. When could he have checked out? As far as Vladimir knew, Thurmond was still in the hospital. Maybe the girl had checked him out. But, when did they get their luggage? Something's really wrong with this, he thought. He decided to spend at least the next day sitting around the lobby in case they showed up to collect their belongings. He certainly had no other way of picking up their trail.

Vladimir was an old hand at this business, but he hadn't been active in the field for a long time. For many years he'd had a pretty easy life as a middle management government bureaucrat, a great cover for passing misinformation to the US, but it wasn't a good way to maintain his field skills. This inactivity, just sitting around waiting to pick up Thurmond's trail, was frustrating. And he had this feeling that the Russians were getting closer to identifying him—nothing solid, just a hunch. He had another vodka.

Chapter 25

I minus 38

Vladimir, feeling a little hung over, woke a little later than normal and went down to the lobby restaurant to have a leisurely breakfast. He kept an eye on the lobby the whole time he was eating, but he never saw Thurmond or the girl.

Garcia, meanwhile, had arrived in Warsaw early that morning and while Vladimir was eating, Garcia was watching the front entrance of the hotel. He'd taken up a position across the street and a few doors down on the bench of a covered bus stop. Bundled up against the cold in the rough clothes and hat of a Polish workman, he didn't think anyone, even Thurmond, would give him a second glance. Earlier he had checked with the hospital to find that Thurmond had been discharged, so he had to assume he'd returned to the hotel. If he left by any of the front or side entrances, Garcia would see him. Now it was time to just sit at the bus stop and wait.

To help legitimize his cover, he lit up a Caro, a popular Polish cigarette. Although Garcia didn't smoke currently, he had in college, so he knew how to inhale and make himself look like a smoker. Wow, these things were stronger than he remembered, he thought. He coughed as he breathed in the smoke. As he sat there, Garcia thought about his career at the CIA and about his secret orders to eliminate the bad guy before Thurmond could question him. He didn't know exactly why that was required, but he knew he had to follow orders. Given where these orders came from, one simply didn't question them. He had sworn allegiance and there was only one punishment for failure.

After eating, Vladimir took up his position in the hotel lobby and started to read the daily newspaper. The lobby was busy this morning, but he was sure he would have no trouble picking out Thurmond and the girl.

Upstairs in their new room, Grant and Sam enjoyed a full room-service breakfast and were discussing the day's activities. Because he was still in considerable pain, Grant had skipped his normal morning exercise routine of stretching, sit-ups and pushups. He was not just sore, but really stiff as well. He'd tried a few stretching exercises when he first got out of bed, but he just couldn't do it.

Seeing that Grant was moving slowly, Sam asked, "Pretty sore, huh?"

Grant responded with a grunt.

"Have you ever tried yoga?" She asked.

"Yeah, that's me. Yoga man," Grant scoffed.

"You laugh, but it's really good exercise for both the body and mind. I know a few positions, want me to teach you?"

Yeah, you bet, baby—soon as my ribs heal up, he thought, but he said, "Not today. I'm really not up for it." Then he said, "We've got to pick things up a bit. We're losing time. I'll bet the President-elect is getting nervous right about now. I know I would be. So here's the plan. We have just one more day, today, to meet with the other contacts before I would have to make another mark and try again. That means another three days here and I don't want to waste that much time. Let's hope at least one of the others shows up today. Since I'm not in very good shape, I need your help. I'd like you to leave about ten minutes before I do. Go to the first meeting place and find a position where you can see me, but not close enough for anyone else to see you. If you see anyone who looks like they're paying me even just a little more attention than the rest of the people around me, let me know instantly on the communicator. Got it?"

Sam nodded and Grant continued, "I'll be ten minutes behind you. Remember, watch me as I approach. If anyone else stops at the same place, let me know ASAP. Let's go over some basic surveillance techniques and then I'll give you some tips to recognize if you're being tailed."

They spent about half an hour covering these topics and Grant also told her where the meet was, describing the area in a lot of detail. He'd decided she should sit in the park just across from the café. When he was finished, Grant stood and said, "Okay, it's time. Off you go. Be careful . . . please. And remember, if you see anything . . . anything at all that would indicate someone is watching either me or you, let me know immediately."

"Got it." Sam said, but she sounded a lot more confident than she felt. She gave Grant a quick hug and then left the room, taking the elevator to the lobby floor.

Vladimir watched as Sam crossed the lobby and left through the front door. So, they *were* here. He decided not to pursue her, betting that Thurmond would follow soon. He knew Thurmond was the person who had to make the meet and that the girl may be just out for a walk or going shopping like American women did. Maybe when he got to America, he'd meet a beautiful American woman and marry her. He would buy a house and be a perfect citizen. The American dream.

Garcia about this time was getting really tired of sitting, also saw Sam leave the hotel. He decided that Thurmond would never leave her alone very long, so he decided to tag along with her. Sam, having no experience in this area, never even glanced at him as she hurried along the busy sidewalk looking for a taxi. She finally saw one, hailed it down, got in and gave the driver an address. Garcia wasn't far behind and was able to quickly flag down another taxi. He handed the driver a US twenty dollar bill and told him to discreetly follow Sam's taxi. The driver didn't reply, just shrugged and took off.

Twenty minutes later, Sam arrived at her destination, paid the driver and looked around. The café was on the corner, just as Grant had described it and, as he said, there was a park on the opposite corner across the street. Perfect. She'd just sit in the park on one of the wooden benches pretending to enjoy the sunny day. From there she could see anyone who approached the café. As she sat there, she noticed it was cold enough to see her breath, but wrapped up in her winter coat and with the sun shining directly on her she was warm enough to sit for hours. It certainly was going to be boring, though, if it lasted that long. As she looked around she could see that it really was a beautiful park with old Sycamore and Oak trees, all with bare limbs this time of year. Sometimes she liked seeing the trees in winter better than any other time of year. In winter she could see the entire structure of the tree; the trunk and all the limbs going every which way. It always reminded her of a black and white print her mother had in the house when she was growing up.

Garcia stopped his taxi almost a block short of where Sam exited hers and was able to observe her as she first looked around and then walk across to the park. He paid no attention to the beauty of the park nor to the warming sunshine, instead he focused completely on Sam's every move. Now she was sitting there like she was just someone out on a cold but sunny winter's day enjoying the morning. Surely, Thurmond wouldn't have sent *her* to make the meet, Garcia thought. No, he was sure that Thurmond would be close by or would show up soon. He paid the driver, got out of the taxi and sat down on the bench at a bus stop where he could watch her.

Grant left exactly ten minutes after Sam. Although he tried to sneak out the side door of the hotel without drawing attention to himself, Vladimir had seen him leaving the elevator and followed close behind. While Grant flagged down a taxi, Vladimir walked half a block down the street, got into his car and followed Grant's taxi when it left the hotel. Vladimir felt lucky that his car had suffered only minor damage when he hit Thurmond and the woman. Although dented and had a broken headlight, it still drove fine.

Grant had his taxi driver approach the intersection by a side street and got out a block away from the café. He walked up the street and entered the café courtyard by the gate on that side, unseen by Garcia. He took an outside corner table and placed an open matchbook standing up in the shape of a triangle in front of him. He had no idea if this would work, but it was all he had. He'd placed the mark in the right spot, he had the matchbook signal on the table and now there was nothing left to do but wait. This was the last of the three days the contact had to show up. He sure hoped it would work. Given the "accident" yesterday, he was particularly alert to anything that seemed out of the ordinary. He could also see Sam across the street watching him. From his position, he couldn't see the bus stop where Garcia was seated.

Vladimir saw Thurmond leave the taxi and go into the café, so he drove past, made a U-turn a little further up the street and parked facing the cafe less than half a block away. From here, he could watch all foot traffic around the café and no one would pay any attention to a man sitting in a car. He observed Thurmond as he took a seat at a table next to the sidewalk and noticed the matchbook. Could that be the signal? Vladimir, looking around, saw the girl in the park. So this is where she was going. She must be watching Thurmond. Covering him? Looking for Vladimir?

Since he was concentrating on Sam, Garcia wasn't in a position to see the café, so he didn't see Thurmond arrive. Nor did he notice Vladimir. Neither did Sam.

The meeting time used to be set for 9:00 a.m., with the window being fifteen minutes before and after the hour. Thurmond, hoping the contact would remember the time and place, had arrived at around 8:30 a.m., so he had a forty-five minute swing. When the waiter came around, he ordered coffee and a pastry. He'd been sitting for nearly thirty minutes sipping his coffee when an older guy at the next table leaned over and asked for a light. Thurmond handed him the matchbook, watched as he lit his cigarette and noticed the pack in front of him: Marlborough's, the right cigarette brand. The man's next comment was in English: "A good day for a walk, but my knee is acting up. How are your knees?"

Grant's response was, "Normally fine, but a little sore today."

"Must be a weather front," the man said with a smile.

"Most likely," Grant responded, smiling back. That was it. The right sequence! Grant stood up and asked the gentleman if he would care to join him at his table. The man replied that he was very kind and that he'd like very much to join him and then took a chair next to Grant. Grant ordered two more coffees. The man introduced himself as Ivan Granowli, an ex-Russian who had lived in Poland for many years.

They chatted easily, with Grant laughing often. This guy told really funny stories, mostly about his youth in the 30's, but some about the war. Even talking about heavy things like war, Ivan was able to inject humor. Anybody seeing them would think they were just friends having a laugh.

After about fifteen minutes, the area around them cleared out and the tone became serious. "Koslowski's dead," Granowli said after looking around to make sure no one could overhear. "So are Kunichki and Poslusny. I'm the only one in the network left in Warsaw."

"Yes, I know," Grant's serious tone matched Granowli's. Both men were now leaning forward with elbows on the table. "I saw Koslowski a few days before he died and I was with Kunichki when she was hit by a car. I had intended to talk to Poslusny today. You might say it's a coincidence that all three died when I got close to them. But, in my line of work, I don't believe in coincidences. I think someone is using me to get to them. The only problem with that is whoever it is tried to kill me also. I'm still trying to work that out. But I do know that you need to be extremely careful over the next few days. You have to be a target too."

"I'm an old man. I can't believe anyone would want me dead. Any information I may have possessed is out of date and, anyway,

I've forgotten most of it. But, as you say, I have never believed in coincidences either, which brings me to you. What do you need of me?" Granowli's accent was heavy, but Grant understood every word.

Still leaning forward, Grant turned his head to the side to look directly at Granowli. "I'm trying to fill out the list of people that helped the US by passing on valuable intelligence information over the past thirty years. Koslowski gave me your name and said you know some that he didn't. I'd like you to tell me their names and how to contact them."

"I can certainly give you all the names I have, but several new people have replaced some of us who have retired. I don't know all of their names or even if they continued providing information. Why do you need them?" Granowli said.

Grant explained, "Anything you can provide will be helpful. As to why I need the names, someone is systematically killing people in the old network that I put together many years ago. I'm trying to find him and it's possible he may be among the names you provide or additional names they might provide. Unfortunately, one of the people we believe to be on his hit list is a very important person in America, a person we can't afford to lose. And we don't have much time—less than a month to find the killer and take him out."

They continued to talk for the next thirty minutes during which Granowli gave all the information he had regarding the small network he had set up. When he was active, he had contacted a couple of the people through newspaper personals ads. Grant memorized the ad copy, deciding to place the first ad tomorrow. He recognized most of the names Granowli gave him from the list Koslowski had given him, but there were three new ones. Of the three, Granowli said he was sure one was a codename and all he knew was where he said he used to work. He said this man was extremely cautious and while he gave Granowli important information about Soviet weapon movements, he refused to tell him anything about himself. Granowli at first thought that was unusual, but since the information the man relayed to him was very valuable, eventually he accepted it.

Granowli also explained to Thurmond about the drop box used with this mysterious person. It was a trash can sitting in the middle of the block of a fairly busy thoroughfare and was immediately adjacent to an alleyway that ran clear through to the parallel street a block away. The way they had worked it, at the informant's insistence, was that whenever he had something to pass on, the informant would place the ad in the personals column. Granowli would get to the spot early, the informant would walk by and drop a bag into the trash can and Granowli, after waiting a few minutes to see that they weren't being watched, retrieved it before anyone else could get to it. It was strictly a one-way communication. At their first and only face to face meeting, during which the informant was clearly wearing a disguise, Granowli had also worked out a unique newspaper ad in case he needed to contact the informant. He had tried it a couple of times, but the man never responded.

During the time the two men were talking, Sam sat on her park bench and looked around, trying to spot someone who was paying too much attention to them. Even though she had received some instruction from Grant, she wasn't a pro and she completely missed both Garcia and Vladimir. She knew she didn't know exactly what to look for so, as Grant had instructed, she just looked for anything out of the ordinary. Garcia and Vladimir, of course, *were* pros in the surveillance business, so they did nothing out of the ordinary, nothing for Sam to notice.

Vladimir, on the other hand, was unnoticed by everyone and watched the entire café meeting with great interest. His job now was to follow the old man home and kill him. After all, he was the only one in the old network left alive who knew about his spying and who had seen his face. He was sure Granowli had given his code name to Thurmond, but that didn't matter. The only way he and Granowli had communicated was through the drop box. Granowli knew only his code name and where he had worked. They had met only once at the beginning, but with his disguise he knew Granowli couldn't accurately describe him and would never be able to recognize him. Anyway, neither Thurmond nor Granowli had any way of knowing he was the one Thurmond was looking for. Also, no one knew where he lived, so even if Thurmond did have his code name and decided he was the person who was killing all the others, there was no way to trace it to him or his new flat in the Moscow suburbs. He had left his job in the Polish ministry some time before and no one there knew where he went. Nor did anyone, including his ex-bosses in Russia, know his new identity.

Remaining slumped down in the driver's seat of his car, he smiled to himself. This was going to work. He would assassinate everyone who knew of his existence and the coup de gras would be when the United States lost their newly elected president just after being sworn in. In the confusion following all the carnage, he would easily be able to blend in. Who knew, in time maybe he could even become a citizen? Also, even though he'd be the only person who knew, he'd be famous. As best he could figure, the people on the podium would include the current President-elect, his Vice-President-elect, all the military leadership, the Supreme Court, plus the outgoing president and vice-president, and all their families. If all went according to plan, they would all die at the same time. There would be mass confusion for days or maybe even weeks. He didn't know what America's plans were for such a catastrophe, but he knew it had never happened before.

Vladimir was so engrossed in his daydream that he nearly missed Granowli leaving the café. He finally looked up to see him walking away down a side street. It was an easy task for Vladimir to follow him home, talk his way inside by claiming he had information Granowli could use to help the American and then kill him. One more person who couldn't identify him. He wasn't sure how many more he had to go, but it had to be down to only a few and none of those had seen his face. He was pretty sure none of them could identify him, but he couldn't afford to take any chances. After all, what's a few more kills? With all that he had already killed, a few more wouldn't really matter. After Granowli died, he'd go back to the hotel and try to pick up Thurmond's trail. The only problem would be if Thurmond left Poland. He'd have no way of knowing where he was going or how. Oh, and that one more nagging problem—Granowli may have described him in his disguise to Thurmond, but that description would be several years old and he doubted very much if Thurmond could recognize him today from that description.

Garcia, in the meantime, watched Sam doing nothing. After an hour he was starting to believe this was a wild goose chase when she got to her feet and walked down the street. He watched her as she approached a taxi that had just pulled over. As the taxi drove past the bus stop, Garcia saw another person in the back and realized it was Thurmond. He'd missed him. He was at the café. How stupid of him not to realize where Thurmond would be. Sam was just a diversion.

Well, back to the Hilton. He hadn't seen anyone else watching Sam, but if anyone was following Thurmond, he wouldn't have seen him. Damn. Now he had to find a taxi to get back.

Grant and Sam talked little on the way back to the hotel. After they were in their room, Grant told her about the meeting and that he'd gotten a new list of names. Since he wasn't sure the secretive code-named informant would answer his ad, Thurmond decided to focus on the other two. At least he knew they had always responded to the ads Granowli placed. It might mean another three days in Warsaw, but it'd be worth it. The first thing they had to do was to check the death records for the past six years or so. No more waiting around on people who were never going to show up. Neither of the two names was listed at DIA as having been killed, but that would make sense. No one at DIA knew they were even part of the network.

***

Granowli, before he died, also told Vladimir the same names he had given Thurmond. There were only three that Koslowski hadn't told him about. Since they were all in the same cluster, he had already known those names and had killed two of those people almost two weeks ago. His was the third name. Although he couldn't be positive, he believed that with the information he had drugged out of Granowli, he had killed *all* the people who might be able to identify him. There may be a few left that would know his code name, but he didn't think anyone was left who could positively identify him to Thurmond or to the Russians. But, just to be sure, he'd better keep tabs on Thurmond, who was turning out to be cleverer than Vladimir first thought.

Thurmond might just identify more people and be able to put more pieces of the puzzle together. If it looked like he was getting close, Vladimir would kill him and his girlfriend, too. Then he remembered this guy Garcia. He hadn't been able to spot him yet, so he didn't know if he was in Warsaw or not. Since he didn't know how much this Garcia knew, it would be very important to make sure he died when Thurmond and the girl died. With all this going on, it might be a good idea to move up the timetable on all the deaths. Vladimir decided to work out a plan to make that happen in the next few days. But first, he had to spot Garcia.

Chapter 26

I minus 37

The next morning both Grant and Sam were up early. Since Grant wanted to continue to limit the time they were together outside the hotel room, he ordered room service breakfast.

Between bites Grant said, "Sam, even though I don't like you going out on your own, we need to split up today. I'd like you to head to the bureau of public records, or whatever that's called over here, and check on death reports for these two people. If you don't find anything, you might have to check the newspaper morgue files. I'm gonna head to the embassy to call General Wheeler on the secure phone with an update."

"Sure. I can do that. Meet back here for lunch?" Sam said brightly.

Grant, stopping a forkful of food on its way to his mouth, said, "Yeah. If you find out either one or both are not listed as having died, then I'll place the newspaper personal ads in the *Gazeta Wyborcza* this afternoon. I can get help from the embassy translating the message into Polish. I've memorized the words, but I don't have a clue how to spell them. After that . . . I guess we'll just wait." He filled his mouth with the very good food.

Soon, after placing the handgun in his inside coat pocket, Grant left the hotel. As usual, Vladimir had parked his car near the entrance of the hotel and when Thurmond hailed a taxi, he stayed close enough behind to make sure he didn't lose him . . . but not close enough to be recognized. However, Grant, on high alert right now, did notice a car swing out and make a daring U-turn, staying behind them. Could be nothing, but he kept an eye on the car all the way to the Embassy. Since they didn't make any turns along the way and the morning commuting traffic was heavy, it was difficult to tell whether the car was following him or was just another crazy Polish driver on his way to work. As Grant's taxi slowed down to enter the embassy gate, the other car sailed on past with the driver not so much as giving Grant's taxi a glance. The car looked like a million others on the road and Grant wasn't sure he could recognize it again. It had a few dents in the front fenders and the grill was busted, but a lot of other cars were banged up, too. Still, he'd keep it in mind.

Garcia, meanwhile, sitting on his bus stand bench, watched Grant leave the hotel and, determined not to miss him this time, frantically hailed down a taxi. As he entered the taxi and told to driver to just go forward quickly until he told him to stop, another crazy driver made a u-turn on the busy street causing traffic to stop quickly, including his taxi. He got a quick view of the driver in profile and by the determined look on his face he was clearly a man on a mission. Man, they drove crazy here. Worse than the beltway back home, he thought. His driver was able to get about a block behind Thurmond's taxi and hold that position. The wild driver was still a couple of cars ahead of him, but was driving more calmly now so Garcia dismissed it. As they approached the US embassy, Grant's taxi pulled in. To avoid detection, Garcia went on past. Half a block further the same stupid driver did another U-turn and as Garcia looked back, the driver parked his car on the other side of the street facing back towards the embassy. Garcia's training kicked in. Was this guy following Thurmond? He'd swung out into traffic right behind Thurmond's taxi and had now had placed his car in position where he could watch anyone arriving or leaving the Embassy. He instructed his driver to go around the block and park on a side street near the corner where he could keep the other car in sight.

After making his way up the Embassy's inside elevator to the third floor, Grant called General Wheeler on the secure phone.

"Wheeler," The General barked as he answered. His voice was, as usual, gruff, making his name sound like a command.

"General, this is Thurmond," Grant paused.

"Great timing, Colonel. I have a meeting in fifteen minutes that the DNI is also attending. When he sees me I know he'll ask for an update."

Grant spent ten minutes updating the General on what he'd found.

"So let me get this straight. You're no closer to solving the problem?" Wheeler was clearly annoyed.

Grant replied calmly, "Well, sir, I'm getting more information, more pieces of the puzzle. I know time's getting short, but I'm not ready to throw in the towel. I think I'm getting closer."

"We're planning the most secure inauguration in history, but the

President-elect insists that it be outside and proceed as planned. There are so many things to cover that I'm just not sure we can make it completely assassination proof. The secret service is running the show and, while they're the best in the world at this stuff, nobody's perfect. Colonel, I've got a bad feeling about this."

"So do I sir, but to solve this we have to take a systematic approach, following each lead as we uncover it. That's what I'm doing," Grant said with more confidence than he felt.

"Do what you have to, but get it done. If you need any help, you know how to reach me," Wheeler growled.

"Yes, sir."

The defense attaché said he had a meeting in town and offered to give Thurmond a lift back to his hotel and Grant accepted. They left by a back door and their ride was uneventful. Thurmond knew the driver was CIA and armed, ready to protect the defense attaché with his life. He felt completely safe and was able to relax and even able to have a social conversation about the upcoming NFL playoffs while in the car.

***

Vladimir assumed Thurmond would exit the embassy through the front door and take a taxi from there. So he paid close attention to see if a taxi came to the embassy front entrance or if Thurmond came out to flag one down. The official embassy cars that came and went had heavily tinted windows, preventing Vladimir from seeing anyone who might be inside them, so he paid no attention to them. After waiting in his car for two hours, Vladimir decided he'd somehow missed Thurmond so he decided to go have some lunch and return to his post outside the hotel. Hopefully he'd find a parking spot on the street where he could watch the entrance.

Garcia, restlessly sitting in the back seat, had been feeding the taxi driver twenty dollar bills every half hour or so to keep him waiting. As the other car pulled out, Garcia instructed his taxi driver to follow, thinking he was unnoticed by the driver of the parked car.

Vladimir had, however, noticed the taxi sitting on the side street, thinking it was unusual for the driver to be idle and not out hustling fares. But, maybe the driver had been up all night and was just napping. Vladimir started his car and pulled away from the curb, staying in the right lane. He kept his eye on his mirror and was surprised to see the taxi pull out behind him. Vladimir immediately became alert. He varied his driving speed, sometimes slowing down much slower than surrounding traffic and sometimes speeding up. The taxi stayed behind him. Not too close, but definitely queuing off his driving speed. Who would be looking for him? Russians? He decided to quickly pull over and stop and let the taxi pass by him. Then he could follow it. When Vladimir's car pulled over, Garcia instructed his driver to continue on down the road, ignoring the car. As the taxi passed his car, all Vladimir could see was someone slumped down in the back seat and couldn't tell whether it was a man or woman.

He started going through the possibilities—it could be the Russians, it could be the girl, or it could be the elusive Garcia. He was sure it wasn't Thurmond. The taxi was there right after Thurmond entered the embassy. He wouldn't have had time to get into position. If it were the girl, she would be no problem for him. If it were the Russians, he might be in trouble, but he couldn't see them using a taxi and also it looked like there was only one person in the back of the taxi. The Russians would no doubt send several. They weren't known for being subtle. It could be this Garcia, but he couldn't be sure. He decided to take the initiative and get close enough to the taxi to see into the back seat. He pulled his hat low over his forehead and accelerated forward, speeding around cars both on the right and the left side of the road.

As he approached the taxi from the rear, Garcia, who'd been watching Vladimir's car, told the driver to get away from the car behind him. His driver sped up and the car behind him gave chase. The taxi driver, being very experienced and skilled in veering through traffic started to put distance between the two cars. This only encouraged Vladimir to drive more erratically, taking even more risks.

After several blocks, the taxi driver came upon a knot of traffic he couldn't safely go around and was forced to stop. Vladimir, in the car behind, saw an opportunity and closed the distance rapidly slamming into the rear of the taxi at full speed. Garcia, who was not wearing a seatbelt, was thrown around the back of the taxi, hitting his head on the left side window hard enough to break the glass and knock him unconscious. The crash completely demolished the trunk area of the taxi, rupturing the fuel tank and starting a fire.

Vladimir's car was disabled, but he was unhurt. Immediately after the crash, when he saw the taxi burst into flames, he abandoned his car and escaped on foot down the block. He walked the rest of the way to the hotel, went to his room, opened a vodka from the mini bar and sat heavily in one of the armchairs. Thankfully they restocked the mini bar every day. He thought about what had just happened. Somehow, someone had identified him. That person hopefully was now dead, but he couldn't be sure who it was or what nation he was working for. It had to be either the US or Russia. No one else was looking for him. He wasn't worried about the crash. The car had been stolen in Krakow a week before and there was no way to trace it back to him. But now, everyone had to die . . . quickly. And he had to find another car.

***

Garcia came to with fire raging all around him. Although not thinking too clearly, he was alert enough to know he had to get out of the taxi. Looking into the front seat he saw the driver struggling unsuccessfully to open his door. He knew the driver would die in the fire without his help. He clambered into the front seat and dragged the driver out the front passenger door, the only one still working. As they moved to a safe distance Garcia could hear sirens coming closer. His head was bleeding, but he felt okay, maybe a little woozy, but not disabled. His first thought was that he had to get out of there fast. He didn't need to be questioned by the police. He had a reasonable cover story, but not deep enough for a police investigation.

He had registered in a small hotel just around the corner from the Hilton. It was only a few blocks away so he decided to walk and let his head clear a bit. Man, that was close. If he'd stayed unconscious even a minute longer, he'd have fried in the fire. He looked around and saw the taxi driver sitting on the curb holding a bloody handkerchief to his face. Garcia went over to him, handed him a wad of currency and quickly started walking away.

After going only a few steps, he first heard the explosion and then felt the concussion as the rest of the fuel in the gas tank ignited. Less than a minute earlier, he'd been in the back seat of the car that was now completely engulfed in flames. It looked like he was right about this not being a coincidence. He was attacked, no doubt about it. But now he knew something Thurmond didn't—he was sure that it was one man he was looking for, not an organization. He had even gotten a partial visual. After the crash, he had noticed the door to the car that hit them was open, so obviously the guy fled the scene. Too bad the bastard didn't die in the crash or resulting fire. That would have saved everybody a lot of trouble.

Chapter 27

I minus 37

Sam came into the hotel room just as Grant was hanging up from ordering lunch. "I ordered for you," he said, standing up.

"Thanks."

Helping her take off her coat he said, "What'd you find out?"

She looked around, a little surprised at his gallant gesture and said, "Well, the death records at Warsaw's version of City Hall were a mess. They're not computerized and they're months behind in filing. The only records they'd let me go through were the ones already filed. Nothing there about either person. So, I went to the newspaper. They were better organized and they had all past issues in computerized databases. I just did a search on both names and came up with one hit. That person died less than two weeks ago. No cause of death mentioned, but homicide suspected. The article said that when the police arrived, the apartment door was unlocked, the rooms were orderly and although there were only a few valuables, the fact that they were left behind indicated it wasn't a burglary. An investigation is ongoing, but there're few clues and it doesn't look good for identifying a suspect. So, where do we go from here?" She hung up her coat in the closet and turned to face Grant.

Grant said, "We keep going forward. I place the personals ad and try to meet the one informant left who may be alive. If that person doesn't show up, we'll go back to the States and continue looking through the files trying to find a clue. In the meantime, the General's got a bunch of analysts going through the documentation we have. Hopefully, they'll find something that'll point us in the right direction. Those guys are pretty good."

Sam, with her hands on her hips, frowned. "I'm not looking forward to going back without accomplishing much during our stay here. Let's hope someone shows. How will the meet work? Is it the same as before?" she asked.

Grant shrugged, "Pretty much the same. It's a four day cycle. I place the ad in the morning paper today and it'll run for the following three days. I start showing up at the meeting place tomorrow and continue for two more days after that. If nobody shows, we struck out."

"Okay, sounds like it's our only shot. Sure hope it works. What do you want me to do?"

"Same as before. You get to the meeting place early and see if anyone follows me."

"Was it always this boring being in the field?" Sam asked with an impish smile.

Grant smiled back. "Not always, but a lot of my work was like this. Long periods of boredom interrupted by moments of frantic activity."

"Well, I couldn't do it. I need more action." She laughed.

Grant looked at her with a sudden grim smile on his face. "Yeah, well wait until this mission is finished before you ask for more action."

They spent the rest of the afternoon in their room alternately reading, playing cards and talking. Grant spent a lot of the time pacing around the room. So much so, that at one point Sam threw her hands up in the air and said, "Grant, would you please just sit down for a while? I know you're anxious and want to do something, but you're driving me nuts." Grant gave a mock grimace and sat.

After breakfast in the room the next morning, Sam left for the meeting place. It was the same café where they had met Granowli. This time, Garcia just watched Sam leave and wasn't tempted to follow her. He was waiting for Thurmond who, he knew, wouldn't be far behind.

Chapter 28

I minus 36

The DNI decided to make one more plea to the President-elect about moving the inauguration to a safer place. He called David Carlisle, the head of the Secret Service detail protecting Mason, to enlist his support. They agreed to make the case together and were now both seated across from the President-elect.

"Sir, we could have the actual ceremony inside the White House and telecast it live to a huge screen on the outside podium next to the capital. The people would get an even better view than they would if you were there," pleaded Barry. "And, we could—"

"Sir, sorry to interrupt," said Carlisle, "but if we move the ceremony, procedures are for it to be in the Capitol Rotunda, not the White House."

"That would be no problem," declared Barry firmly, thinking it would be pretty easy to secure that area.

Mason sighed and leaned forward in his chair. Putting his hands in the air, palms facing each other about shoulder length apart, he said, "Look, guys, I'm not going to start my term in the highest office in the land being a coward. What message would that send to both our citizens and our enemies? We'd look like we couldn't control things in our own capital, which I think would encourage increased terrorist attacks on Americans and American interests overseas. Maybe even on our own soil. They'd assume we're an easy target. No way. Not on my watch." Mason leaned back and crossed his arms over his chest.

Carlisle decided to jump in. "You know, sir, we have done everything we can to make this a safe inauguration. We've placed metal detectors in the only access points attendees can go through to get to the stands. We will have trained agents from both the Secret Service and the FBI watching every person who enters the area, we've placed bullet proof glass in front of the podium and, in fact, in front of the whole dignitary seating area. We'll have choppers in the air, more than two hundred uniformed police and nearly that many plain-clothes officers mingling with the crowd. But even with all that, I'm worried. Sir, are you sure you won't reconsider?" he pleaded.

"With all those precautions, someone would have to be insane to attempt anything," Mason countered.

Carlisle replied, "Exactly, sir. That's what we're worried about. In this era of suicide bombers, no one is safe. A bomber can pack so much Semtex or C4 into such a small space, or even on themselves, that it would level a city block. And the metal detectors won't pick it up. Anyone could conceivably just waltz on through them disguised as an overweight supporter here to watch the ceremony. Remember, it's outside, so overcoats will be commonplace. We're struggling with how to detect hidden devices in large crowds, but we don't have foolproof measures."

"What about the see-through screening devices they use at airports?" Mason asked, still with his arms crossed. Now he crossed his legs as well. Both Barry and Carlisle notice the body language.

Carlisle explained, his frustration showing through, "Sir, there will be thousands of people watching the ceremony . . . we can't possibly screen every one. It'd take hours. Also, it's January . . . we sure as hell can't ask everybody to take off their coats. If somebody on the lunatic fringe is hell-bent on blowing us all up, we can't predict what they'll do or how they'll do it. They wouldn't follow the normal patterns that we can prepare for. We're stretching our staff to really think outside of the box, but we're all rational and we can't think like someone who isn't. So, please, sir, think about it."

Mason, sensing Carlisle's frustration, seemed to relax a little and uncrossed his arms. Less stridently, he said, "David, I have. Look, I know I'm a target and I do have some anxiety about it. As we get closer to the inauguration without finding who is behind this, I'm getting even more anxious. Not just for myself, but for my family who'll also be on the podium. But, I've made my decision. We're going with the original plan. I know it's risky, but I'm not going to act like a coward. That's final. Now what will the day look like?"

Carlisle sighed and then answered, "Well, sir, you and your wife will join the current President and First Lady for brunch in the White House. You should arrive around ten a.m. After brunch, both couples will be driven to the inauguration in separate armored limos. We've arranged a parking area immediately behind the dignitary stands for your cars, as well as for the cars of the Supreme Court chief justice and a couple of your cabinet members. Everyone else will park in a remote lot and be bussed in. I know some of the cabinet members and other dignitaries might be upset at having to ride a bus, but we have to do it this way. We'd appreciate your support in this.

"After the swearing-in ceremony, which, as you know, will be conducted by the Supreme Court Chief Justice, you and the First Lady will be escorted to the Presidential limousine and lead a motorcade from the Capitol area to the White House. Sir, although some newly sworn-in presidents have, in the past, gotten out of their car and walked part of the way up Pennsylvania Avenue, I would strongly advise you not to do that. Please plan to stay inside the car with the windows up the whole way. You should arrive at the White House around one-thirty p.m. At the same time, immediately after the ceremony, the former President and First Lady will be flown home in Air Force Two. At the moment the swearing-in is complete, the former President's personal effects will be taken out of the White House and yours put in place. By the time you arrive, it will be your home."

"So the exposure time will be limited to no more than an hour and a half and I'll be in a protected car part of that time? What about the Popemobile? Can we borrow that? Sorry, just kidding," Mason said with an attempt at humor.

Carlisle chuckled and said, "The Presidential limousine is heavily armored and you'll be fairly safe as long as you're inside."

At this point Barry interjected, "But sir. An hour and a half is a long time. Anything can happen. You also have to attend inauguration balls that evening—I think five in total. You'll be exposed there also."

"Look, I can't hide forever. The best shot we have, no pun intended, is to solve this before the inauguration. I'll make a decision about walking part of the way later. Let's just hope Thurmond finds this guy before it's too late. I gotta go; I'm out of time."

Barry and Carlisle answered in unison, "Yes, sir."

In his car on the way back to his office the DNI placed a call to General Wheeler. "We couldn't talk the President-elect out of it. The inauguration is going on as planned. We all better hope that Thurmond finds this madman first."

"We've got the best man on the job. If this guy can be stopped, he'll do it. He has to. The alternative is unthinkable . . . ." The general's voice trailed off.

Later that day, Riley left a short message on the voice mail system: "Just heard that the inauguration is on as planned. Don't know if that's important, but you said to report anything I heard." Riley felt sure he was reporting too much unimportant information, but he wanted to make sure the guy wasn't disappointed and that the checks would continue. And, yeah, he knew in his gut that he should be more concerned about why this guy wanted all this information about the President-elect, but it was a dog-eat-dog world and he had to look out for himself. It was all about the money. Between the money this guy was paying him and his regular paychecks as a government driver, he was already building up a nice little nest egg. Yessir, that condo in Florida was a sure thing now.

He knew it wouldn't last forever, but maybe when this guy stopped paying him, he could still keep his job as a government driver. It paid really pretty well and, if he worked there long enough, he'd have a retirement check for the rest of his life. Steady pay with a retirement sure beat the hell out of working all hours as a PI, never able to save a dime and ending up having only Social Security to live on. Also, nearly all of his PI work was following low-life people and taking ugly pictures for divorces: long hours, low pay and too long between assignments. All in all, he saw himself in a pretty sleazy occupation. Easy decision; if at all possible, he'd stay a driver.

Chapter 29

I minus 36

Thurmond left ten minutes after Sam and this time it was like a parade. He hailed a taxi right outside the hotel. Close behind, Vladimir flagged down an empty taxi and told him to follow the taxi ahead. Garcia, at his usual post sitting at the bus stop, saw Thurmond leave and in his haste to grab a taxi, completely overlooked Vladimir. Now there were three taxis, one after the other, less than a block apart. Both Vladimir and Garcia had their eyes glued to Thurmond's taxi and the traffic was heavy so they didn't notice each other. Thurmond, because of what happened last time he went out, was alert and watching to see if he was being followed. Unfortunately, since traffic was so frantic and with every third car on the road an identical looking taxi, it was impossible for him to tell one from another. Taxis were all around him, zooming in and out of traffic, most of them carrying only one passenger and most of the passengers were male. So much going on that, even with his experience, Thurmond completely missed both of the other men.

Traffic thinned somewhat when they entered the street the café was on. At that point, he was only a couple of blocks from the café, so Grant started looking towards the meeting place and paid less attention to the other cars on the street.

Sam, meanwhile, sitting on the same bench in the park, saw Grant exit his cab and enter the café. She noticed two more taxis stop down the block, not more than thirty yards from each other. No one got out of either taxi. That was curious, she thought, so she continued watching them.

In the traffic madness, Vladimir's taxi had been passed by Garcia's on the way, so he was now in the taxi at the rear of the procession. Leaning forward to hand the driver some cash, Vladimir realized that the passenger exiting a taxi just ahead of him looked a lot like the guy he thought he had killed in the crash the day before. Damn. How did he survive that fire? If it was him, these guys had nine lives. Now what was he going to do? Not having a lot of other options, he decided to lay low in the back seat of the taxi and watch

117

what the guy did. Vladimir couldn't believe it. They guy just sat down at a bus stop less than half a block from the café. What the hell was he doing? Was it the same guy as before?

Sam watched as a man dressed in ordinary workman's clothes wearing a snap brim hat finally got out of the foremost taxi. The taxi drove away and the man walked up the street about half a block and sat at the bus stop closest to the café. The hat was pulled so low that at this distance she couldn't see his face. She thought it strange, though, that the guy got out of a taxi and sat at a bus stop. Maybe he just decided that the taxi was getting too expensive and he was going to take a bus the rest of the way. Not sure what he was doing, she decided to keep an eye on him. At the same time, she noticed the second taxi was still double parked near the end of the block. That's interesting, she thought. Why is he just sitting there? Surely she was reading too much into these things. She must be getting jumpy. Just the same, Grant said to notice anything out of the ordinary, so she kept watching both the man at the bus stop and the taxi parked down the street.

Grant, unaware of it all, had a coffee and pastry in front of him and was completely focused on the upcoming meeting. This was the part of the operation where Sam had to earn her keep by watching his back, he thought. If she saw anything unusual, she was supposed to let him know. Knowing that she was watching everything else would let him concentrate on the meeting and not worry about movement around him. As a precaution, in the taxi he had taken the 9MM out of his jacket pocket and tucked it into the back waistband of his pants. He left the spare magazine in his coat pocket. Although it was a little uncomfortable, with the gun close at hand he was confident he could defend both himself and Sam. He was calm. He felt he was getting back into the groove.

After fifteen minutes of everyone just sitting, Vladimir had had enough. He pulled out the silenced 9MM he had bought from a minor gangster weeks earlier in Moscow. It was not a brand he recognized, just some older Eastern European or Russian model, but it was untraceable. He leaned forward over the front seat as if he wanted to talk to the driver and with just a very quiet pfft sound, shot the driver at the base of his skull. He casually got out the street side door, opened the driver's door, pushed the driver to the side and got behind the wheel. He rolled down the driver's side window and accelerated down the street coming quickly to a stop just in front of the bus stop where Garcia was sitting. He managed two quick shots out the driver's side window at Garcia. In his hurry to get to his next target, Vladimir didn't take time to make sure the shots hit home but he did see the man fall on the ground. He immediately accelerated and drove quickly the half block to where the woman was sitting. Slowing but not stopping, Vladimir reached out the window with his left hand and fired two shots at her. Pfft, Pfft. He then floored the taxi and rocketed down the street disappearing from view. The only sound anyone else heard was the roar of the taxi's engine and the squeal of tires.

Garcia was surprised when the taxi screeched to a stop directly in front of him. But his training kicked in. Fearing the worst, he dropped to the ground and rolled, hoping to throw off the aim of anyone who might try shooting at him. Two bullets slammed into the bench where he was sitting just seconds before. He watched as the taxi barreled off down the street. "What the hell?" he thought. Then he ran.

Sitting at one of the café's outside tables, Grant heard the taxi tires screeching, turned towards the sound and watched as the taxi then tore off only to pause again twenty yards from where Sam was sitting. He also saw a man rolling on the ground in front of the bus stop. The man looked just like every other workman in Warsaw, so Grant was puzzled. He watched as the man got up, look for just a moment at the taxi going away from him down the street, then sprint in the opposite direction. What the hell? he thought. Completely alert now, the hair on the back of his neck stood up. He then looked at Sam, saw her holding her hand to her neck and immediately leapt to his feet. Because of his injuries and bulky overcoat it was an effort for Grant to jump over the short wrought iron fence surrounding the outside seating area of the café. But over the fence he went anyway and ran, gun in hand, to where Sam was sitting.

Sam also saw the whole thing play out and was completely thrown, not knowing what to do next. She realized it had happened so fast she didn't register the faces of either the taxi driver or the guy at the bus stop. When the taxi driver slowed near her, she was so distracted by the man at the bus stop rolling on the ground, she didn't notice the taxi driver reach his hand out the window and shoot at her. She only realized what happened when the bullets struck the wooden bench she was sitting on, splintering the weathered wood and sending shards of wood into the side of her face and neck. By the time she recovered, the taxi was gone. Did I just get shot? she thought as she reached up to touch the stinging pain in her neck. She hadn't even stood up and was still sitting there stunned with her hand on her neck when Grant arrived by her side.

"Are you alright? You're hit, let me see." He checked her neck. There was blood, but it looked superficial.

"I don't think I was hit by a bullet, just wood fragments," Sam stammered.

"Can you walk? How bad is it?"

"Yes, I'm sure I can walk," she said with a catch in her voice.

Grant helped her up and said, "Okay, then let's get out of here before the police arrive. We'll check you out more thoroughly back at the hotel. Here, hold my handkerchief over the wound to stop the bleeding."

They quickly moved through the far side of the park and walked another two blocks before Grant slowed down.

"Here, let me take another look at that. You might need to see a doctor."

Getting her voice a little more under control, she said, "No, I don't think so. It doesn't really hurt that badly, just stings a little."

After examining Sam's neck and face more closely, Grant concluded that she was right. It was just superficial and she wouldn't need to see a doctor.

"That was a close call. Too close," Grant said. We know for sure now that someone is after us. At least you. Not sure whether they even saw me. You were a pretty easy target sitting out in the open like that and that's my fault. Damn, I must really be rusty to expose you like that. I *know* you're not trained for this shit. How could I do that?" Grant paused for a moment and when Sam didn't reply said, "Now that you've become a target, we're going to need new tactics to keep you safe. We'll work on those this afternoon. What was up with that guy at the bus stop? Did he get shot at too?"

"I don't know, I couldn't tell. By the time I saw that he was down, the splinters were hitting my neck. I didn't even see who shot at me. He was in a taxi, though, that much I know."

"Well, whoever he was, he sure got out of there in a hurry. You're lucky the splinters didn't hit your eye. Could have caused a lot more damage. Let's get back to the hotel and try to sort through all this." Grant took her arm and they walked away looking for a taxi.

Meanwhile, Vladimir was over a mile away looking for a convenient place to ditch the taxi. He had to get another car. Taxis were just too much trouble. He drove to a quiet alleyway a few blocks from the train station, locked the car doors and walked away, leaving the driver lying in the front seat. Anyone who saw the taxi would think the driver was just taking a nap. It would be a couple of hours at least before the body was discovered. By that time he'd be long gone. He entered the train station and bought a one-way ticket to Krakow. He was on his way to steal another car so he could be back in Warsaw by tomorrow morning. He still had more to do. He had no idea if he hit either the man at the bus stop or the girl. Piece of shit gun. He had to go back to get rid of Thurmond. He had wasted enough time. If the girl had survived, he knew she wouldn't be far from Thurmond, so he could get her anytime. Anyway, he was sure she couldn't identify him, so there was no real hurry with her.

The only problem was that he didn't know anything about the other man. It had to be either the Russians or this Garcia guy, but if so, where was he staying? How could he find him? If it *was* Garcia, was he working with Thurmond or acting on his own? CIA maybe? After mulling it over for another half an hour, it hit him how to get Thurmond where he wanted him. He was sure Thurmond had gotten the contact information for all the informants, including his, and was watching the personals. He'd just place an ad calling for a drop. He'd make it at midnight. If, as he thought, Thurmond had gotten his contact information from Granowli, he would know the details. If he saw the ad and showed up at the meeting place, Vladimir would kill him on the spot. He could be back in Moscow the next day, planning his trip to the United States.

While he was looking out the train compartment window, Vladimir thought about what he might want to do in America. Over the past thirty years, he had lived frugally. With most of his ordinary living expenses paid by his Soviet controllers, he'd been able to put away a considerable sum of money in a bank in Switzerland, funds that were hard to trace. Just before he left for America, he'd have it transferred in small increments to multiple banks around the country. After this whole thing was over he'd travel all over America. He'd certainly see New York. Maybe he'd splurge once and rent a limo to drive him around. America was full of rich people and he had to play the part to fit in. Then, maybe, Chicago. Also, Miami—yes, he had to see Miami. He'd wait for winter to go there. Then San Francisco— it was a famous city, though he wasn't sure what for. Hawaii; absolutely, Hawaii. Once he became a citizen, he could, if he wanted, get a passport and travel to all the places around the world he ever dreamed of. He would be a rich American tourist. He smiled at the thought.

Chapter 30

I minus 36

Back at his hotel, Garcia sat thinking about what happened. Obviously he'd been spotted and taken completely by surprise. But by whom? The guy Thurmond was after? Probably. Was he trying to get all of them at the same time? Garcia had a lot of questions, and not many answers. He was gonna have to be a lot more careful in the future. Funny, though, he was sure no one could recognize him with his workman's clothes. How did the guy get on to him? Could the man that had crashed into him in the taxi have recognized him? It was time to change his disguise, and time to start shooting back.

Grant and Sam eventually flagged down an available taxi and after arriving at their hotel, went in through the side door and used the stairs to avoid being spotted from the lobby. In their room, Grant took another look at Sam's wounds.

"You'll be alright," he said. "But, we need to pull out a couple of splinters. Got any tweezers?" He looked at her.

"Yes, in my makeup bag. I'll get them," Sam said without meeting his eyes.

Tweezers in hand and Sam seated in front of him, Grant said, "This might hurt a bit. Want a drink first?"

"No, just pull them out," Sam replied. She winced when he pulled the first one out. "Sorry," he said. "Two more to go." She met his eyes this time, her reserve slipping.

"I'm really sorry," he repeated.

"No, just finish it," she said, so quietly it was almost a whisper. "I'm just being a baby."

"No you're not." Grant put his hand on her shoulder, looking into her eyes for a moment.

After the splinters were removed, Grant sat across from Sam leaning forward with his elbows on his knees and his hands together. In a serious tone he said, "Okay, Sam, you now know how dangerous this is becoming. You just had an attempt on your life. You've been identified and targeted and I'd really like to send you home." Grant looked down at his hands and shook his head. "Unfortunately, I'm still not up to full capacity and I need your help here," he said, looking back up at her. "But we've gotta keep you out of harm's way, so here's the drill. We have to stick around here for a couple more days to see if any of the contacts show up. Out of the hotel room I want you to be in busy places. No quiet streets, no parks, no sitting by the window in restaurants. When you're not in the room, stay around crowds. I don't think he'll try anything where lots of people can see." His penetrating blue eyes searched hers.

"Look, Grant," she sighed, regaining her control. "I've done a combat tour in Iraq. I've faced danger and gunfire before and have come out okay. This guy, well now he's just pissed me off. I want him."

"I want him too," he said urgently. "But he knows us and we don't know him. He could walk right up to either of us and we wouldn't know it was him. And, don't forget he's killed over two dozen people. That makes him really dangerous . . . he's got nothing to lose by killing us," Grant continued in a softer, gentler voice, "And I have an added responsibility; I'm supposed to be protecting you."

Sam scoffed. "No, you're not supposed to be protecting me. I'm supposed to be assisting you," she responded a little more hotly than she intended.

Grant paused a moment, sighed and looked into Sam's eyes. "Okay, you've got a point. Sorry." He stood up.

"Apology noted," Sam responded sternly. Then she continued in a quieter voice, "and accepted." She stood and walked over to Grant, intending to give him a quick hug to show she was no longer offended. But what started out as a quick hug turned into a longer embrace with Sam resting her head on Grant's shoulder. It felt good to both of them and neither was anxious to move apart.

Finally moving away, Grant said gently, "We'd better put something on those cuts."

That broke the moment, but they both knew something had just happened between them that could change their relationship. Though neither of them would have felt comfortable saying it out loud, both Sam and Grant had a warm feeling about that.

Chapter 31

I minus 35

Grant placed another ad in the personals early the next day, hoping to reach anyone who might be looking. At this point he wasn't sure who was left alive in Warsaw. Obviously, the shooter was here, but who else? Best he could figure, the person he was trying to meet yesterday when the shooting happened was the only one that might be left. Oh, yeah, there was one more: the mystery person known only as Vladimir. However, since this guy never responded to any of the ads Granowli placed, there was no reliable way to contact him. Grant decided to place the ad anyway. Maybe this Vladimir would see the ad in the personals and respond with his own. He decided to start reading the ads today. If he could get in touch with this guy, he may have some helpful information. He phoned the paper and asked to speak to someone who knew English. It only took a few minutes to dictate the ad.

The next morning Grant confirmed his ad was in the morning paper and told Sam he was going out to meet the contact. He suggested Sam stay put in the hotel room.

"Make sure you take the gun," Sam responded. "I'm a little nervous about you going out there alone."

"Can't be helped," he responded. Then he put both hands on her shoulders and looked directly into her eyes. "Remember the rules. I'd rather you stay in, but if you do go out, stay in crowds and on the main street." Sam nodded, saying nothing.

During the time Grant was gone, Sam spent most of the time reading. She had tried TV, but couldn't understand anything that was said. She was running out of English reading material, though. Maybe she'd see if she could find a bookstore that sold books in English. The hotel was located in a busy commercial area and there had to be a bookstore around here somewhere. She'd ask the desk clerk later.

Meantime, Garcia, still dressed like a local laborer, but with different clothes and a large, fur, Russian-style hat, watched as Grant came out of the hotel's revolving doors and got into a taxi. Garcia grabbed the next taxi in line and told the driver to follow Grant's cab. The driver looked back over his shoulder and asked in heavily accented English, "Is this a joke?"

Garcia responded by handing the driver a US twenty dollar bill and saying, "Does this look like a joke? Just follow that cab." The driver took the money and accelerated quickly, throwing Garcia into the back of his seat. Off they went down the street with a cloud of blue exhaust smoke trailing after them.

Garcia noticed that they were heading the same direction they did yesterday, but this time he'd be ready. No sitting at a bus stop. Keeping a close eye on the traffic around him, he was sure he wasn't being followed. A block from the café, he had his cab go around the block to the far side of the park before letting him out. Then he wandered slowly through the park keeping Grant in sight. Garcia, unaware that Sam had also been shot at yesterday assumed she'd be covering Grant so he kept a sharp eye out for her. He doubted she'd be at the same bench two days in a row, but foot traffic was light and the park was the only vantage point where one could blend in and still keep the café in sight. As he walked through the park, he watched Grant drinking coffee and eating a pastry at the café. Garcia was chilled and the hot coffee looked good. There was no sign of either Sam or the guy who shot at him yesterday. After nearly an hour, Garcia watched as Grant stood up, left some currency on the table and hailed down a passing taxi. Obviously, the contact was a no show.

Chapter 32

I minus 33

Two days had passed since Grant posted the ad and, still, no one showed up at the meeting place. While at the embassy getting his ad translated, Grant made arrangements for a translator to read the personals each day, looking for the right response. The third morning Grant got a call from the translator, who simply said an ad in this morning's paper contained the message, 'The same place, midnight tomorrow.' Just what Grant was looking for.

In his excitement, he almost shouted to Sam. "Vladimir just made contact. I'm really glad now that Granowli gave me the contact info even though it was only a one-way communication."

Sam came into the room from the bathroom. She was wearing tight-fitting jeans and a soft gold sweater that complimented her dark hair. Stretching, she said casually, "Great. Where and when's the meet?"

"The usual place was an alleyway off Poznanska," Grant replied trying to keep focused. He hadn't seen her in attractive clothes like this before. "Guess I'll follow the routine Granowli used." Opening up his Warsaw map, he continued. "If it's not too far from our hotel, I think I'll walk. I'll have a better chance of seeing if I'm being tailed. Here it is," he said, trying not to be distracted by Sam, who was standing close. He noticed she was wearing a subtle, but really nice perfume. "He said the meeting place was twenty meters north from the corner of Poznanska and Nowogradzka where an alley came out onto Poznanska. There should be a trash can right on the corner of the alley. Sure hope it's still there. Even if it isn't, I should be able to find it okay." Man, she sure looked good this morning. He remembered the hug.

Assuming she would cover him, Sam asked, "Do you want me to get there before you or to follow you?"

He shook his head. "Not this time, kiddo. This is a solo mission."

"Grant, it's not safe," she argued with her hands on her hips. "You know this guy's out to get you and you have no idea who it is or what he looks like. For all you know, this could be a setup."

"I know," he said, making a frustrated gesture with both hands out in front of him. "But, if we're both walking, we're both targets. If this is a setup, it'll be easier for me if I don't have to worry about you."

"Oh, you think I can't take care of myself?" Sam asked.

He looked at her to see if she was kidding. She wasn't. Grant sighed, dropping his hands. "Look, Sam, that's not it at all. If I'm attacked I just don't want to have to be concerned about anything other than defending myself." He took a deep breath. "Like it or not, I care for you and, well, if you were out there and shots started flying, thinking about you would be a distraction. That's what wouldn't be safe. For either of us."

Sam just looked at him with a small smile. Then tilting her head to the side, she said, "A distraction, huh? Ok, but, it's going to be hard for me to wait until you get back. Any idea of how long you'll be gone?"

Grant resisted the urge to smile back. "Well, if all goes according to plan and he shows at midnight, I'll need up to an hour to talk to him. Given the lead time and the time to walk back to the hotel . . . guess it'll be two hours or so."

"That'll be a long two very long hours for me." This time it was her turn to take a breath. "And, Grant, I care for you, also, so please stay safe and return in one piece, okay? Remember our cell phones do work here, so call me if you need anything."

"You can count on it," Grant replied sitting down.

They spent the rest of the morning in their hotel room, Sam finishing her book, Grant poring over local maps and thinking about all the times he'd been in dangerous situations. Considering all that had happened, this meet tonight could be extremely dangerous. He knew he'd have to be on high alert.

They ordered room service lunch and because they were missing good old American food, they feasted on cheeseburgers, French fries and Diet Cokes.

After they had called for room service to pick up their trays, Sam turned to Grant and asked, "Grant, I really need to talk with you about, uhhh, us. What did you mean when you said earlier that you cared for me? You mean like a friend?" She looked down at her hands.

Grant paused a long time before answering, "Sam, even in the short time we've been together on this mission, I've grown very fond of you."

"C'mon Grant," she said. "I have no idea what 'fond' means to you. The way I use the word, it's like 'I'm fond of red wine.'"

"No, it's not like that," Grant stammered, then paused again for a long time. He took both her hands in his. "Look, Sam, I've loved one woman in my life. At least I thought I loved her at the time. That didn't work out very well for me. I've met a few women since and they seemed just out for a good time." He smiled slightly. "Okay, maybe it's because I met them in bars. But, you're different. You're not only beautiful and smart, you're, I don't know, different."

"Really," Sam drawled, smiling.

"No, not like that. It's not that you're weird or anything. You're special. You're sweet. I don't know . . . . You're different."

Sam just looked at him, eyebrows raised.

"You're gonna make me say this, aren't you?" Grant took a breath and let it out slowly, looking deeply into Sam's eyes. "Okay. Sam. It seems I'm falling in love with you."

Sam's eyes widened and her mouth opened in surprise. Pulling her hands away from his and bringing both of them to her mouth, she said, "Oh, boy. Wow. Not exactly what I thought you were going to say."

"Oh, look Sam, I'm sorry." Now *he* was uncomfortable. "I was talking out of line. Please, let's just forget I said that, okay? Can we just go on the way we were? Can we just change the subject?" Grant said, looking around the room. Anywhere but at Sam.

Sam paused this time, making sure her words were just right. She took his hands again and looking back up into his eyes quietly said, "Grant, I said it wasn't what I thought you would say, but, believe me, it was what I hoped you would say."

"Oh jeez, you really had me scared. Thought you were going to throw up or something," Grant exclaimed, looking more than a little relieved.

She laughed. "Oh Grant, I'm falling in love with you too, you dumb ass."

They both stood and embraced. This time, there was no pretense of it being just a friendly hug. This was an embrace. A full body hug.

After a moment that seemed to stretch forever, Grant lifted Sam's head from his chest and kissed her . . . a long lingering kiss.

Chapter 33

I minus 32

That night, as Grant leaned against the side of the brick building just across from the trash can, he couldn't help feeling exposed. There was a streetlight above the trash can and Christmas lights on the old-fashioned lamp posts, but the dim light didn't really penetrate into the alleyway very far. There was no other lighting and no moon shone above. Looking into the alley, he couldn't see anything beyond fifteen feet or so. He knew he was vulnerable, but what choice did he have? This meeting place was set up for exchanging information, not for face-to-face meetings. His choice would have been a far more public place in broad daylight or at least a place where he would be less highlighted by the light. But, Grant reasoned, the contact really didn't have any choice. There was no way he could put an ad in the paper that said, "Meet me in the lobby of the Marriott at noon. We'll do lunch." He had to use the standard code or no one would realize it was him. That intellectual rationalization, however, didn't help his nerves.

A few people passed in the first fifteen minutes Grant was there. Not as much as one person even looked at him. Grant was getting concerned that the contact wouldn't show. As he was standing facing the street, he heard a small scraping sound down the alley behind him. He was tempted to ignore it and not take his eyes off the street, but a nagging feeling caused him to turn towards the sound. Just as he turned, although he didn't hear anything but the impact, his face was stung by brick fragments chipping off the building he was just leaning on. A silencer—not good, Grant thought. He immediately dropped to his knees and drew his weapon, using the corner of the building to hide behind. Grant couldn't see anything but he knew someone was there. All he could hope for was that the assailant would take another shot. In the dark he'd be able to see by the fire from the muzzle where the shot was coming from. He'd just open up on that spot. The little 9MM had limited range, however, so he had to get within forty feet or so to be sure of hitting his target.

Vladimir, meanwhile, was tucked inside a back doorway exiting onto the alley about thirty feet away. He couldn't believe he missed. The perfect setup and he missed the shot. This damn Russian piece of shit gun. He should have gotten another one after he saw how bad it was when he shot at the woman. Now that Thurmond knew he was there, the game had just changed. Thurmond was a dangerous man. All DIA agents were dangerous. If he pursued this, Vladimir knew that if Thurmond was armed, and he surely would be, he might not survive. It looked like retreat was the only option. He could see that Thurmond was backlit and he knew he was in the dark so Vladimir backed out of the doorway and trotted softly the direction he had come. His freshly stolen car was less than a block away.

Grant, now behind the wall, both hands on the gun in the classical military firing position with arms bent at the elbow, gun pointed upwards, had a decision to make. Should he engage the guy by trying to get a clean shot, or should he back off and hightail it out of there back to the hotel? The problem was, if he left, would he ever be able to find the guy again?

Retreat was a word not normally in Grant's vocabulary, but he didn't really have much choice. Being backlit by the streetlight he was a sitting duck if he leaned out to fire a shot. It would be one way of drawing fire, but it might be fatal. He decided to turn around and beat it back to the hotel.

Vladimir, now running full speed down the ally, turned the corner. His car was ten meters away. He was safe, he thought.

As Vladimir entered his car, the passenger side glass shattered and shortly afterward he heard the very loud report of a large caliber gun. "Who the hell was shooting at him?" he thought. It couldn't possibly be Thurmond—he was clear down the alley on the other street. Did he follow him? He couldn't have gotten here this quickly.

Garcia, meanwhile, having followed Grant from the hotel, had decided to circle around to the back, and as he was walking down the street, had seen a man leave a car and walk down the alley. There was something familiar looking about the man. Also, he was staying in the shadows and was acting like he was trying to go unnoticed. Garcia decided to watch him. A few minutes later he saw the same guy running back to his car and Garcia realized where he'd seen him before. This was the guy who had demolished his taxi. As the man got into his car, Garcia fired. He was quite a distance away for a handgun, even a Glock .40 caliber, but his first shot hit the passenger side window, sending shards of safety glass into the car. His next shot went into the pillar behind the passenger window. His third shot, he was sure, hit the target.

He was using law enforcement hollow points so he was amazed to see the car pull away from the curb and rocket down the street. He could have sworn he'd nailed the guy. The big gun roared as he fired twice more, but the car continued speeding away. He didn't really give a shit if Thurmond had been hit or not, but he thought he ought to know, so he ran quickly down the alley keeping in the shadows. When he got to the corner, there was no sign of Thurmond. He must still be alive, but Garcia didn't know whether or not he'd been hit. He could see where a bullet impacted on the side of the building so if the assailant only fired once, Thurmond should be okay. He had to get out of here fast before the police showed up. Someone surely had called after hearing his big .40 caliber go off several times. Nothing left to do but go back to his hotel and wait for morning. He sure wished he knew more about the driver, though.

Later, back in the hotel room he shared with Sam, Grant finished telling the story of the evening events.

"You could have been killed," Sam said. "Why did you just stand under the light like that?"

"I needed to make sure he would see me."

"Obviously, he did. You're lucky he's not a good shot. Come to think of it, guess I'm lucky too. If he'd aimed just a little to the left when he shot at me, his bullet would have gone right through my neck."

"Hmm. You might be on to something there. His shot at me went to the right as well. Maybe the gun pulls right. Not sure how that helps us, but who knows. At least we can assume now that the person code named Vladimir is our mystery killer. Wonder if he is working for someone else or just himself. If just for himself, why? What's he trying to accomplish?" As he usually did when thinking things through, Grant started pacing around the room. The he continued. "And, why now, after all this time? Damn. Nothing but questions." Another pause, then shaking his head said, "Well, we'd better get some sleep. I'll need to call General Wheeler tomorrow morning and tell him about Vladimir. We may not know who he is, but we should be able to review all the information he's fed us over the past twenty years or so. Maybe there's a clue in there somewhere. First thing in the morning I'd like you to check out flights home. Don't book anything just yet, but I think we ought to go home and continue there. I'll ask General Wheeler to have someone pull out everything we have that refers to Vladimir and have it ready for us when we get back."

Sam, who'd been quiet, giving Grant time to work through his thoughts, now said, "Okay, Grant. I'll get on the airline schedules first thing in the morning."

They said good night and after a short embrace they retired to their separate bedrooms and both were asleep within fifteen minutes. It had been a long day for both of them.

Garcia, meanwhile, had returned to his hotel and after a short thought about how seriously he might have wounded the assailant, he, too, fell asleep.

Chapter 34

I minus 31

At 1:00 a.m. Vladimir was parked about five kilometers away from the hotel examining the wound in the back portion of his upper right shoulder. It was really painful and bleeding pretty badly. He knew he needed to have it looked at, but it was obviously a bullet wound and any doctor he went to in Poland would report it to the police. He knew a doctor he could count on who, for a couple hundred US dollars, would treat the wound and never make a report. Unfortunately, this doctor was in Moscow. He'd have to pack and bandage the wound as best he could and get back to Moscow immediately. He just hoped he wouldn't lose too much blood before he could get to the doctor. He drove back to the Hilton, went to his room, wrapped the small amount of ice he found in his mini bar inside a hand towel and pressed it to the wound. That should slow down the bleeding.

After that he called the airline office and booked an early morning flight to Moscow. He could sleep for about three hours before he had to leave for the airport. He also made a mental note: while in Russia, get a better gun, but not another Russian-made gun. The black market always had plenty of weapons, even American made.

The wound in his shoulder, while not life threatening, was painful, so he washed down four ibuprofen tablets with a vodka from the mini-bar. That should help. He fell asleep quickly, but slept fitfully until the alarm sounded a few hours later.

When he awoke three hours later, he took three more ibuprofen, this time with water. He then stuffed part of a washcloth into the wound, trying to cut off the bleeding and bandaged it as best he could by taping a piece of plastic bag over the washcloth. That should keep the blood from leaking through until he got to the doctor that afternoon. Even with the ibuprofen it was still really painful, though. On the flight to Moscow Vladimir thought about what all this meant to his plans. He knew he'd need a few days to recuperate so he couldn't do anything right away about Thurmond and the other guy who shot him. He was confident they wouldn't be able to track him back to Moscow. But time was running out.

He had to come up with a new plan for Thurmond. He thought about it and concluded that Thurmond couldn't go much further contacting people on the list because everybody was dead. Thurmond didn't necessarily know that, but when no one showed up at the meeting places, he would eventually have to give up and go home. Maybe he could find him in Washington. Maybe Thurmond would be at the inauguration and he'd take care of him there. It was highly likely Thurmond knew his code name, but he couldn't know his real identity and would never be able to find him. Even after it was over and he knew he killed the new President, Thurmond would only know him by Vladimir and he was pretty sure Thurmond had never gotten a visual on him. That wouldn't be enough to find him in a country as big as the United States. No, he really didn't have to worry about Thurmond.

The other guy, however, the one who shot him, did get a look at him and might be able to identify him. But, he didn't know who that person was, so there really wasn't anything he could do about it right now. Not what he'd hoped for, but maybe the best he could get under the circumstances. His first priority was to get bandaged up before the wound got infected.

Chapter 35

I minus 31

Thurmond slept until 6:30 a.m. then got up. Sam was in her bed still asleep so he quietly showered, shaved, dressed, wrote a note telling her what he was doing and left the apartment. He got a cab right outside the hotel and, fifteen minutes later, was entering the US Embassy. No one saw him leave—Vladimir was on his way to Moscow and Garcia was still sound asleep. He started to call General Wheeler when he realized that with the time difference it was just before midnight in Washington. So instead he called the night duty officer at the DIA ops desk. Grant explained what he was looking for in the files and asked him to leave a private brief for General Wheeler. He told the duty officer, a LTC Bailey, that this was extremely confidential and that the brief should not be copied or logged and be marked "Eyes Only" for General Wheeler and that he, the duty officer, should not mention this to anyone else. LTC Bailey, used to such requests from field agents, assured Thurmond that he would do as requested.

Grant didn't have anything further to do at the Embassy so he went back to the hotel. When he got to the room he found a note from Sam on the table saying she was going out to buy a book and that he shouldn't worry because she was sticking to busy sidewalks. Grant smiled at the note and decided to go downstairs to the restaurant for a late breakfast. There, he ordered a full American breakfast of three eggs, scrambled; three pieces of bacon, crispy; buttered toast, dark; and a carafe of black coffee, American style. The hot coffee was served right away and he sipped slowly, waiting for his breakfast to be served. He thought about all that had happened and how lucky he was to have survived the attempts on his life. Although he was still pretty sore, he was much better than he had been and even though he'd been shot at last night, he was still alive. He cheered at that thought and when it was served, he thoroughly enjoyed his breakfast.

Sam, at the same time, was meandering slowly between the racks of books at a store about four blocks down the street from the hotel.

The store had quite a few English language books and it was taking her some time to see all they had. She had no clue that she was being watched from outside the store.

Garcia, at his usual post at the bus stop, had seen her leave the hotel and had followed her to the book store. He knew she might recognize him if he went into the store, so he was content to just lounge on the corner across the street until she came out. Sam finally picked out a book, paid for it at the front counter and walked back to the hotel. The December air was cold and the stores lining the street were fully decorated for Christmas, bringing a cheery look to what otherwise would have been a string of dreary, soot-stained, old Soviet-era buildings. Sam enjoyed her walk without once suspecting that Garcia was not too far behind her. As she entered the hotel lobby, Grant was just exiting the restaurant and they met up with each other at the elevator.

"Everything go okay?" Grant asked.

"Completely uneventful," Sam replied.

"Good. Let's go upstairs and plan our next move."

Garcia, just outside the hotel entrance, watched Sam and Thurmond meet and enter the elevator. He resumed his position at the bus stop. At least it had a bench. He sat and lit another of his local cigarettes. Not so bad this time. Maybe he was getting used to them. All this waiting would get on the nerves of most people, but in his career with the CIA Garcia had spent a lot of time just sitting and watching.

He wondered again about Vladimir. He was *sure* he hit him, but didn't know how serious it was. That .40 caliber slug would make a huge hole and would almost certainly require a doctor's care. Wonder what he'd do about it? Now that the guy knew he was being stalked, Garcia knew he would be even more dangerous. Clearly he had to be careful; the bastard had already tried to kill him once. It would have been perfect if he had been able to kill Vladimir last night. Next time. On the positive side, though, he was certain that neither Thurmond nor Sam had a clue that he was tailing them. He took another puff.

Back in their room, seated on the couch, Grant and Sam began planning their next steps.

Granted said, "Sam, we gotta get this guy before he gets us. He's obviously on the offensive and sees us as a threat. He's killed nearly everyone in the whole network and my guess is that he'll continue to stalk the rest until they're gone. I think I'm on that list and now I think you are too. And, don't forget the 'big-guy' back home."

"But, at this point, what can we do about it?" Sam asked, her concern obvious.

Grant, sounding confident, said, "First, we're going to place the ads in the paper. Then we're going to sit and wait, hoping someone shows up."

"And if they don't?"

Grant shrugged. "Well, I'm hoping that the analysts can find something about Vladimir in the files. If we can find out where he worked, we can go there, talk to people he might have worked with and see if we can identify him. At least get a real name. I know it's a needle in a haystack, but it's all we've got."

"We know he uses Vladimir. Maybe they'll recognize it."

"Not likely. I've never known any informant to use his code name at his cover location. It's too dangerous and they're all told when they're recruited to only use the code name with their control officer."

Sam sighed. "Okay, better call the paper and place the ads," she said.

Chapter 36

I minus 30

"Well, we have a month before we move into the White House. How're you feeling now about being First Lady?" The President-elect and his wife were having breakfast in the dining room of the Blair House. They had been there about a week now and could see the White House from the dining room window. It was unusual for the President-elect to move into Blair House, but given the circumstances the Secret Service thought it would be the best place to keep him safe.

"I'm really nervous, Teddy. I never dreamed I'd be in the spotlight this much. There are photographers everywhere I go. It's almost like being a movie star. And I'm still not comfortable with the Secret Service surrounding me all the time." Mason's wife, Becky, was 38, a few years younger than he. She was a slender, beautiful woman with blond hair and brilliant blue eyes. They had met in Ann Arbor when he was in law school and she was a junior at University of Michigan. While not exactly love at first sight, their relationship developed quickly, with Becky moving into Mason's apartment only three months after they met. By the time he finished law school, Becky had finished her undergraduate work, graduating with honors, earning a BA in Political Science. They were married that June. Mason was elected to the state senate that November. Although both wanted children, Becky was unable to conceive and, after much soul-searching and heart-felt conversation, they decided not to adopt.

"Better get used to it. It's gonna be that way for at least four years," Mason laughed.

"Teddy, I'm really worried about this possible assassination attempt at your inauguration. How real do you think it is?" Becky was clearly nervous.

"Well, I think it's a pretty slim chance that anyone could slip through the massive security procedures that are being set up. However, both DIA and CIA are taking it very seriously, as is the Secret Service. We have agents in Eastern Europe right now searching for clues to the identity of the guy who's killing our

139

informants, and we have some evidence that shows it's the same person who's threatening me."

"But what if it's more than one person? What if it's a large group of terrorists using the other killings just to focus attention elsewhere—as a diversion? How could we ever find all of them?"

Mason reached out and took her hand. "Hey babe, that's a lot of what ifs. First of all, we have no intelligence that indicates a terrorist country or organization is involved in any way. The best guess is that it's a rogue agent with a grudge against America. What we don't know is whose agent he is—ours or someone else's. It doesn't really matter though; the process for rooting him out is the same." He took her other hand and continued quietly, "Look sweetheart, there's nothing more that can be done and I have a lot of other things to deal with. This one I just have to leave to the pros. And besides, we don't even know if I'm targeted. The best we can say is that I *might* be and it *might* happen at my inauguration."

Becky looked unconvinced and released his hands. "I know you're right, Teddy, but I do worry about it. It just always seems to be on my mind."

Mason took a sip of coffee, then, changing the subject, asked, "How are the interviews going for your new staff?"

Becky opened her eyes wide and replied, "I didn't realize how many people work for the First Lady. I'm amazed that I have my own press secretary, even. I think I'm going to keep several of the people who are already in place. They're experienced and not political. Several of them have worked for two or more First Ladies."

"Glad you're making progress," Mason said and then stood up, leaned over and gave his wife a quick kiss. "Well, I've got to run. I have a full day and won't be back until around dinner time. Remember, we have a formal dinner to go to tonight. The limo will pick us up here around seven. Dinner'll probably run late—you might want to think about a nap this afternoon."

She laughed. "Just go. I can take care of myself. Have a wonderful day, and . . . please be careful."

After Mason left, Becky sat at the table enjoying another leisurely cup of coffee thinking about all that was in front of them. She sure hoped the next four years would be free from terror attacks and wars. She knew that sending Americans to die in war would weigh heavily on her husband. He was a strong man, and even though he was a staunch conservative and supported a strong America, hearing about casualties in Iraq and Afghanistan really got to him. She couldn't imagine how he'd feel if he were the one who had ordered these soldiers to war, to their deaths. An involuntary shudder shook her as she sat at the table looking across the street to the White House. It was at times like these when she questioned whether being President was really worth it. Well, a little late for that now.

Chapter 37

I minus 28

Two days had passed since he placed the latest ads with no one showing up at any of the meeting places. Thurmond was beginning to think he'd have to go back to the States with no leads and no motive. He knew the guys at HQ had been poring through the files and had identified a lot of material that was attributed to Vladimir, but, so far, none of it gave any clue to his identity. They'd continue to sift through the files and General Wheeler had told Grant he'd be notified if they found anything worth reporting.

Grant, with his hands in his pant pockets, was pacing again. "Sam, we'd better keep thinking about next steps. If the guys back home don't come up with anything in the next couple of days, we're gonna have to go back empty handed. Other than continuing to review every piece of information we have in our files, I really don't know where to turn after that." He stopped pacing and looked out the hotel window at the brick building next door, then he turned towards Sam and continued, "Seems like I've been saying that a lot lately, but I'm not used to failure . . . and this is one mission that can't be allowed to fail."

Sam, who'd been watching him pace, shrugged and said, "Grant, I'm sure you'll think of something. You know, if we do go back, maybe you can convince the President-elect to move the ceremony to a safer place."

Grant shook his head, "Not likely. The DNI has been pushing really hard, but the President-elect is standing firm and has now completely taken it off the table. No further discussion." He continued to stand, hands in pockets with his back to the window.

"That doesn't seem reasonable," Sam said.

With another shrug, "He doesn't have to be reasonable—he's going to be President. What he says goes."

"Hmm, yeah, I suppose you're right. On another note, what do you want to do today? I'm getting tired of just sitting around this hotel room."

"Yeah, me too. Want to go shopping?" Grant asked.

Sam smiled. "A man wanting to go shopping? Wow, never thought I'd hear that from you."

"I don't *want* to go shopping, but I thought *you* might. I'll just tag along for safety reasons. Also, I'd really like to see if Vladimir is still watching us. I have to assume he is and if he is, I might be able to spot him. If we stick to busy streets he won't try anything. Also, if we walk, he'll have to be on foot also and that will make him easier to spot."

Sam continued smiling. "My own personal bodyguard. I feel like a movie star. Okay, sounds good to me, let's do it. I'm normally not much of a window shopper, but I'm really restless. Let's go." She stood up and grabbed her purse. "I just have to comb my hair."

They left the hotel and walked down the street and without either of them seeing him, Garcia followed at a discreet distance. He stayed on the other side of the street where he could easily keep them in sight. Being across the busy street meant that they might give him the slip, but it would also make him less obvious and more difficult to spot. The street was filled with traffic, both cars and trucks, and was lined on both sides with parked cars. He didn't believe there was any chance they could spot him through all that. He could tell that Thurmond was being cautious and checking surreptitiously to see if he was being followed. Garcia was sure Thurmond hadn't gotten a good look at this Vladimir character so he knew he'd only be looking for obvious signs rather than a face. He knew Thurmond would never suspect he was in the area so he wouldn't expect to see him. Whenever Thurmond stopped to look in a shop window, Garcia would keep shuffling slowly forward without turning his head in Thurmond's direction. He knew that an easy way to keep an eye on what's going on around you was to watch reflections in glass windows . . . and there were a lot of them on this street. You could see other people while they thought you were just looking at items in the shop. It usually worked pretty well and he was reasonably sure Thurmond was using that to check everybody out.

The day passed uneventfully. Sam went into several shops but all she bought was a scarf as a present for her mother. They had lunch at a cozy restaurant just off the main street. The restaurant was gaily decorated for Christmas with lights, candles and greenery adorning every table. Garcia stayed outside across the street, buying a sausage and sauerkraut in a bun from a street vendor. He sat at a bus stop bench eating his sausage and watching the restaurant door. It was gray and overcast and was easily the coldest day since he'd been in Poland. Even bundled up as he was, Garcia was beginning to get cold. With a shudder he thought, why don't these people just go home?

After a long leisurely lunch, Sam and Grant chatted as they strolled along the boulevard. They went into a few more shops, but didn't buy anything else. It began to snow lightly so Grant suggested they return to the hotel and have something warm to drink at the bar.

When he saw them turn around and walk back to the hotel, Garcia was relieved. He was freezing by that time and just wanted to get to his hotel and warm up. If Thurmond was crazy enough to go out later tonight, he was on his own. The weather forecast was for snow, a lot of snow, and very cold temperatures, which meant that just sitting outside at the bus stop would be intolerable. He'd stay in tonight, enjoy a nice dinner in the little hotel restaurant and be back at his post tomorrow morning. A little less than a block from Sam and Grant's hotel, Garcia turned into a side street and walked the half block to his hotel.

Just as Sam and Grant were going through the revolving doors into the Hilton, Grant's cell phone rang. It was General Wheeler.

"Thurmond," Grant said answering the phone.

"Thurmond, Wheeler, how long will it take you to get to a secure phone?"

"The embassy is about twenty minutes away, General. I'll call you as soon as I get there."

"Good. This is important." Wheeler hung up without saying goodbye.

Grant folded his phone and put it into his coat pocket. When he looked at Sam she asked, "General Wheeler?"

"Yeah, I have to get to the embassy right away. Wanna come?"

"Sure," Sam answered. "I don't want to sit alone in a hotel room."

Grant and Sam went back through the revolving doors out into the snow. They waved to the first taxi in the queue just up the street and told the driver their destination. Since Garcia was warming up and nursing a scotch in the little lobby bar of his hotel, he didn't see them leave. Twenty minutes later when they reached the embassy, Grant took Sam to the third floor secure area, signed them both in and called General Wheeler.

The general answered on the second ring with his customary "Wheeler"

"General, this is Thurmond."

"Thanks for getting back to me so soon. You're on a secure line?"

"Yes, sir," Grant said.

"One of the analysts going through the files found something that might lead you to Vladimir," Wheeler said. "We've traced several of the documents which show Vladimir as the source back to the same department. These documents were received over several years, so our analysts believe it may be the department he worked in. Also, some of what he supplied has, over the years, turned out to be fake. We don't know whether he faked the documents just to be able to supply more stuff, or whether he was directed to provide us specific misinformation. He might have been a double agent. I don't know how much that helps, but it sure does point us in the right direction. You might want to write down the department name and location. Maybe you can find someone there who can recall something. A long shot, I know, but it's the best we've come up with."

"General, could you check with the CIA to see if they have any trusted assets in Krakow?"

"Sure. If they do, I'll set it up so that they contact you at the hotel. I'll tell him to use the code name Billie. I'll also call you on your cell and just say 'okay' or 'no dice' to let you know what to expect."

"Thanks, General. we'll be heading to Krakow tonight."

"Good luck, Thurmond. Stay in touch."

Grant turned to Sam and filled her in on what the General told him, then said, "Okay, at least we have *something* to go on. Let's get back to the hotel and see if we can get a flight tonight to Krakow."

Sam thought for a moment and said, "You know, we could drive. It's only a hundred and fifty miles or so."

Grant took a moment to stand up and think about this. "Well, it's still snowing, but it might be a way to give Vladimir the slip, just in case he's still tracking us. The snow is supposed to get heavier later tonight but we could be there before then. Also, a car would be useful in Krakow. Let's do it. I'll see if I can get the Defense Attaché to take us to a rental agency."

When Grant asked the Defense Attaché to recommend a rental agency, the officer told him there was no need to rent a car, he could just check out an embassy car and keep it as long as he'd like. They picked up the car, a black four wheel drive Chevrolet Trailblazer, at the rear of the embassy and drove back to the Hilton. It was early enough that despite the snow there were still plenty of cars on the streets. Since Grant couldn't be sure he wasn't being followed, he parked on a side street a block or so from the hotel.

He checked the area out pretty thoroughly on the way back to the hotel and didn't see any sign they were being followed. When they arrived they went in through the side entrance and up the back stairs to their room. They packed their bags and checked out by phone, using the credit card Sam had given them when she arranged for this room. They went back down the stairs to the side entrance. Grant told Sam to wait inside the hotel and, when she saw him pull up, to come out quickly and he'd load the bags into the back. It all worked well and they were soon on their way to Krakow with no sign that they were spotted leaving. The attaché officer had given him a map and directions and said he would call ahead to the Grand Hotel, reserving a room for each of them. He paused and looked into Grant's eyes for only a moment when Grant told him they'd only need one room. Grant just met his stare.

The drive to Krakow took over four hours. Traffic was light, but the roads had not been plowed and the snow was piling up. Even in the dark it was easy for Grant to see they weren't being followed, so he began to relax a bit. During the drive, Grant and Sam talked some more about their past and Sam asked what led him to join the Air Force.

Grant, keeping his eyes on the road said, "My father went to Annapolis as did his father and, although no one insisted I had to go, I just felt like my dad would be proud of me if I went to a military academy. Unfortunately, he died while I was in high school and never got to see me in uniform."

"If they were Navy, how did you end up in the Air Force? I know you went to the Air Force Academy," Sam asked. In the dark she was able to see Grants profile, lighted slightly by the glow of the instrument panel lights. She liked what she saw and knew he couldn't see her staring. She smiled.

"Well, I chose the Air Force because I wanted to fly and I was told that a much higher percentage of Air Force Academy graduates went to flight school than did Naval Academy graduates. I also wanted to have a family and didn't want to spend as much time away from home as they Navy types do. You know the old saying, 'Sailors belong on ships and ships belong at sea.' The ironic thing is that with the career path I chose, I spent very little time at home, far less than a typical naval aviator."

"That leads to the obvious question—why aren't you a pilot? Did you ever go to flight school?" Sam asked.

"No, I didn't. One of the things the academy did for us was to bring in people to talk about the different career fields available. Nothing but flying interested me until I heard the guys from intel talking about all the things you could be involved in as part of the intelligence community. I had a chance to spend a couple of hours with them and by the end of that time, I was hooked. I never looked back. After graduation, I spent over a year in specialized training and was assigned to the National Reconnaissance Office, the NRO. It was okay for a while, but I really wanted more action, so I wrangled a job at DIA where I insisted on anything but a headquarters staff job. There were less than a hundred field agents, so it took a little while to work into one of the slots. I stayed with them until I retired."

She was intrigued. "How do you start setting up a network?"

"Actually, the first slot to open up was a new one created to establish a network in Lebanon. I told you about that one. That's the only network I really grew from scratch and, given the circumstances, it was never too successful. When I got back to the States, I was given a very small network based in Eastern Europe and grew it. When I took it over, there were two informants. I managed them and reported to a handler in DIA. As I got promoted, I was given other informants to manage, I recruited others and by the time I retired, there were about sixty people in my network. It was *very* productive and we received a lot of helpful intelligence, continuing even after I retired. I'm sure there was some junk in there also, but that was for the analysts back at HQ to sort out."

Sam shook her head slightly from side to side. "Wow, it must have been interesting. That's a world I know nothing about."

Grant risked a quick sideways glance at Sam. "Well, neither you nor anyone else were *supposed* to know anything about it. That's kinda the point of a spy network, you know. The best way to keep something from being compromised is to make sure you keep everything at the 'need to know' level and that's what we did." Grant was smiling now.

Sam chuckled. "I get your point," she said.

Grant turned back to once again stare at the road. "It was always an interesting field, but the work was often either boring or, like the other night, you get more excitement than you want."

Just before 10:00 p.m. they approached the outskirts of Krakow. The directions provided by the attaché were right on and they had no problem finding the hotel. Grant easily recognized it from his stay a couple of weeks ago. They used valet parking and as they were walking to reception, Grant reminded Sam of their cover as tourists traveling together, saying they would be in the same room. "Two beds," he said before Sam could reply, "and I have pajamas." They registered in Sam's name. As far as they could tell, only the General knew they were in Krakow.

Chapter 38

I minus 27

Early the next morning, back at his usual post, Garcia brushed the snow off the bus stop bench and was sitting, sipping a cup of hot coffee while he kept an eye on the front door of the Hilton. It was bitter cold. By noon, he was growing weary and took a short lunch and warm-up break inside a diner, not far away. He sat by the window where he could just barely see the front door of the hotel. By the end of the day he was getting worried. Had they slipped out while he wasn't watching? He'd give it another day or so before he took any action to find out.

After two more days of seeing nothing and freezing his tail off, he decided to check in with the DDI to find out if she'd heard anything. Half an hour later, he was at the Embassy using a secure phone. During that conversation he learned that General Wheeler had updated the DDI right after his conversation with Thurmond. Thurmond and Sam were in Krakow. Damn. Somehow they had given him the slip. Why the hell hadn't the DDI called him? Well, he'd be in Krakow by nightfall. His guess was that Thurmond would stay in the same hotel as the first time, so, as soon as he got there he'd check to see if he was registered. If he'd used another name, Garcia would just have to wait around trying to spot him without being spotted. Damn, this was getting old.

Vladimir, meanwhile, had made his way to his very discrete Moscow doctor who gave him a local anesthetic, dug out several bullet fragments, put in eight stitches, gave him some bacterial cream to apply twice a day and told him to keep the wound clean. He also told him that any physical stress could rip out the stitches and start the bleeding again. Vladimir paid the doctor and left. The whole thing had taken less than half an hour.

Back in his suburban flat, Vladimir started planning his next steps. Even though it wasn't going exactly as he'd hoped, the overall plan was still valid and he was sure it would work. Less than a month to go and he'd be free and clear.

He briefly thought about calling off the assassination, but knew his future depended upon getting rid of everyone who might be able to identify him. He still had his former Russian controller to take care of, but that would be easy. Thurmond would be more difficult, but not impossible. The hard part would be identifying and killing the other guy, this Garcia. That's what he needed to work on. Especially since the man was clearly after him and was trying to kill him. He had to be working for the Russians and Vladimir had no way of knowing how much the guy had communicated back to them. Maybe the guy even described him. Killing all the others was just part of the job, but killing that guy would be a pleasure.

The next morning Vladimir began making plans to go to the United States. His new passport and identity papers had been easy to come by. Russia was full of illegal activities and identity forgery was everywhere. It had cost him less than one hundred US dollars and it was excellent work. Of course, he had to kill the forger. Couldn't have any loose ends. Looking now at the passport, Vladimir couldn't tell in any way it was a forgery. He was now a citizen of Poland. His plan was to use a Russian passport to get into Poland again and then use the Polish passport to fly from Warsaw to New York. He also had a US passport and a driver's license from the District of Columbia, also obtained from the passport forger, and would use that as ID for the train from New York to Washington. He'd use the time before the inauguration to set up bank accounts and arrange for some money to be transferred from his Swiss bank to his new banks in America. Then in about three weeks he could go anywhere he wanted. He opened the bottle of vodka he had bought on the way home and took a large swig. Had to keep the pain at bay, right?

Chapter 39

I minus 26

At breakfast the next morning, Grant and Sam were discussing how to approach finding someone who worked at the old Soviet department identified in the Vladimir files. They were interrupted by the ring from Grant's cell phone.

"Everything's okay," the General said, then hung up. Let anyone who might be listening in on the cell transmission try to figure out what that means, he thought.

After hanging up, Grant looked up at Sam and said, "Apparently we, at some point, are going to have a visitor who might be able to help us out."

"What do we do until then?"

The question went unanswered because at that moment a woman who looked to be in her thirties approached their table and said, "Hi, I thought that was you. It's me, Billie. I couldn't believe my eyes. It's you! Just sitting at a restaurant table in Krakow. I haven't seen you for years. How are you?" She remained standing.

Grant stood up to greet her and said, "Oh, hi Billie. It's great to see you." He gave her a quick hug and continued. "We were just finishing up and going for a walk. Would you like to join us?"

Billie gave a quick look at Sam, then returned her gaze to Grant and said, "Sure. It's beautiful outside. The sun is out and is starting to melt the snow already," Billie said.

Once they were outside walking along the sidewalk, Grant chuckled, "It's a good thing the General didn't choose Robert. It would have been a bit awkward."

"Yeah, these old Generals always assume an operative's a guy. They seem so surprised when I show up. Now, how can I help you? I received no background on this at all. All I got was your name, location and your picture." She glanced again at Sam and said, "And I thought you'd be alone."

Grant gave her his sort of smile. "I was wondering how you recognized me. This is Sam. She's part of this operation and you can talk freely in front of her."

The two women shook hands and Billie said to Sam, "Tell me, Sam, what exactly do you do for the Colonel?"

Seeing that Billie had put Sam in a difficult situation, Grant answered before she could say anything. "Sam is my partner in this operation. She's got my back and keeps me out of trouble."

Billie just said, "Okaaay."

Grant glanced at Sam and saw she was no longer smiling.

To break the tension, he decided he'd better get right to business. As they strolled, he filled Billie in on what he needed, not telling her anything more than he was trying to find the identity of someone in a particular department. He then asked her if she had any contacts who might be able to help. Billie said she did have some current contacts at the Ministry of Defense and she'd see if they knew anyone in logistics who had been there long enough to help. Grant gave her his cell phone number and she agreed to call him as soon as she got the names.

After Billie left, Sam turned to face Grant and said, "I could have answered her, you know." Then she chuckled and said, "I wonder what more she would have said if she knew we were sharing the same room?" Grant smiled, glad Sam could see some humor in the situation.

Billie called back in less than two hours.

"You, my friend, are in luck. We're having lunch today with someone who might be able to help. See you at noon at the café next to your hotel."

"Roger." Grant replied.

"Looks like she found someone who might be able to help. We're meeting them for lunch," Grant told Sam.

"That was quick."

"Quick is good. We only have three weeks to find and stop this guy." Grant said.

Sam said, "Yeah, assuming it's him. What if the two things are unrelated and we're spending all our time looking for this Vladimir guy only to find out he's not our man? We'll have wasted a lot of time on a wild goose chase."

Grant hesitated a moment before he answered, "That would be bad. He's our only lead. If we don't get him or it turns out to be someone else, then we'll only have one opportunity to catch them and that's at the inauguration. That's *way* too late and would probably be disastrous. We just can't let that happen. It has to be Vladimir and we have to find him . . . and that's what we're going to do." He sounded confident.

Precisely at noon, Billie entered the café with a man who looked to be in his fifties. He was fairly ordinary looking, about 5'9" and stocky with dark hair graying at the temples and a huge mustache. Billie came over to the table where Grant and Sam were sitting, gave them a friendly greeting and introduced her companion. "Vasaly has worked as a supervisor in the Ministry of Defense logistics section for over twenty years. He knows everyone who worked there during that time and can obtain work history records for you to review. He will need you to brief him on anything you know that could help point him in the right direction. He speaks excellent English. I've told him you're both reporters, so he knows that you're doing background research for a story." Billie lied so easily it was clear why she was considered one of the best at her job.

They had a quick lunch where they talked a little, mostly about the weather, then went outside and walked down the street. On the street where they couldn't be overheard, Grant explained what he was looking for and the section where the documents originated. He said he was working on a story about the brave people who aided the US during the Soviet occupation of Poland. Billie's contact seemed to buy the story and told Grant he knew everyone in that section and, although there had been some turnover in the past ten years, many of the same people were still there. Grant asked if he could provide employee records for all that had left employment in that time and the man said he could do that and would have them by tomorrow noon. Grant asked if he could offer Vasaly compensation for his time, but Vasaly refused, saying that he was happy to do anything that would show how brave his countrymen were during the Russian occupation. They agreed upon a time and place for the exchange and Grant and Sam walked back to their hotel.

The next day, after meeting with Billie's contact and receiving the files, Grant and Sam divided up the records to review. Even sharing the job, it still took a full day to go through them. Discouraging to both of them, when they were finished, they were nowhere close to identifying Vladimir. They had earmarked fifteen people that fit Vladimir's profile and it could be any one of them. All fifteen were within the age range they believed Vladimir would fit into and had worked in the section during the time frame in which the documents were dated.

Grant took in a deep breath and let it out slowly. "Okay, Sam, let's divide these up and make notes. I'll take the ones you've already been through and you take the ones I've reviewed. When we're finished, we can discuss the notes and maybe one of us will see something the other missed."

It took four hours to go through the fifteen records a second time. When they were finished they both had pages of notes.

"Maybe the best way to do this is to throw out the ones we think are least likely to be our man," Sam suggested.

"Good idea. Okay, who's first?" Grant clasped his hands behind his head and arched his back, stretching his legs out in front of him. He was not looking forward to just sitting around talking, but knew they had do go through the notes.

They spent the next couple of hours discussing the ones they thought were least likely and culled the list down to three people, any one of whom could be Vladimir. All three were born, grew up and were educated in Russia and were placed in these jobs when Poland was part of the Soviet Union. Two went back to Russia within three years of the Soviet Union collapse and the third quit suddenly about the same time. They had forwarding addresses in Russia for the first two, but not for the third. However, they all had to give permanent home addresses in Russia when they were hired, so at least they knew where the third guy came from originally. Grant figured that was enough to start on.

"Looks like we'll have to try to track these guys down to see if they're still alive. Did we ever get visas for Russia?"

"Yep. Have you ever been to Russia?" Sam asked.

"Not through the front door," he replied. "Went in a few times through Odessa. Met up with our underground contacts and showed them how to set up an effective network, communication links, stuff like that."

"Do we have any CIA or DIA people in Russia that could help with this? Or maybe just someone at the embassy? It seems like we're running out of time trying to do all of this by ourselves. We don't have to tell them why we want to know, but if they could just get current addresses for these three people, we could take it from there."

He liked the way Sam was taking the initiative. She's being a great help, he thought. Then he said, "Great idea. And you're right, we don't need to tell them why we need to know, just that it's a request from DIA. Also, we can do this on an unsecure line because we just need them to provide us with current addresses. That saves us a trip back to Warsaw. It's a little late today—I'll call 'em tomorrow morning." Grant paused. "Well, it's been a good day. Whatta you say we go find something to eat."

"Another great idea. I'm famished," said Sam, hoping dinner would include a nice bottle of wine.

Paying for dinner, which had included several very nice local dishes and a really good bottle of wine, Grant thought, I'm sure racking up expenses. Well, the General is just going to have to approve my expense reports. If we're successful, he won't even notice and if we're not . . . well, if we're not the General will have bigger things to worry about than my expense account.

That night, in their room, they took turns in the bathroom changing into their pajamas. Grant watched, trying not to stare, as Sam came out of the bathroom after changing. Her pajamas were flowered flannel with a button up shirt that covered everything. But somehow, on Sam, they were the sexiest PJs Grant had ever seen. He was incredibly physically attracted to her, he realized. Emotionally, too.

The next morning they met again with Billie and her contact just down the street from the ministry to return the records.

Grant said they had narrowed down their search to three of the most interesting people and asked if there was any additional information he could provide for those three. Still thinking they were doing research for an article, Vasaly was more than willing to help as much as he could.

"You know, if it would help, I could probably make a copy of the badge photographs for those three," he said.

"You have photos of these people?" Grant exclaimed.

"Yes. Everyone in the ministry has to wear a badge when at work. The badges have access codes and photographs. I can't give you the badges, but I can get you copies of the photographs. In addition to the personnel files you've seen, we have a security file on everyone. In the security file is a copy of their badge picture. The photos you get may not be the highest quality because I'll have to make them on an ordinary copy machine."

"That would be very helpful," Grant said, trying to keep his face neutral. "How soon could we get them?"

"I could have them by lunch time."

"Great. I'll buy you lunch. And thanks for all you are doing to help us," Grant replied.

After Billie and Vasaly had left, Grant turned to Sam and said excitedly, "I can't believe our luck. Pictures. That's so much more than I had hoped for. This is really gonna help."

By noon, Grant had pictures of all three men. He couldn't believe his luck.

Chapter 40

I minus 23

The embassy staff in Moscow said they'd be happy to help the Colonel locate the three men and they did not need a formal request through DIA. Grant gave them both the permanent home addresses for all three and the forwarding addresses for the two he had.

Later that afternoon, the embassy called him back to say they had been unable to locate any of the three, but a neighbor of one of them said he thought the guy had died. For one, however, the permanent home address given at the time he arrived in Poland was false. There was no such street now or ever in Moscow. Since the permanent home address was the one shown in his identity papers when he was hired, that meant the papers were false. Turns out, it was the same guy who had quit suddenly and left no forwarding address. Grant was becoming convinced that this guy, Sergey Baskov, was Vladimir. Confirming that, however, was going to be difficult. Well, at least he knew what the guy looked like. Well, at least he knew what he looked like several years ago. Fortunately the department required new badge pictures every few years and this one was taken less than a year before he quit. The picture he had was really grainy but Grant was pretty sure he would recognize the guy if he saw him in person. Assuming he wasn't disguised. It was one more piece to the puzzle. A big piece, though.

Grant turned to Sam and said, "It looks like we'll have to go to Moscow to get any closer to finding this guy. I'd better update General Wheeler and, hopefully, he'll agree to update the DNI. I only have my cell phone and I don't know if the DNI knows the protocol for unclassified conversations. He might unintentionally say something that would alert anyone who happened to be monitoring cell phone calls.

A minute later, Grant was on his cell phone dialing the General's number. It was mid-morning in Washington and the General was at his desk in the Pentagon.

After the General answered Grant said, "Good morning, this is Thurmond. I'm on my cell phone so this will be brief." Grant knew the general would pick up the unsecure cell phone reference and not use titles or refer to the actual operation during the conversation.

"Thurmond, how're you doing? Where are you? What's going on?"

"I'm in Krakow researching the story and it looks like I can find out more information in Moscow. So, with your permission, I'll be heading there tomorrow."

"Fine. Do what you need to do in order to get the story. Remember the deadline is closing in and you need to wrap up over there pretty quickly."

"I understand. I'll call you from Moscow with another update in a day or two."

"Sounds good." With that, the general hung up.

He turned to Sam. "Pack up, Sam. We're leaving. I wanta be in Moscow tomorrow morning so we have to drive back to Warsaw this afternoon and return the car to the Embassy. Please see if you can get us into a hotel close to the Warsaw airport and on an early morning flight out of there to Moscow."

"Will do. I should be able to book the flights by phone within the next few minutes. Where do we go from there?"

"At this point, I really don't know. I do know, however, that we only have two or three days to spend in Moscow. If we're not any closer to finding Vladimir by then, we'll have to go back to the States."

Sam called and quickly booked two business class tickets on a LOT-Polish Airways non-stop flight leaving Warsaw the next morning.

"It's done. We stay tonight at the Hilton airport hotel. We leave at 9:00 a.m. tomorrow morning and arrive Moscow at 3:00 p.m. I just bought one-way tickets. By the way, I also booked us a room at the Marriott Grande hotel in Moscow on Tverskaya, wherever that is. She said it was in the middle of the city."

"Thanks, Sam. We'll get a taxi at the Moscow airport. The driver'll know where the hotel is. Ready to get on the road?" He turned toward the door.

At the same time that Grant and Sam were heading out of Krakow towards Warsaw, General Wheeler called the DNI.

"Sir, it's Wheeler."

"General, hope all is well. What's up?" Barry responded.

"I just heard from Thurmond. Is this line secure?"

"Yes. I'm on my secure line in my car. I have a meeting with the CEO of BlackTropics, a contract intelligence and operations outfit we use sometimes to help us out. Know them?"

"Yes, sir, I do. Be careful. These guys are good, but they sometimes exceed the scope of their assignments."

"Yeah, we've found that out the hard way a couple of times already. This is just a keep in touch meeting, so it should go well. I'm meeting the CIA DDI there. She'll be joining me for the meeting. BlackTropics is going to update us on their new skills and people. What've you got?"

"As I said, Thurmond is in Krakow and has picked up quite a bit more detail. He's narrowed the search down to three possible men, one of which might be dead. He's on his way to Moscow to check out the other two. The good part is that he was able to get photographs of all of them. I'll get another update in a day or two."

"That's good news. How close is he, do you think?"

"Well, Moscow station wasn't able to determine the current location of either of the two remaining men, so it will take some luck for Thurmond to go much farther. I've told him he only has a few more days before I want him back here."

"Thanks for the update, General." The DNI pressed the off button on his phone and picked up the BlackTropics briefing folder to read on the way to the meeting.

***

That afternoon, when Vladimir picked up his messages, he learned that Thurmond was not only on his way to Moscow, but he had Vladimir's photograph as well. Moscow was a big place, so he wasn't too worried about Thurmond seeing him, and without his current name, there was no way for Thurmond to find out where he lived. But, the photo could be a problem back in the US. If it were passed around to all the security people, it would make it very difficult to slip through during the inauguration. Vladimir knew, then, that Thurmond had to die tomorrow and the picture had to be destroyed. Since Vladimir was wounded, he was worried he might fail if he tried, so he called an acquaintance in the Moscow underworld. He told him he wanted someone eliminated.

His acquaintance told him it would not be a problem, but that it was a cash-only business. Vladimir told him that was fine. He knew crime was so rampant in Moscow, no one would ever be able to pin it on him. Hired killings were commonplace, happening almost every day somewhere in the city. And although Thurmond probably couldn't find him, Vladimir knew there were only a few flights coming into Moscow from Krakow. Thurmond should be easy to spot and identify to the gangsters. He passed that information on to his connection and they settled on a price.

The plan was for all of them to start meeting every flight from Warsaw that afternoon. Vladimir knew that the quickest way to Moscow from Krakow was LOT airlines through Warsaw. He was certain that they would choose that route. After identifying Thurmond, they would follow him and take the first opportunity to gun him down—and the girl as well, if she were with him. Nothing elegant, just mass fire power. If this Garcia was still tailing Thurmond, he might even be able to spot him and take him out also. That would be a good day.

***

Garcia checked into his hotel in Krakow late that evening and by 7:00 a.m. the next morning, he was outside what he guessed was Thurmond's hotel watching the entrance. It was a pretty loosey-goosey way to run surveillance, but it was all he had. Grant and Sam, having left the same hotel a little over two hours before, were in Warsaw, changing planes for their flight to Moscow.

Upon arriving at Moscow's Sheremetyevo airport, Grant and Sam filed off the plane and went down the hallway to customs and immigration. There they presented the immigration forms they had filled out on the plane and waited in a long line for their baggage to be delivered and then waited in an even longer line to get through the immigration check point. When they finally got to the immigration officer, they answered all the questions asked, said they were traveling together, that they were only here for a few days on vacation and would be leaving together. The bored-looking officer stamped their passports and waved them through.

After another long walk, they passed through automatic doors timed to admit only one person at a time and saw what looked to be hundreds of people waiting for other travelers. Because they knew no one would be meeting them, they just walked straight through the crowd looking for the taxi stand. Vladimir had guessed right and saw them immediately. He pointed out Thurmond and the girl to the men who were with him, handed one man an envelope filled with cash, and then walked the other direction to the parking garage. This part of his job was over; the gangsters would take it from here. He was delighted at his progress.

There were three men following Grant and Sam and they had no trouble keeping them in sight. A fourth man was waiting outside in a car parked near the taxi stand. They were all heavily armed under their long, bulky coats.

Chapter 41

I minus 22

Grant and Sam went through the airport lobby exit doors and were greeted with a blast of frigid winter air. The temperature had to be below zero and the wind was strong and gusty. The sky was gray and overcast and light snow swirled around them as they stood there. Welcome to Russia. After taking a moment to get their bearings, they managed to locate the taxi stand and told the man in the kiosk at the head of the line they needed to get to the Marriott. The guy opened the door of the first taxi in line and shouted what Grant assumed to be their destination to the driver and immediately went back inside his small warm kiosk. The driver, loath to leave the warm car, offered no help in loading their luggage into the small trunk. Grant told Sam to get out of the wind into the taxi while he loaded the luggage.

Finally heading down M10 on their way towards Moscow center, the traffic was heavy and Grant couldn't tell whether or not they were being followed. But they were. The four men had picked up their trail as soon as they got into the taxi and were only two cars behind. All four were hoping for an early opportunity to end the workday. Their only task today was to kill the two people in the taxi in front of them. These were thugs—experienced killers, but not sophisticated hit men, and they had no plan other than to find a good spot and open fire. Before they had pulled out to follow the taxi, one of the four, for a two hundred Ruble note, had received their destination from the man in the taxi kiosk and they were anxious to complete their work before they got to the busy streets around the hotel. Not that they cared about being seen, it just might make things more difficult on small streets.

After travelling about four miles, the man in the front passenger seat said, "Pull up beside them." The car surged forward and pulled up next to the taxi.

Grant noticed the car keeping pace with the taxi. His training kicked in and he was immediately suspicious. When the car pulled alongside of their taxi, he saw four burly men, all staring at them.

The windows in the car were all rolled down. It was way too cold for a ride on the freeway with windows rolled down, even for Russians.

Grant shouted at the taxi driver, "Get out of here!"

The driver looked in his rear view mirror and, not knowing what Grant was saying, just shrugged and kept driving at the same speed. Grant reached forward and grabbed the driver by the shoulder and made motions with his hand, hoping the driver would know that he wanted him to pull to the right and slow down or speed up, whichever—just change course.

As he did that, two of the men in the car next to him lifted up guns and opened fire. That got the taxi driver's attention and he instantly slammed on the brakes. Sam was sitting directly behind the driver and when the driver braked so suddenly she flew forward, hitting the back of the driver's seat hard. Grant reached over and pulled her down to the floorboard and covered her with his body. They were unarmed and there was nothing they could do but cower on the floor and hope they didn't get hit with what had become a shower of bullets hitting the taxi. They were both instantly covered with shards of glass from the window that the bullets had shattered. During the fusillade, the driver was obviously hit because he screamed once and then slumped over the steering wheel. By that time, the taxi was almost stopped and was drifting slowly to the right of the road. The shooter's car was stopped twenty feet ahead and was beginning to back up slowly, dodging oncoming cars. Grant sat up, reached forward, muscled the unconscious driver over to the passenger seat and climbed over the seat to get behind the wheel. He immediately accelerated, passing the other car far to the right, using the road shoulder to put distance between them and the shooters. The thugs opened up again and Grant could hear some of the bullets making impact with the left rear of the taxi.

"Sam, you alright?" he yelled.

"Yes, no hits. Damn, I wish we were armed. Where are you going?" Sam answered from the back floorboard.

"I have no idea. Just away from these guys. Stay low—hug the floor and I'll try to lose 'em."

Grant drove like a madman, weaving in and out of traffic. The bad guys kept coming and were only about forty feet behind, but not having a clear view of Grant and Sam had at least stopped shooting. Grant couldn't believe they'd survived the onslaught. Not a window was left in the taxi, but he knew it wasn't over. As long as these guys were on their tail, they were still in danger. He was sure that if they got within range, they would open up again. And this time, being in the driver's seat, he was too exposed. He had to stay away at all costs. He had the old taxi floored now, still weaving through traffic, leaving a trail of blue exhaust smoke behind. It looked like they were coming into the more populated areas of Moscow now. Maybe he could escape on one of the side roads. It was risky, though. He had to let them get close enough that when he jerked the car to the right onto one of the exits, they wouldn't be able to make the turn. Even if they stopped and backed up, it would take a few seconds and he could use that time to dodge through alleyways and side streets until they lost him.

Here goes, he thought. Seeing an exit coming up, he slowed the car slightly, trying to judge the distance just right. They were now less than ten feet behind and coming up fast on the left with their guns brazenly sticking out the windows. When they were almost beside him, he swerved sharply to the right, missing the exit surface a bit and bouncing over turf until he got back on the exit roadway. As he hoped, the other car reacted too late and missed the turn. Grant screamed through the stop sign where the exit joined the cross street, made a tire screeching right turn and rocketed down that street for two or three blocks. He looked in his rear view mirror hoping they were clear, but instead he saw the thug's car just turning right onto the same street. As he thought, they had stopped and backed up to the exit. He had two blocks on them; maybe he could outrun them on the side streets.

He took a left on the next street, then a right into an alley about halfway down the block. He thought about pulling into one of the driveways off the alley, but the taxi would be too easily recognized. He had to ditch this car soon, but not just yet. At the end of the block, he turned left and saw that he had miscalculated. The thugs had turned down the same street he was exiting onto and were now only feet behind. How the hell was he going to lose these guys? Not having any idea where he was, he shot straight through a stop sign at the cross street and pushed the accelerator to the floor. As he bounced over the rough intersection he nearly went airborne and when he bottomed out on the other side of the cross street, his tail pipe and muffler separated from the bottom of the car and each other.

They both bounced off the pavement into the air and immediately into the path of the following car full of thugs.

The muffler bounced harmlessly off the front grill, but the tailpipe went right through the front windshield, between the driver and front seat passenger, impaling the chest of one of the two men in the back seat, instantly killing him. The driver began applying brakes to slow down the car, but the remaining man alive in the backseat yelled for him to go on, to catch up with the taxi. He then reached across his dead companion, opened the back passenger-side door of the car and unceremoniously kicked the dead man and the tail pipe out of the car and closed the door. His clothes were a little bloody from reaching across the body, but he didn't really notice. He was completely focused on catching and killing his target.

Grant, seeing that the smoke from the exhaust was increasing and now, hearing the car roaring without a muffler, knew the taxi was on its last legs. He *had* to lose these guys. He noticed they had slowed momentarily and, although they were coming on fast, they were now almost two blocks behind him. He made a quick left turn onto another side street and then an immediate right into an alleyway. This was a very nice neighborhood for Moscow, where all the houses were two stories and all had a garage behind them facing the alley. Halfway down the alley he saw an open garage door and, to his relief, he saw the garage was empty. Grant pulled the taxi into the garage, shut off the engine, exited the car and quickly pulled down the garage door. A few minutes later he heard a car roar by in the alleyway. The car didn't stop so it looked like they weren't spotted. The next question on his mind was how much time did they have before the residents of the house confronted them? Or called the police? They were just going to have to chance it because being discovered by the residents was far less dangerous than dealing with the gangsters.

As he stood there thinking about what to do next, Sam, looking a little dazed, opened the back door and got out of the taxi. Grant turned to her, took her into his arms and said, "You okay?"

"Yeah, a little shook up, but not injured," she replied.

After holding her close for a couple of minutes, Grant relaxed his grip a little and started brushing the glass out of her hair.

"Grant, that was close. Who were those guys?"

He continued brushing the glass away and shook his head as he answered. "Don't know for sure, but my best guess is that they're working with Vladimir. Maybe we were wrong and he's not acting alone. Or maybe they're just goons. They obviously picked us up at the airport and waited for the right moment to attack. At first, I thought it was just some thugs trying to rob American tourists. But, why would they open fire? Who knows, maybe that's how they work over here. It's a rough environment right now. I've heard that Moscow can be a dangerous place for tourists. But, the suspicious side of me is fairly strongly convinced that Vladimir either has some accomplices we didn't know about or he hired some people to make the hit. I'm going to operate on the latter assumption for now."

"So what do we do now?" Sam asked.

He had stopped brushing and was holding her by both shoulders. "Sit tight for at least half an hour and then see if this car will still run. If it does, we need to find someone who speaks English and get directions to our hotel. We'll find a small street two or three blocks before we get there and ditch the car. Then I want us to walk separately to the hotel. The bad guys will be looking for two people together. You go first and check in. I'll keep you in sight and follow. Fortunately it gets dark early here, so it'll be harder for those guys to spot us."

Grant then went around to the front passenger door, opened it and checked for a pulse on the taxi driver. None – he was dead. He lifted the body out of the car and laid it on the back seat. He then took off the bloody seat covers uncovering the tattered, but clean original passenger seat and put them in the trunk. Sam would sit up front with him.

After forty minutes, Grant opened the garage door, walked down the alley both ways trying to spot a car with people in it, and when he didn't see one he came back and found that the taxi would, indeed, start. Although it was smoking badly and was very loud without a muffler, the car seemed to operate okay. Grant drove on down the alley, crossed two streets and finally turned right onto the third street he came to. Seven blocks later, they saw a small restaurant on the corner.

He turned to face her. "Sam, you're going to have to go inside, see if anyone there speaks English and, if so, get directions to the Marriott."

"What if they don't speak English?" she asked.

166

"Then we'll just keep looking. We don't know where we are and we don't have a map. I've heard that many people in Russia were taught English during the Soviet era, so I'm sure we'll find somebody."

Sam was back quickly. The lady greeting customers spoke reasonable English and Sam was able to get good directions to the hotel. They roared off in the smoking taxi and saw the hotel in the distance within twenty minutes. Grant turned left about two blocks before reaching the hotel, then left on a small street and pulled to the curb. It was dark on the little street and there was no traffic.

"What now? I'm freezing," said Sam.

"Let's get our luggage out of the trunk and walk to the hotel. If we can avoid going through the front entrance it would be best. Never know who's watching. When we're a block away, you walk by to see if there's a side entrance. There probably is at least one; it's a big hotel. I'll watch you all the way and follow a few minutes later. I just want to see if anyone recognizes you and follows you into the hotel. If not, I think we're in the clear."

"Got it," Sam said. She opened the handle on her roll-aboard and started walking towards the hotel.

The Russians, meanwhile, had parked their car at the other end of the hotel and were watching the main entrance. For fifteen minutes they had circled the area where they lost sight of the taxi and, not seeing anyone, had come straight here, hoping to get them as they entered the hotel. They were on the wrong side to see Sam enter the hotel and, even if they had, they might not have recognized her. As Grant had suggested, they were looking for the taxi and two people traveling together.

Grant followed Sam by five minutes, giving her enough time to check in and get the room key. She met him as he went in through the side door. All went smoothly and they were in their room a couple of minutes later.

"Nice room," Sam commented. "I'm surprised."

"It should be. How much did you say this was costing the American taxpayers?" Grant said, looking around.

Sam gave a smiling grimace. "About $450 a night. Plus, we got upgraded to a junior suite. It's beautiful."

"Right now I would settle for anything as long as it was warm," Grant said.

"First dibs on the shower," Sam said, lugging her bag into the bedroom.

While Sam showered, applied the minimal makeup she used and got dressed, Grant called down and ordered dinner for them both to be delivered to the room in forty minutes.

After Grant took his turn in the shower and put on fresh clothes, they split a half bottle of wine they found in the mini bar. Neither of them recognized the label.

"Wonder what this costs?" Grant asked, meaning the wine.

"Probably ten times what it's worth," Sam replied, wrinkling her nose after taking a sip. "It's not very good."

"First thing tomorrow morning, I have to get to the embassy and secure us some weapons. This is way too dangerous for us not to be able to protect ourselves. If today's attack was an isolated mugging, we probably won't need 'em, but if not . . ." Grant let the sentence trail off, the meaning obvious.

He then said, "Sam we might want to alter your appearance so you won't be recognized. It might make you less of a target."

"Grant, if you think I'm going to cut my hair and dye it red or something, you have another think coming. No way. If it would help, I could wear it down, though. That changes my appearance some."

Grant agreed that Sam should wear her hair down for the rest of the trip. That was the way he liked it best, anyway.

After a not so bad dinner in their room, they talked tactics for a while and decided on any early bedtime. Grant pulled out the sofa bed in the living room and Sam retired to the bedroom. After he was under the covers, Grant laid there wondering how Sam would look if she did cut her hair short and dyed it red. He smiled, deciding that Sam would look great no matter what her hair looked like. Grant slept soundly that night. He had no way of knowing that the criminals were aware of where he and Sam were staying and were watching closely. If he'd known they were that close, he would never have slept so well.

Chapter 42

I minus 21

"Sir, I think I've lost them. I spent all of yesterday in Krakow watching their hotel, but neither of them have left in the last twenty-four hours. I came back to Warsaw this morning. Have you heard from them?" Garcia asked the DNI. He had flown back early this morning and was calling from the Embassy.

"Garcia, if you're in Warsaw, you're at least a day behind. I got an update this morning from General Wheeler. He says Thurmond is in Moscow looking for Vladimir. You sure you're up for this?" Garcia could tell the DNI was pissed and wisely decided to say nothing. The DNI continued, "Get your ass on the next plane. They're staying at the Marriott downtown. I haven't heard from them since they arrived, so I presume the plan hasn't changed. Moscow's bad news these days and I don't want Thurmond there without backup. Maybe you ought to contact him and let him know you're there and available to help."

"Not sure that's a good idea, sir. Thurmond made it pretty clear he doesn't want my help." Garcia was cautious.

"I don't give a shit what Thurmond wants, but it's your call. If you don't contact him, then don't let him out of your sight. If anything happens, I want additional fire power. Got it?"

"Yes, sir. I'll be there in a few hours." Garcia said, relieved to still be on the case.

Garcia sat for a few minutes after hanging up, trying to figure out the best way to support Thurmond without being detected. He didn't know what Vladimir had planned, but he knew it wouldn't be good. He had to make sure Vladimir died before he made it to the States. He looked around the office. Man, these embassy types had a cushy job, but sitting at a desk all day would drive him crazy. Well, time's a wasting, better get going.

Garcia had come to the Embassy straight from the airport and was already packed. He spent a few minutes with one of the Embassy's administrative assistants and was booked on a flight to Moscow in two hours. He used a staff driver to get from the Embassy to the airport and easily made his flight to Moscow.

He went straight from the airport to the Embassy. He needed a weapon. As he was coming out of the cultural attaché's office, he literally bumped into Thurmond.

Surprised, Thurmond stepped back and seeing who he had bumped into his expression went dark. "Garcia, what the hell are you doing in Moscow?"

"Ah, just here to follow up on a few things. What're you doing here?" Garcia responded too casually.

Thurmond studied Garcia for a moment. "Let's find a conference room or an office where we can talk," Thurmond suggested.

"Good idea," Garcia said, wondering if Thurmond was finally going to bring him in to the operation.

They each got a cup of coffee and settled into nice, high-backed leather chairs in a secure conference room. Thurmond thought it too coincidental that Garcia just happened to be in Moscow the same time as he and Sam, but he knew Garcia would never bring him in on a CIA operation. Instead of asking, he opened the conversation with, "Look Garcia, you know what I'm working on. Some things have happened and, well, if you're going to be in the area for a few days, as much as I hate to say this, I might need your help."

Caught off guard, Garcia nodded. "I'll be here for a couple of days. Where are you with this? You know where to find him?"

"Not exactly. According to his original employment records, he used to live here. It's a needle in a haystack situation. I'm here; he *may* be here. If he is here, I have no idea where he is. However, there may be complications. It may not be just one person we're looking for." With that, Thurmond explained about the attack yesterday.

"Man, you know it could be just bad luck, but I wouldn't take any chances. How about I join your team and we work together to find this guy?"

"No thanks. I think I can do this alone, but I want to be able to call on you if I need help. Okay?" Grant said.

"Always the cowboy, right Thurmond? Alright, I'll stay out of it, but don't blame me if you get your ass slammed. You really need backup."

"I've got backup. Sam's here." Grant leaned back and crossed his legs.

Garcia barked out a dry laugh. "Sam's not trained for this shit. You know that."

"She's been in combat, Garcia. She knows how to handle herself." Although Grant sounded confident, he wasn't sure Sam could handle backup. That's why he wanted Garcia on call.

"Being in combat with other soldiers around you isn't anywhere close to the kind of one-on-one work we do."

"Said like someone who's never been in combat. Look, man, she'll be fine."

Garcia leaned forward to give added emphasis to what he was about to say. "Thurmond, you can't trust your back to someone with that level of experience," he said. "You're not just risking just your life, you're risking hers as well. Don't do this, man."

"We'll be fine," Thurmond said with equal emphasis.

They stared at each other for a moment, saying nothing.

"It's on your head, man," Garcia finally said disgustedly. "But take down my phone number in case you need me, cause I'm sure you will. Just hope it's not too late."

They stood, exchanged numbers and then left the Embassy in separate cars. Garcia knew Thurmond wouldn't call him and would be looking to see if he was followed, so he asked the driver to take him to any downtown hotel that wasn't the Marriott.

Chapter 43

I minus 21

After Grant left the hotel, Sam had called down for a room service breakfast. After calling, she took a quick shower, got dressed, and was just finishing applying makeup when she heard a knock on the door. She went to the door and said, "Yes?"

"Room service." A cheery voice called out in broken English.

Sam unlatched then unlocked and opened the door wide without thinking to look through the peephole. Before the door was even fully opened, two huge men slammed back the door, pushing Sam into the room and onto the floor. While one of them closed the door, the other was on her before she could make a sound, placing his large hand over her mouth.

She could barely breathe, but never one to give up, she fought as best as she could. She got in a few scratches to the guy's face before he was able to tie her hands down. But, even with her using all her strength to resist, it took them less than a minute to tie her up. They told her that if she screamed, they would kill her instantly and, given what had happened yesterday, Sam believed them. One of the men picked her up and sat her down roughly in a chair. The other was already checking out the rest of the suite. When he returned to the main room, he said something in Russian to the guy who was now standing if front of her.

He leaned menacingly over Sam and asked, "Where is the man?"

"What man?" stammered Sam. Her only hope was that she could convince them they had the wrong room.

The man in front of her reached forward grabbed her hair and said, "Don't lie to us. You will only die if you lie to us."

"He's out," she nearly shouted. "He won't be back today. He's gone to St. Petersburg to meet with someone." She was trying not to cry.

"I told you not to lie to us," The man said and then hit her hard in the stomach with his fist. She doubled over in the chair gasping for air trying not to throw up. He then pulled her up by her hair and said, "Now tell us the truth."

Sam, tears running down her face, was barely able to talk, but she managed to gasp, "I'm not lying. Why would I lie to you? We have nothing to hide. We're just here to see the sights." She was really frightened. This was different from being in combat. In combat she was armed and was a fair distance from the people who were shooting at her. Here she was unarmed and face to face with two huge men. She didn't know what she should do, but she knew she had to get them out of here before Grant came back; otherwise they'd both be dead. Sam began remembering the questioning part of the SERE training she took before being deployed to Iraq. What did they say during the resistance phase? Just play along when questioned? She was remembering a little more. Tell plausible lies with just enough of the truth mixed in for it to sound reasonable. But never give up others to save yourself.

The man was saying, ". . . and if you don't tell us we will wait here and kill both of you."

"Okay," she said, breathlessly, "I'll tell you. We got here yesterday and someone shot at us in our taxi on the way into the city. My friend is at the main police station trying to describe the men in the car. He got a pretty good look at them. He called a little while ago and said he's bringing the police back here to talk with me. They should be here in the next few minutes," she nodded, warming to her own story. "If they find you here they'll arrest you. I think you have maybe four, five minutes tops to get out of the hotel. Tell you what I'll do. If you leave now, I won't even tell them you were here and I won't cooperate with the police when they question me. You'll be safe."

They laughed. "We will leave now and you are coming with us. Get up!" With that, he grabbed her by her upper arms and roughly heaved her to her feet. They opened the door and dragged her towards it.

She started yelling as loudly as she could, but stopped as soon as the guy that was manhandling her turned around and pulled a gun from under his coat and spat out, "Silence! If you keep yelling, I will kill you right here."

She believed him, so she remained quiet. They went through the door and down the hall to the stairway. They walked down the four flights to the garage access door, went into the garage where they headed towards a black boxy car. Sam couldn't tell what kind it was and would probably never recognize it again. Sam felt real fear. She had no idea what these men would do to her, but she knew it wouldn't be fun. She'd had briefings before going into combat about what to expect if captured in Iraq. She briefly wondered if this would be the same. She hoped not.

As they were pushing Sam towards the car, Grant drove into the garage in the nondescript Embassy pool car he had checked out. He went up the ramp and turned onto the second parking level. As he rounded the corner, he saw a group of people ahead of him and closing in, he recognized Sam. Seeing what the two guys were doing to her, Grant had to make an instant decision. He could either let them go and follow them or extract Sam now. There were problems with following them. What if he lost them in traffic? Sam would surely not survive and with these goons, who knew what they'd do to her. No question. He'd get her out of this here and now. Attacking them might be a problem, though. He didn't know if they were the same guys who shot at them yesterday. If they were, they'd probably recognize him if he got close enough and they'd either use Sam as a shield or would kill her immediately.

He knew he had to go straight at them and get Sam away as fast as he could without her getting hurt. And he had to do it now. If these guys got her to their car, it would be really tough to get Sam out. He couldn't just open fire without risking hitting Sam. Grant slammed the accelerator to the floor and with squealing tires headed straight at them. They immediately turned and headed back to the hotel entrance which was about fifteen yards away, but at that moment, Sam decided she'd had enough and kicked the guy hauling her in the groin. He bent over and Sam using strength she didn't know she had, pulled free. She started running as fast as she could and since she didn't know who was in the car coming at them, she ran away from it. The two guys stopped going towards the hotel and started chasing her, guns drawn. When it got about ten yards from them, the car screeched to a stop and to Sam's great joy, Grant jumped out with a gun in his hand. The two goons started firing towards the car. Grant used the door as a shield and started firing back. He completely emptied his thirteen round magazine in the direction of the bad guys. He immediately popped the spent magazine and slammed a new one in.

The two guys both went down, one of them groaning loudly and the other was silent. Grant ran directly towards them wanting to disarm them first, then check on Sam. He never left a gun close to someone who just shot at him—even if they looked dead or disabled. When he got there, he saw one man who he was sure was dead and the other was obviously severely wounded. He picked up both guns, checked the men to see if they had others, then stood and called to Sam. Sam was already running towards him. She flew into his arms and he held her close for just a second. They heard a moan from one of the men at their feet and Grant said, "We need to do something about these guys," and released his grasp on Sam. He quickly untied her.

"What do we do?" Sam asked. Rubbing her wrists where the bonds were.

"First, we check to see if anyone saw this happening. I doubt if they have cameras in the parking garage over here, but look around just in case. If no one saw what happened, I'll try to get CIA to help clean this up. If we can patch up the guy who is wounded, we might be able to question him and find who put 'em up to this. We can dump 'em somewhere later."

Sam panicked. "We're not going to just torture and kill the guy who's alive, are we?"

Grant, trying to calm her down said, "No, we'll patch him up and question him, then drop him off at a hospital. We'll just tell them we found him on the side of the road. He sure as hell won't say anything. It may not be a problem because he might die anyway. I'll call the CIA guy at the Embassy and see if they can help. If not, we'll use a pay phone and place an anonymous call to the police saying we heard gunshots in the garage and when we looked, there were two men lying on the floor. Then we'll just hang up. No way can they trace that call back to us."

Grant then called the CIA station chief. "This is Thurmond. We've had an incident and need assistance. There was a shooting in the garage of the Marriott that needs immediate attention."

The station chief immediately picked up on the urgency and said, "Stay put until my cleaner crew arrives. We'll transport you to a safe house and remove the mess. If anyone comes around and asks what happened, just plead ignorance. Just tell them you just came into the garage to pick up your car and saw the mess. You didn't see anything. You didn't hear anything. Got it?"

"Got it," Grant replied.

"If the police get there before my crew does, call me back immediately and I'll abort the mission. You guys then will be on your own to get away." The CIA station chief hung up.

In the eight minutes it took for the CIA team to arrive, no one came into the garage. Apparently no one heard the shots. Grant sat Sam in the front passenger seat of the Embassy car, got behind the wheel and pulled it into an empty parking slot. It took a little less than two minutes for the two men to be loaded into a van, the garage floor cleaned and for everyone to be on their way to a local safe house. One of the people from the Embassy was a doctor who immediately began an IV drip on the surviving man and said, "I don't know if he's going to make it. Those hollow points made a hell of a mess, but this guy's a moose and he may survive. We won't know for at least four hours and it may take twenty-four hours before you can talk to him. The other one's dead."

"Yeah, I figured that," Grant replied.

The safe house was, by Russian standards, an unusually large suburban home in an upscale neighborhood about fifteen miles from downtown Moscow. While Grant went with the CIA doctor, Sam stayed on the main floor to make arrangements for their stay. The CIA crew took the wounded man down to the basement which contained what looked to Grant like a double hospital room. He was stripped down and placed into one of the beds. He then secured the man to the metal bed frame with handcuffs. The doctor changed the IV bag and injected something into the line.

When the doctor was finished, Grant asked, "What's going to happen with the other body?"

"Don't worry about it. It's being handled as we speak."

Grant nodded, relieved to know he didn't have to do anything with it.

He went back up to the main floor and joined Sam in the living room.

"They said the top floor is ours," she informed Grant.

"Well, there's nothing left for us to do here, so let's go check it out," he said.

They went up to the third floor of the mansion to find a large, beautifully furnished living suite, complete with kitchen. Exploring, they found a living room area, a dining area, and two bedrooms, both with en-suite bathrooms.

They returned to the living room. "Wow, this is nice," exclaimed Sam, sitting on the sofa.

Grant sat next to her. "Yeah, sure beats the hotel. There's even beer in the fridge. And there's no way anyone has of knowing where we are. The hotel cover is busted, so this is as good a place as any to stay. Have to figure out how to get our personal items from the hotel room, though."

"They told me they were taking care of that. They left a guy behind who will go to the room, pack up everything and drive your car here. I gave him my access card. They said he would check us out and settle the bill. The hotel took an imprint of your credit card when we arrived, so there shouldn't be a problem," Sam said.

"These guys are good. Unfortunately, they're going to want to be there when we question the guy in the basement." Grant sighed. "Guess I ought to bring Garcia in on this. Oh, by the way, I didn't get a chance to tell you but I ran into him at the Embassy."

Sam looked surprised. "You did? What's he doing here?" she asked.

I don't believe him, but he said he was here on other business. Looks like we'll have his company while we're here." Grant paused a moment, then continued. "Maybe he can be useful. I just hope they don't try to use this incident to take over."

Sam sighed. "Well, I'm about ready to let them. While this apartment is nice, I'd much rather be sleeping safely in my own bed in the good ole US of A. We've been here less than two days and I've already been shot at and kidnapped."

Grant leaned towards her and put his hand on her arm. "Look Sam, now that Garcia's in on this, you might as well go back home tomorrow. He can cover my back for the rest of the time I'm here. I'll be home in a week or so, as soon as I find out who's behind all this."

"No way. I'm not going to abandon you just because of a little discomfort. I'm going to be wherever you are, Garcia or not. I was just being whiney. I'm sorry, it won't happen again." Sam squared her shoulders.

Grant smiled at her. "After what you've been through, you're allowed a little whining. Sure you don't want to go back home?"

"Absolutely certain," Sam replied with more confidence in her voice than she had in her heart.

"Okay, then." Standing up he said, "I'd better call Garcia and bring him up to speed," He called Garcia, pacing as he described what happened and told him where they were. Garcia said he'd be there in an hour.

Chapter 44

I minus 21

Grant and Sam spent the better part of three hours with Garcia, giving him all the details they had. When they wrapped up, Garcia said he had some things to do on another case and would be in touch later that day. He also suggested they stay put until he returned.

After Garcia left, Grant discovered a fully-stocked kitchen refrigerator and pantry and made them each a huge deli sandwich, which they washed down with a beer. They retired early into their separate bedrooms. As tired as he was, sleep still eluded Grant. He thought over and over how lucky Sam was that he drove into the hotel garage at that moment. If he'd stopped for anything on the way back he would have missed her and he knew she would probably not have survived. Who knows what they might have done to her in order to get information about him. He was not used to the emotions he was feeling about Sam. He wondered about how she really felt about him. It was not unusual for two people working very closely together in hazardous conditions to be attracted to each other, he knew that. But is that all this was? Or could it be more? He had to find out as soon as this mission was over and they were safely back home. However, first, he had to *get* her safely back home. With that, Grant drifted off to sleep.

The next morning, Grant was up early and was standing at the bay window overlooking the snow-covered street, drinking a cup of coffee. His thoughts were on the mission and how he didn't feel they were making enough progress. With less than three weeks to go before the inauguration, he still didn't know who Vladimir was or how to find him. He went over the things he did know: Vladimir was a code name. The name he used on his original employment papers was false and his real name was unknown. Other than a very old fictional Moscow address, where he lived was unknown.

They only had one lead—the guy in the basement—and he might die before they could question him. Even if he lived and was willing to give answers, he may not know anything. He might just be a killer for hire. If so, almost certainly Vladimir had paid for this hit in cash and this guy would never know where he lived. Their only lead could be a dead end. Then what? Keep searching in Moscow? Where? Go back home? And do what? Damn! He had nothing but questions. His frustration was evident on his face when Sam walked into the room. His back was to her so she stood there for a moment, watching him.

"Grant, you look so tired and worried. Didn't sleep well?"

He turned away from the window to face her. "Oh, sorry. I was deep in thought. Just frustrated by our lack of progress. I don't like failing . . . especially in this case."

"Well, maybe we'll learn something by questioning that guy. I understand the CIA interrogator will be asking the questions in Russian. Hopefully that'll help," Sam said. "And another thing – I'm not sure I want to be there when you question him. I've heard the stories about that stuff. Really don't want to be part of it."

Grant nodded. "Probably for the best." Then he changed the subject. "Ready for some breakfast? Coffee's fresh and strong. Garcia will probably be here inside of an hour and then we'll get a determination from the doc if that guy can talk yet. I did check to make sure he survived the night. I understand the doc gave him drugs last night to keep him asleep and the nurse said he didn't wake up."

Sam fried some fatty, bacon-looking stuff they found in the refrigerator and made some toast while Grant scrambled four eggs. He remembered all safe houses he'd stayed in through the years and none of them were as grand as this. Wonder why they maintained such an elaborate dacha? Probably for political informants or former Soviet higher-ups who wanted to defect. Hell, they've probably had this since the old Soviet Union days, he decided.

Garcia didn't show until about 9:30.

"Where the hell you been?" asked Grant.

"Uh, just had some stuff to take care of. What's the status on our John Doe downstairs?"

Grant decided to let that pass. "He's still kicking, but I don't know when we can question him. The doc should be here soon to examine him and let us know," Grant replied.

Garcia said, "Yeah, the doc and the interrogator are riding together. They planned to leave the embassy shortly after I did. They should be here any minute."

"Good. The sooner we get some information the better. Coffee's in the kitchen." Grant said, without offering to get it for him.

I agree, Garcia thought as he headed into the kitchen. Things were finally starting to move for him. Now that he was involved, he'd slyly work to stay a step ahead of Thurmond. He had to get to Vladimir before Thurmond. He had his orders.

Grant heard the front door open and close and said, "That sounds like them coming in now. Grab a cup of coffee and let's get downstairs."

When they got to the basement, the doctor was leaning over the wounded man listening to his chest with a stethoscope. When Grant asked how he was doing, the doctor just held up his hand for silence and continued his examination. He listened, poked, prodded, and looked at the gunshot wounds carefully. All in all he took about fifteen minutes. Grant, Sam and Garcia waited impatiently, but kept silent. Finally he turned to the trio and said, "Looks like he might make it. He's still not out of the woods, but I think you can ask him a few questions. The only ground rule is that if I say stop, you stop. Clear?" the doctor said firmly.

"You got it," Grant said to the doctor, then turned to the interrogator and said, "We need to find out who this guy is working for. If it's an individual, we need his name and contact information. If it's an organization, we need to know which organization and his contact information within that organization. I also want to know where they were taking Sam. They clearly had some place in mind and I want to know where it is. If they were taking her to talk to someone else, find out who. See how much of that information you can get and, if he's still able, we'll go on from there."

Garcia added, "And make sure he gives you real names, not just the street names these guys use to sound tough."

The interrogator nodded. Meanwhile, the doctor had given a stimulant drug to the guy to wake him up. The interrogator leaned over the still-groggy man and spoke in Russian. He got no response. He spoke louder and made aggressive hand gestures. Still no answer. This went on for about twenty minutes with the man not uttering a sound. Suddenly the interrogator leaned close to the guy's ear and said something gruffly while at the same time pressing on one of the bandages. The man moaned, but still didn't say anything. One more time the interrogator pressed on the bandage, but much harder this time. The man screamed out something in Russian.

The interrogator nodded and said something the others in the room didn't understand but what was obviously a question. The man replied in Russian. The interrogator turned to the trio and said, "He's not being very cooperative, so this is going to take some time. You guys might as well sit down for a while." He then turned back to the bed.

Sam, who was getting decidedly uncomfortable with the direction this was going said, "I think I'll go upstairs and have another cup of coffee."

Although not particularly bothered by the questioning tactics, Grant said, "I'll join you."

"You guys go on up. I think I'll stay here for a while. I'll let you know if he starts talking," Garcia said.

Grant and Sam headed to the stairs just as the guy let out another loud moan.

After they had poured themselves each a cup of coffee, Sam asked quietly, "Does it have to be this way?" She was looking down at her coffee cup.

Grant moved close. "I'm afraid it does, Sam. This is our new President we're talking about. If this guy has information which'll keep the President safe, we need to know it. Whatever it takes. Even the CIA has rules, though. It won't be too bad for the guy. If he just starts talking, the pain will stop. They won't do any real harm to him, but it will be painful if he holds out. If he'd been successful in kidnapping you, I can assure you they wouldn't have been as humane in their treatment of you."

"I shudder to think of what would have happened." She looked up into his eyes. "By the way, thank you very much for coming to my rescue. Just like a movie hero," she teased with a small smile.

"Thurmond, Grant Thurmond," Grant said, giving his best impersonation of Sean Connery. Sam's smile widened.

The questioning continued for two hours, during which time they learned that this guy was just a contract killer working for a small-time Russian Mafia figure. All he knew was that someone paid to have Grant and Sam killed. The kidnapping was impromptu after they found that Grant wasn't in the hotel suite and after Sam told them he was bringing the police. They figured they'd take her to their boss and use her as bait to get Thurmond down there. Then they could kill them both. The interrogator had gotten the wounded guy's name and both the name and location where the boss could be found.

At that point, the doctor stopped the questioning so that the guy could rest. He told Thurmond that, if necessary, they could continue the interrogation after the guy slept for four hours.

Upstairs, Grant turned to Garcia and said, "That interrogator is good. Where did they come up with him?"

Garcia responded, "I understand he's ex-KGB. Came over to work for us about ten years ago. His cover is a job with the cultural attaché as a translator."

"Makes sense," Grant replied. "Okay, we know how to contact his boss. I think we oughta pay him a visit."

"You're kidding, right?" Sam exclaimed.

Grant flicked his eyes toward Sam. "No, I'm *not* kidding. I think Garcia and I ought to go find this guy and convince him to talk." To Garcia he said, "How much money do you think the CIA could come up with to buy the information?"

Garcia shrugged. "Well, I don't know. A few thousand, probably."

"Can you make arrangements to get it? The sooner the better. Five thousand ought to do it. I'd like to talk to the boss this afternoon."

"Well, that's pretty quick. I assume they have that much on hand. I'll see what I can do. I'll head to the Embassy now and call you when I find out."

"Thanks," replied Grant.

After Garcia left, Sam turned to Grant and said, "Grant, this is foolish. You're going into the snake pit filled with vipers who are being paid to kill you. What makes you think they won't shoot you as soon as they see you?"

Grant replied matter-of-factly, "I'll have Garcia with me. Besides, they won't be expecting it. He may be curious enough to let us talk, and, don't forget, we're going to offer him money for information."

Sam couldn't believe Grant was serious. "And why wouldn't he just shoot you two and take the money. That way he completes his contract with Vladimir and gets your money, too," she threw her hands up into the air for emphasis.

"You have a point. But what other choice do we have? We can't go in there with an army and shoot the place up. I need him to tell us who hired him. He might be able to give us a physical description and, if we're really lucky, tell us the name of the person he talked with. Sam, we have nothing else. We have to take this risk."

"Then I'm going, too. Three guns are better than two," Sam said.

Grant shook his head. "Uh uh. No way. Look, we need someone standing by. That has to be you. Someone we can call if we need anything. We have to have you here to coordinate back up if we need it."

Sam paused a minute, then, sounding unconvinced, said, "Okay, but you call me just before you go in and as soon as you get out. Also, at the very first sign of trouble, you let me know. Can we have a CIA team standing by?"

Grant, relieved the questioning was over said, "Garcia's heading back to the Embassy. Give him a call and see what can be set up. In fact, maybe they can be assembled and waiting not too far from where we'll be. Tell 'em to bring plenty of firepower. If we get ourselves into something the two of us can't handle, we're gonna need more ammo flying. Also, tell him to bring a few extra thirteen round mags for our Glocks. We've got plenty of rounds, but if we need them, we sure won't have time to fill a magazine."

"I still think this is a bad idea," Sam said as she started dialing her phone.

Chapter 45

I minus 19

Both Garcia and Thurmond were on high alert as they approached the building where the thug said his boss could be found. Although they had worked together a couple of times in the past, it was a long time ago and it was hard to trust your back to someone you haven't been close to. At the entrance they stopped for a minute.

"How do you want to play this?" Garcia asked.

"We just walk straight in and ask for Kozlov."

"And if they give us any trouble?" Garcia played it straight but he was thinking, oh great, more cowboy stuff. Just like Thurmond. But this was information Garcia needed, too, and he wasn't going to let Thurmond out of his sight. Not now.

"Just make sure your gun is locked and loaded. If we have to, we'll shoot our way out of the building. Let's just hope we don't have to. I at least want to be able to question Kozlov."

"You're calling the shots. My team is about three blocks away and standing by. Let's boogie," Garcia said.

"One more weapons check," Thurmond replied.

They turned towards the building where it would be difficult for anyone to see what they were doing, and double checked their weapons. Both had rounds in the chamber and were ready to fire. They put them in their right overcoat pockets.

The address they were given matched the numbers on the front of what looked like an old warehouse in a rundown commercial district on the outskirts of Moscow. They had already checked behind the building and found an old loading dock that looked as if it hadn't been used in years. But it had doors leading out and they knew if they needed to, it could be an escape route. They tried the front entrance door and found it unlocked, so they went into the reception area. One man who looked to be in his mid-thirties was sitting in an old easy chair, blocking the hallway which Thurmond presumed led to the other offices. He looked up, then stood up and spoke gruffly in Russian. He was huge.

"Sorry, we don't understand. Do you speak English?" asked

185

Thurmond in a pleasant voice.

"What you want?" the man shot back.

"We have some business with Kozlov," Thurmond replied.

"What business?" the man asked in the same demanding tone.

"We need some information and we have US dollars to pay for it."

"How much dollars?"

Garcia shook his head. "Come on, we'll only deal with Kozlov. Where is he?" he said.

The man hesitated for a minute, looked at Garcia, then at Thurmond, then shouted in Russian to someone down the hall. A man came out from one of the rooms and joined the first one. He was just as big as, maybe bigger, than the first guy. The body odor was almost overwhelming.

"Stay here," the first man said to Thurmond and Garcia. The second man then crossed his arms and blocked their path as the first man went down the hallway.

This is going to be easier than I figured, thought Thurmond. Maybe too easy. He looked at Garcia and nodded slightly. They both put their hands into their coat pockets.

After about a minute, the first man came back and motioned for Thurmond and Garcia to follow him. The second man followed them down the hall. With the first guy in front and the second guy in back, they were sandwiched in . . . not a good place to be if something went down. Thurmond was sure both men were armed to the hilt, but, so far, no guns were showing.

They went quite a ways down the hall before the first man stood aside and motioned them into a large room. They entered and saw a man with long, dark straggly hair sitting behind an old metal desk. There was only one small window high up on the left wall which was so grimy it let in little light. The semi-dark room was filled with boxes and the only place to sit was occupied by the guy behind the desk. Once Thurmond and Garcia were inside, the original two men were joined by two others standing by the door.

Five to one odds weren't great, but it could be worse, thought Garcia. Thurmond was having similar thoughts. As he looked around, he saw that they were in a room with only one exit. And that exit was guarded by four thugs. If this thing went south, they were going to have to go through a lot of muscle to escape. Both Thurmond and Garcia kept their right hands inside their coat pockets.

As their eyes adjusted to the semi-darkness inside the room, they could see that the man at the desk had an AK47 fully automatic rifle lying on the desk in front of him. They were one hundred percent certain it was loaded and that he wouldn't hesitate to use it if he felt threatened. It was going to take all their negotiating skills to get out of here alive.

Since the guy was just sitting there staring at them, Thurmond said, "We need information about one of your customers."

"You have US dollars?" the man asked.

"Yes."

"Show me."

"Answer some questions first," Thurmond said.

"No. I see my money first," the man shot back.

Thurmond nodded to Garcia who brought his left hand out of his coat pocket holding the cash.

"Give it to me," the man said, reaching across the desk.

Garcia pulled his hand holding the money back. "Not so fast. Are you Kozlov?"

"Yes. Now give me my money."

"I need to know you have information worth paying for before I give you the money." Thurmond said.

"Or, I will just shoot you and take the money," The man said, smiling and showing yellow teeth. As he was talking, he reached his right hand up and rested it on the automatic rifle.

Thurmond said with a shrug, "Then this will be all you get. Cooperate with us and there'll be more. Consider this just the down payment." Thurmond nodded to Garcia who threw the banded stack of bills onto the desk.

Kozlov grabbed the bundle, leaned back in his chair and made a show of slowly flipping the bills with his finger. After about a minute, without looking up he said, "What do you want to know?"

"You were hired to kill a man and a woman two days ago on the way into Moscow from the airport. The attempt failed. You then tried to kidnap the woman, but that also failed. We captured one of your men alive and he told us you were the boss and he just followed orders. He had no knowledge of who hired you." Thurmond explained and then asked, "The man who hired you, what was his name and how do you contact him?"

He opened a desk drawer and put the money in before answering.

"This will be a short meeting. First of all, I did not try to kidnap anyone. Secondly, I cannot give you his name and I cannot contact him. He contacts me. End of story. Now get out of here, I am losing patience with this game."

"You haven't answered any of our questions. You haven't earned any of the money. If you don't give us the information, we'll take our money back," Thurmond said forcefully, putting his finger on the trigger of the gun in his pocket.

In the instant it took for the man to lean forward and pick up the rifle, both Thurmond and Garcia had their guns out and opened fire— Thurmond first took out the guy behind the desk and then spun around to help Garcia with the four guys at the door. The goons were down in less than four seconds. It happened so fast, none of them had even drawn their guns. Garcia reached around behind the desk and retrieved the money and as they fled towards the door, they could hear shouting and feet running on the wood flooring. It sounded like at least a dozen men were closing in on their location in the office. At that moment, the door jamb was splintered by automatic weapon fire. Thurmond looked around the doorway to see several men down the hall.

The one with the automatic weapon was kneeling in the center of the hallway. Thurmond took him out with two shots, one to the throat and one to the chest. Garcia joined him at the doorway, kneeling and shooting next to Thurmond who was standing, the standard high-low position they had both been trained for. The thugs weren't very smart fighters. One by one they came into the hallway to try to get a clear shot, and one by one, Thurmond and Garcia took them down. Finally there was silence. The hallway was choked with smoke and the smell of cordite was a visible haze in the air. They had each gone through three thirteen-round magazines. They quickly left the room and were out the front door in a few seconds without any further gunfire. As they ran down the street, a car screeched to a stop at the curb. They saw one of the CIA backup team at the wheel so they jumped in and the car immediately shot forward taking them out of harm's way.

"Just like old times, heh?" Garcia chuckled as they sped away.

"Yeah, the bad old times," Thurmond responded. "But, we still don't have a clue who this Vladimir is."

"Well, at least I don't have to explain where the money went. I'll just return it to the station chief." Garcia actually sounded cheery.

Chapter 46

I minus 18

"What now, coach?" Sam asked. They were back in the safe house having an early breakfast of toast, eggs and coffee.

"Damned if I know. Seems to be standard answer number one these days," Grant responded, taking a big bite of toast.

Sam put down her fork and turned to face Grant. "Grant, yesterday was pretty scary for me. I could picture you not coming back. It wasn't good and I barely slept last night. Kept having nightmares. There would be a big hole in my life if something happened to you," she said.

"Sam, you know I've grown very close to you, but I can't talk about that right now. It's dangerous for us to be distracted. When I think about you I can't seem to concentrate on anything else. And I need to focus all my attention on this problem. Can we put this conversation on the back burner for the next couple of weeks, just till this is over?" Grant replied earnestly.

"Of course we can—if you promise to bring it up again later." Sam smiled.

"I promise." And with that, Grant reached over and pulled Sam close. They held each other for several minutes. "I'll look forward to it," he finally whispered, his lips close to her ear.

They spent the next several hours talking about what they knew about Vladimir and complaining about how much they didn't know.

At around 10:30, Garcia showed up and they ran through everything one more time, hoping he'd pick up on something. When they concluded, Garcia said, "I'm sorry, Thurmond, but I just don't see anything to go on. Tell you what I'll do. I'll try to get one of our friendlies in Russian intel to do some checking. Maybe he can find something in the files to point us somewhere. It's a long shot, but it's all we got."

"Is he SVR?" Thurmond said, using the abbreviation for the Russian Foreign Intelligence Service.

"Yeah."

"Thanks," Thurmond replied. "We can only hang around for

another couple of days or so. Can you get right on it and urge your informant to hurry?"

Garcia shrugged. "I'll do what I can. I have to go through the station chief—it's not my informant. I'll tell him it's a priority. My boss'll back me up if needed."

With nothing to do until they heard back from the CIA informant, Grant and Sam spent time at the central library pouring through the Moscow and the many surrounding suburb and town telephone directories looking for the only name they had connected with Vladimir: Sergey Baskov. They weren't even sure he was their guy. It turned out that it was a popular name, with hundreds of entries. They copied the information for all of them, but knew there was no chance they could follow up with that many. It was a frustrating drill and they emerged each day with cramped hands from writing so much.

During this period, Grant tried several times to reach Garcia, but he didn't answer his phone. The Cultural Attaché said he hadn't seen him for a couple of days and had no idea where he was. Grant thought that was odd, but there was nothing he could do about it— Garcia didn't report to him.

Finally, after three days, Garcia called Thurmond.

"Thurmond, it's Garcia."

"Where've you been, man? Did your guy find out anything?" Grant asked, frustrated.

"Been busy on other matters. The guys couldn't find a single mention of anyone code-named Vladimir, nor any more than you already have on Baskov. The address they found was the same fictional one that you had. But they did confirm that Baskov was on their payroll for many years. He's got to be your guy."

"Did he tell you if this Baskov was still on their payroll?" Grant asked.

"He said, no, that they had cut him off several years ago and, as far as he knew, the guy just disappeared. He also said that if they found him he was facing some sort of internal indictment. He didn't know or, at least wouldn't tell me, any details."

"Well, it's good to get that confirmed, but it doesn't really help us. Sam and I've been copying down the addresses of everyone in all the phonebooks we could find named Sergey Baskov. There are hundreds," Grant said.

"Too many to run down. It would take us months to interview all of them. At some point, one of them would call the police who would then start checking us out. That wouldn't be a good thing," Garcia replied.

Grant made his decision. "Well, I'm not going to sit around Moscow wasting any more time. Sam and I are heading back to the States tomorrow. I'll go to the Embassy later this afternoon and update General Wheeler on the secure phone. Shit. We've only about two weeks to solve this and we're nowhere." And the DNI's gonna be pissed, Grant thought.

"You guys go ahead back; I'm going to hang around here for another day or so finishing up some other business. See ya." With that, Garcia hung up and headed out for his meeting. Have to make sure I'm not followed, he thought, looking around.

Grant turned to Sam and said, "I'm going to head to the Embassy to call General Wheeler on the secure phone. Want to come along?"

She looked up from the paper she'd been studying. "No, don't think so. I'll stay here and make our reservations home. Any preferences?"

"Nope. But, if possible, just get us back by tomorrow night. Oh yes I do have a preference. Book us in Business Class," he said heading towards the door.

"You got it. See you later," Sam replied as Grant walked out the door.

Chapter 47

I minus 15

"General Wheeler, please. This is Colonel Thurmond." It sounded strange for Grant to say his rank again after all this time. Not bad, just strange.

"I'm sorry; the General is on leave this week. He'll be back Monday," the voice said on the other end of the secure line. "Would you like to leave a message or call back then?"

"I'll call back, thanks," Grant replied. Wheeler on leave? He never went on leave.

He decided to call the DNI directly. Time was running out and he'd better let him know about his lack of success in Moscow. He dialed his direct number.

When Barry answered, Grant said, "Sir, this is Colonel Thurmond. Just wanted to update you on where we are." Grant gave the DNI, who was in his car on his way to an early morning meeting, a thorough analysis of the situation. "And, sir, we just don't have any further leads," he concluded apologetically.

Barry sighed audibly. "What's your next move?" the DNI asked.

"Well, right now we're planning to return to Washington tomorrow. Widen the search. At some point we know he's gonna to be there. My guess is he'll have to get there soon in order to get everything planned. We don't even know what he's gonna to do or where he's gonna to do it. We only have a date. I know we're concentrating on the inauguration ceremony, but it could be any time during that day. The President's whereabouts are usually pretty widely known, aren't they?"

"Inauguration day is long for the President-elect. He starts early and ends late. He's in a dozen locations where he might be vulnerable. Get back here as soon as you can. I want you to lead a coordinated task force to try to stop this maniac. I'll alert CIA, DIA, NSA, the FBI and the Secret Service that you'll be contacting them for support. I want every agency involved with all of them supplying you team members." The DNI was emphatic.

Grant was impressed with the Director's forcefulness. "Thanks, sir. We'll need all the support we can get. Oh, by the way, as I mentioned, I got Garcia involved in this. He's actually been a big help. I'd like him to be the CIA lead on the taskforce."

Now it was the DNI's turn to be impressed. He said, "Done. Anyone else in particular you want?"

"I'll think it through on the plane coming back. I'll fill you in on the plan as soon as I return."

"Thanks. Gotta go, I'm here," and the DNI hung up the phone without waiting for Grant to reply.

Five minutes later, after having dropped the DNI off at FBI headquarters, his driver left a message on an answering machine. It was a long message that detailed everything he'd heard. Vladimir picked the message up before Grant had arrived back at the safe house. So, Thurmond had survived the attack and had taken retribution. Damn! Oh well. Vladimir couldn't be bothered with that now. There was nothing more he could do and he had a lot to set up before leaving for America. His flight was in two days.

Chapter 48

I minus 13

The flight back to the US was crowded, even in business class, so Grant and Sam sat separately. They couldn't talk through the plan. After landing, Grant reminded Sam that they needed to return to the DIA apartment near Key Bridge when they. It was one place they could be safe. With all that had happened to her recently, Sam readily agreed.

During the flight, Sam alternately dozed and read a novel she picked up at the airport prior to boarding. Grant, however, spent most of the flight looking out of the window and thinking about what to do next. By the time they arrived in Washington, Grant had a plan outlined in his head. Tomorrow would be used to contact each agency and asking for a lead person from each. If he could get quick action on that, he'd have a meeting tomorrow afternoon to talk through the plan with the agency leads. They would probably need a day or so to pull together their other team members and Grant wanted to have a complete task force briefing the following afternoon—two days from now. They had a lot to do and no time to waste.

Grant spent the next morning contacting all the appropriate agencies—CIA, DIA, FBI, NSA, Secret Service, State Department and the District of Columbia police department. He also contacted an Air Force agency responsible for all DOD spy satellites. He wanted to make sure they had satellites in position and relays set up to closely monitor the entire inauguration site for any suspicious activity. They all agreed to send representatives to a joint taskforce meeting that afternoon. The D.C. Chief of Police volunteered a meeting room, but Grant had already arranged for a freshly swept room at FBI headquarters. The FBI was located in the J. Edgar Hoover building on Pennsylvania Avenue and had a secure entrance where everyone was logged in and out. Grant wanted to keep good records of everyone who had access to the information he was about to provide.

Precisely at 3:00 p.m., the meeting started. Grant stood and addressed the group of eighteen people. "Thanks for coming on such short notice, but when you hear what's going down, you'll understand. First of all, the information you are about to hear is highly classified and is for your ears only. Do not discuss this with anyone not on this taskforce, . . . no one who hasn't been read in." Grant paused a moment to let that soak in, then continued. "We have information that points to an assassination attempt on the President-elect on inauguration day, possibly at the swearing-in ceremony itself." A murmur went up from the people in the room.

Grant continued, "We've spent the better part of two months running down clues from all over Eastern Europe and Russia. However, our target is extremely elusive. Although we refer to him by his code name, Vladimir, we do have another possible name, but we believe that name is false and that his documentation was forged. What this means is that we have very little to go on. We do have a grainy badge picture, which we believe is him, but it's several years old." He clicked on a slide with Vladimir's picture. "We'll get copies of that picture to everyone who'll be screening visitors, but not until inauguration day. I don't want him to know that we have his picture. We need to get it into the immigration computers to compare against biometric chip pictures of everyone entering the country, but I don't know if we have time for that. Other than the picture, we only have a probable target, the President-elect, and a date, January 17th. I say probable because we are acting on solid, but unverified intelligence.

He cleared his throat and scanned the faces in the room. They were attentive and quiet. "I have to add that I'm having serious doubts about finding this Vladimir prior to the inauguration. If that turns out to be true, I don't have to tell you that we're looking at a very dangerous scenario. I intend to meet with the President-elect and make a strong plea that he consider moving the inauguration to a more secure location. I've been told, however, that he has been asked several times and has consistently said he will not hide from America's enemies. I think, in this case, that is an unwise decision and I'll tell him so later today. Assuming that I don't get my head handed back to me on a platter, let's plan to meet here at 0800 tomorrow and I'll fill you in on what happened."

The rest of the meeting went well, with each agency accepting assignments and tasks and agreeing to meet the next day. The guy from State approached him after the meeting and said he'd see if he could get the photo of Vladimir into the customs and immigration system overnight. He said he couldn't promise anything, but he'd give it a shot. He also said he'd request that immigration authorities all have the picture and be required to visually check out all arrivals who did not have a biometric chip picture imbedded in their passport. He said that might take a couple of days but it was the best they could do. Grant thanked him and said that if he ran into any stalling or roadblocks the DNI could help clear them.

Chapter 49

I minus 12
January 8th

As Vladimir left his small, dingy apartment for the last time, he carried a medium–sized, roll-aboard suitcase and a small pouch containing his new Russian identity papers and passport. The man said it was an authentic passport that would stand up to scrutiny by both the Russians and the Americans. He assured him the biometric chip imbedded in the passport was also authentic and contained photographic information about Vladimir, so the scan would go fine. When they scanned the passport, Vladimir's current picture would come up. He had already mailed his other papers, the US identity he planned to use afterwards, to a post office box in Fairfax, Virginia. In fact, he'd had the man make up two identities, both showing him as a US citizen. He'd pick them up when he arrived. Would it work? Well, he'd find out soon enough. His flight was in just over three hours. Amazing, a direct flight from Moscow to Washington, D.C. in Business class. On an American airliner. He looked forward to the in-flight meals and free vodka. Or, maybe he'd drink American bourbon.

He had less than two weeks to pull everything together and he'd need all of it. He had to scout out the layout of the inauguration ceremony, assemble the necessary components, buy explosives and craft the device. Fortunately, the detailed layout and timetable of the ceremony would be printed in the newspapers well in advance. That would help a lot. He smiled. Stupid Americans. The old Soviet Union would never take chances like that. He didn't know what it took to buy explosives in America, but he didn't think it would be too tough. He'd read about American farmers buying sticks of dynamite. What about dynamite powder? TNT? Could he buy C4 or other plastique explosives? Well, he'd find out when he got there. His internet research indicated that he could. If not, he had the formula to make strong explosives from fertilizer. Not the ideal way because it was so bulky and required a large container, but he knew it would work.

197

His newly printed business cards showed he was an explosives expert with a demolition company specializing in bringing down buildings. He'd been able to create that company over the internet. He set it up in a place called Montana. The map showed it to be pretty much isolated, well west of Washington. His story was that he was in Virginia on a job to bring down an old building. He thought he'd go to Roanoke and Charlestown, West Virginia to buy the explosives, but not too much in one place. He wouldn't want anyone to get suspicious.

He had decided to rent one car using his temporary US identity, both of which he'd abandon later, and also to buy another car using his permanent US identity. That way, no one would be suspicious about a Russian renting a car. He'd accumulated quite a bit of money, so that wasn't an issue. He thought that if he rented a car, then afterwards, after the inauguration, he could just abandon it and then use the car he bought to get away. That way, if anyone remembered him buying explosives and could describe the rental car, it wouldn't lead to him.

He would end up with a new car, enough money in the bank to last the rest of his life, assuming he was careful with it, and an ironclad identity. His permanent identity came from a long time Soviet-era mole who had returned to Russia several years after the Soviet collapse. He'd been planted when he was a teenager, went to college in the US, was a citizen, paid taxes for many years and then, when the wall came down, wanted to return to Russia. The Russian government was accommodating and took him back, but told him to just quit his job, sell his house, then assume his Russian identity and return to Russia through Canada using his Russian passport. There would be no record of an American leaving the country and not coming back. After a while, someone might check. When he had first hatched this scheme, while he still had access to Russian intelligence files, he's searched the data base and picked out the ID. He knew the old American identity was still valid, so Vladimir had taken it. He even had a social security card. He was certain the Russians no longer even remembered the identity existed, so he was safe there.

If he ever needed another US identity, he'd do it the way they'd taught him as he was being trained years ago in Russia. He'd read the obituaries in the newspaper, identifying a recently deceased person who was about his age and use that identity. Usually they contained the place of birth. He would then write to the bureau of records in the state where the guy was born and, posing as the guy, request a copy of his birth certificate. After he received the birth certificate, he would use that to get a driver's license. Without a passport, which might be too risky to get, he wouldn't be able to travel outside the US, but with a birth certificate and driver's license, he could get credit cards and have a completely fool-proof identity. He hoped he wouldn't have to go through that process, but knew he could if necessary.

All the details were lined up. Take out the new president, assume his new identity, and enjoy a new life in America. Perfect. Oh yes, and one small other detail that could be taken care of later. Get rid of Riley.

Chapter 50

I minus 12
January 8th

"Yes, sir, I understand your position, but I really think you ought to reconsider," Grant said, perhaps a little too forcefully, to the President-elect. They were sitting at a conference table in the President-elect's office. The DNI was also there.

"Colonel, this is something I have to do. I'm asking . . . no, I'm telling both of you not to bring this up again. Understand?" The President-elect said with finality in his voice and a grim look on his face.

"Yes, sir. We understand. We'll continue our efforts to find this man, while at the same time strengthening security at the ceremony. We're also working on tightening security at all your functions after the swearing-in, including the balls. Following your instructions, we will try not to inconvenience the public any more than we have to," the DNI responded.

"Thanks. Keep me up to speed on how you're progressing. Now, if there's nothing else, I have a busy schedule." Mason said standing up, clearly dismissing Thurmond and Barry.

As they walked away the DNI turned to Grant and said, "Colonel, do whatever is necessary to stop this assassination. If you run into any barriers or get pushback from *anyone*, call me immediately. I'll take care of it. This is my highest priority right now so I'll take your call no matter where I am or what I'm doing. I'm available by cell phone twenty-four hours a day."

"Thank you, sir. I'll do what I can and keep you informed of where we are every step of the way," Grant said.

It was past six p.m. by the time Grant arrived back at the apartment and Sam was already in the kitchen preparing dinner.

"Smells good. I didn't know you could cook," Grant said entering the kitchen.

"Well...I can," Sam replied, laughing.

Grant smiled. Living with Sam, even though they weren't sleeping in the same room, was getting really comfortable. He asked,

"What are we having?"

Sam put him off a bit by saying, "First, you have to tell me how your talk with the President-elect went."

Grant sighed, "As predicted. He said he wouldn't move the ceremony and told both of us not to bring it up again. So, we won't."

"How'd the DNI take it?"

"What could he do? He just said 'yes, sir' and we left."

Sam moved closer to Grant and put her hand on his upper arm. "I know you're disappointed, Grant, but it sounds like there was really nothing you could say to change his mind. What's next?" she asked.

Changing the subject, Grant simply smiled and said, "Dinner. I ask again, what are we having?"

Sam laughed and moved back to the oven, checking the timer. "Oh, it's something my mother used to make. She called it comfort food. Chicken breasts covered with a cheese and wine sauce. All baked in the oven. Sort of like a casserole. Then dished up over rice," Sam replied.

"Wow, sounds great. When do we eat?" Grant asked.

"In about fifteen minutes. Why don't you open a bottle of wine?"

"Great idea. Red or white?" Grant asked.

"White would go best with dinner. There's a bottle of Chardonnay chilling in the fridge," Sam said waving in the direction of the refrigerator.

Grant got out the wine, opened it and poured two glasses, handing one to Sam.

"Oh, this is good," Sam said, tasting her wine.

"Yeah, it sure is. This is really nice, coming home to dinner cooking and a good glass of wine," Grant paused just a moment before continuing, "especially sharing both with you."

"Well, thank you, sir," Sam replied lightly, looking up into his eyes. "And it's very nice sharing it with you." Then Sam turned serious and her smile faded. "But, Grant, what are we doing to do about finding that man?"

Grant had had enough of Vladimir for a while, so he said gently. "Not tonight, Sam. I need to get away from it for just this one night."

She paused a beat before saying, "Ok, fair enough. Let's eat."

Chapter 51

I minus 5
January 15th

A week had passed during which, the group met at least once a day, sometimes working together late into the evening. They had come up with many enhancements to the security process surrounding the inauguration, but they all knew that nothing was foolproof. The original plan had everyone going through airport-like metal detectors, but one of the team brought up using the new whole body imaging technology and body scanners. That would allow examination of the body through clothing to see if anyone was carrying explosives, not just metal guns.

When Grant had discussed this with the President-elect, he immediately said no, that they showed way too much, and took too long to get everyone through. He thought that too many of the guests, especially at the balls, would object. So they were back to just the metal detectors for all the balls and for most of the people at the ceremony. They did have one device brought in, though, thinking that as they watched everyone come in if anyone looked suspicious they'd move that person over to the body scanner. Profiling? Maybe, but Grant didn't care. They would do whatever it took. They would have both male and female operators on the scanner, so no individual would be seen by the opposite sex. Yes, Grant was told, the scanners were that good.

They just had to keep going over all the potential scenarios hoping that the group, along with the backups at their individual agencies, would cover the one Vladimir might pick. If he did, he was dead. The word was out: don't let this guy escape; if you have to, shoot to kill; take no chances. Yes, they would love to question him, but this guy was way too dangerous for the heroic measures that might be needed to take him alive. They had photo experts enhance the grainy badge photo and age it to the current time. They printed both on the same sheet and had distributed it to all police officers, secret service agents and anyone else in security who would be on duty that day. The original photo was so bad, though, they weren't sure anyone would recognize the guy. Since the sheet they handed out had both the old photo and an aged photo, they hoped there wouldn't be too many false identifications.

Using the DNI as leverage, the guy from State did get the photo into the immigration system, along with an 'arrest on sight' order, but the process had taken almost two days. The delay was because State decided to reprogram the scanning computers to do pattern recognition on the passport picture of everyone entering the US. That decision resulted in long lines, but, well, when you are trying to protect the next President, it was worth having everyone spend an extra couple of minutes in line. But, let's face it, thought Grant, Vladimir might have slipped into the country by now.

Having no information to the contrary and, since they were only five days from the inauguration, he had no choice but to assume Vladimir had gotten through and was at large in the US. As each day passed he was getting more and more concerned for the President-elect's safety. He had completely forgotten that he, too, was on the assassination list.

Chapter 52

I minus 5
January 15th

Vladimir had no problem entering the country, arriving the same day as Grant and Sam, well before his picture was in the system. Months ago, online, he had rented a house north of Leesburg, Virginia, located just off Charles Town Pike, Route 9, right before the road crossed over the state line into West Virginia. The house was set back from the road and was shielded by overgrown shrubs, trees and scrub brush growing in an unkempt yard. Although the house was small and run down, it had a large garage, which suited Vladimir's needs perfectly. Someone in the past had painted over the only window and inside, the ramshackle garage was very private. It was rural enough that no one would pay him the least attention. The next few days were critical. He had a few more supplies to get. One item, in particular, might be difficult to find, so, just in case, he had an alternative plan.

One of the things the Russian mobster had provided, in addition to trying to kill Thurmond and the girl, was the name of a Russian criminal contact in the US. Vladimir had requested that the guy obtain a block of C4 explosive and have it delivered, not mailed, to his address in the US. He had paid Kozlov five thousand US dollars for this. He told the guy he needed it the day after he flew into the US and it had arrived right on time via a courier service. Also, he had found it surprisingly easy to buy conventional explosives to supplement the C4. He now had enough to suit his needs and, since he had used his other forged identity for all the purchases, none of it could be traced to his permanent US identity.

Over the next couple of days, Vladimir completed the rest of his purchases, finding everything he needed . . . except for the one item he needed the most. So, he kept looking, calling over two dozen places. With one day to spare, he found the last item in an auto salvage yard just outside Charles Town, West Virginia, just a short drive from his house. It was large and bulky enough that he couldn't pick it up in his rental car, so he called a local rental car agency in

Charles Town and, using the US identity he planned to discard, rented a pick-up truck for the day. No traces. He drove his rental car to the Charles Town rental agency, picked up the truck, drove to the junk yard, bought the item and took it back to his garage. He then returned the truck to the rental agency, picked up his car and drove home. The whole trip took him less than an hour and a half. With the way this had to come down, he knew he wouldn't get much sleep over the next couple of days. What the hell, he'd have plenty of time to sleep once this was over. Just two days to go.

Vladimir spent nearly all day preparing the item he bought—a gas tank for a late model Lincoln Town Car. He made sure no gasoline fumes were present and cut the tank in half along the seam made when the two halves were originally welded together. He packed one half of the tank full of the conventional explosives, added the C4 and set up a remote-controlled fuse. The C4 would be the first to explode. It would be a large enough blast to detonate both the conventional explosives and the gasoline in the other half of the tank. He then welded a thin separator plate, effectively sealing the explosives from where the gasoline would be, and then he carefully welded the gasoline tank back together. When he was finished, it looked perfect—no one could tell it had been tampered with. No one could tell how lethal it would be when he pushed the RF transmitter.

It was nearly midnight when he finished. He then called his PI contact, Matt Riley, who, since he was sound asleep when the phone rang, was a little groggy when he answered the phone.

Sitting up in bed, Riley said, "Yeah?"

"We need to talk," replied Vladimir in his best American voice.

"Who's this?" Riley asked uncertainly, not recognizing the voice.

"Your employer." Vladimir replied.

A slight pause as this registered in Riley's sleepy brain, then, "Oh, hi. Not much to report."

Vladimir got right to the point. "I need to know the exact plans for inauguration day. Has he covered them with you?"

"No, but all the drivers have a briefing by Secret Service tomorrow morning in Barry's conference room."

"Okay. Here's what I want you to do," Vladimir explained. "Some time in the afternoon when you think your boss will be in his office for a few hours, you're to call him saying you're sick and have to go home. You should also say that you've arranged for a backup driver to take your place. I want you to tell him that there will only be about an hour gap in his driver coverage. Then I want you to come to my house so we can talk about your final payment and letting you get back to your life. Your assignment will be over at that point. Sound okay?"

"Sounds good. I must say, though, this has been a good assignment. Thank you for hiring me." Riley was awake now, thinking of the extra cash.

"You have done a good job and you will get a bonus when we talk. So, tomorrow, call me after you've told him you are sick and I'll give you directions to the house."

"Thanks. See you about 3:30 tomorrow."

They both hung up and Vladimir smiled. A surprise bonus, indeed.

A bonus, huh? thought Riley. Great.

***

At the same time as Vladimir was hanging up, Garcia was saying into the phone, "Yes . . . yes . . . no, I understand, I won't fail . . . . Yes, it's under control. I have full access to the task group's work and I'm deeply involved in every move. There's no way he can escape alive . . . . Yes, I'll keep you informed." Garcia knew his future was on the line. He had to make sure this assassin would not live to tell his story. If he didn't succeed, Garcia knew his CIA career might be over and he might have to walk away and give up the life he now had. He'd stashed away enough money to live modestly for the rest of his life and had a couple of alternate identities he'd used when he was undercover. The CIA thought he'd followed standard procedure and destroyed the passports and other things like driver's licenses, all of which were real and would pass any scrutiny, but he hadn't. Also, there was no way they could trace the money he had supposedly paid informants over the years which, instead, had ended up in his bank account. Just like that five grand from the embassy last week. Interesting how all this worked out. It will be just as interesting to see how it will all end, he thought.

Chapter 53

I minus 1
January 19th

Matt Riley called Vladimir at 3:10 p.m. saying he'd told Barry he was sick and going home and that an alternate driver would be available in about an hour. Vladimir gave him directions to his house.

Riley pulled into the driveway just before 4:00 p.m. Vladimir, who'd been watching from his living room window went out to greet him.

"It's good to finally meet you in person," Riley said, smiling and shaking Vladimir's hand.

Vladimir smiled back and said, "Yes, we should have met before now, but I've been extremely busy. Come into the house where we can talk."

When they were seated in the living room, Vladimir asked, "What are the arrangements for tomorrow? I will be taking your place driving the car and I need to know everything."

Riley explained the details and then asked, "Why're you taking my place? I've been wondering what you're up to."

"It has been a dream of mine as long as I can remember to be backstage at a presidential inaugural. When I was small, my father took me to one, but we were standing far away and I couldn't really see very well. Since then I've been living overseas and have never seen another one. This is my chance to see the ceremony up close and maybe even shake the new president's hand. I am very excited." Vladimir nodded and smiled enthusiastically.

Living overseas, huh? thought Riley. That explains the slight accent.

"Well, you paid me a lot of money just to be up close," he said,

"It will be worth every penny. Now, do you need a ride somewhere?"

Riley shrugged. "Yeah, I need a ride home. No place else to go."

They stood up to leave. Riley headed to the door with Vladimir behind. Vladimir picked up the engineers hammer he had place next to the sofa. Riley never knew what hit him. The heavy hammer smashed through his skull, killing him instantly. Vladimir dragged the body to the back bedroom. He searched the body, looking for any form of identification and, finding only a wallet, removed it. He then left the room, closing the door behind him. He had paid six months' rent in advance for this place, so it would be months before anyone found the body and even longer, if ever, before it would be identified. By that time, Vladimir thought, I will be long gone and the identity I used to rent this place will be untraceable.

He had a lot of work to do, but it would have to wait until that evening. Right now he had to get back to the city and pretend to be the replacement driver for Barry.

Vladimir, having been told by Riley where to park and wait, was leaning on the fender of the Town Car at 6:50 p.m. when Barry walked up.

"Are you my new driver for today?" Barry asked Vladimir.

"Yes, sir, and maybe for tomorrow if your permanent driver is still under the weather," Vladimir replied in a near perfect American accent. All those months in Soviet language school were finally paying off.

"Fine, please take me home, then you're through for the night. Pick me up early tomorrow, no later than 5:00 a.m." Barry got into the back seat and Vladimir closed the door carefully.

After dropping the DNI off at his home, Vladimir headed to his rented house. The drive lasted nearly an hour and once there, he pulled the Town Car into the garage and began to work. First he had to remove the gas tank presently on the car. Then he would replace it with the one he had constructed earlier containing the explosives. No matter how thoroughly the car was searched, no one would be able to find anything wrong. It would look perfectly normal from underneath, even if lifted into the air. However, the amount of explosives contained in the tank would flatten nearly everything within fifty yards. The detonator was rigged into the C4 which, when it exploded, would set off the conventional explosives. The tertiary explosion of the approximately ten gallons of gasoline in the other half of the tank would add even more to the devastation, and that explosion should set off the tanks in the other cars parked next to it.

He knew now that there would be at least six other limousines parked in close proximity. It would create utter chaos and allow him to just walk away to his new life. Of course, in order to be safe, he had to be at least seventy five yards away before setting off the explosion. He assumed, since Thurmond was so involved in finding him, that he would also be present and be taken out by the blast. With any luck, this Garcia would be there, too. But, if he wasn't, he didn't pose much of a threat to his future. There would be no one left who could tie him to his past. He would be safe in America, living far away from Washington, D.C.

Chapter 54

Inauguration Day
January 20th

The President-elect awoke very early and looked over to the other side of the bed where his wife was still asleep. She was so beautiful and with her face at rest, she looked no older than thirty. He leaned over and kissed her awake. When she opened her eyes, he said softly, "I'm more in love with you now than I've ever been." She smiled and replied through a yawn, "I love you, too." She then rolled onto her side facing him, put her arm around him and kissed him, softly at first, then with more passion. They made love.

When they were finished, they both rolled over onto their backs and he said, "Well, are you ready to become the First Lady? We have a full day and a long night ahead of us, but I am so excited that I just can't sleep anymore."

"You are such a typical man," she replied, laughing. "You take advantage of a poor helpless girl, who's a bit star struck at getting so much attention from the President-elect, then just roll over and want to leave."

He laughed. "You are far from helpless. Come on, let's get going. I can't stand just lying here. I've got to move around. Think I'll go to the gym and work out before I hit the shower."

"Okay, okay. I get it." she replied, still laughing. "Let's go."

An hour later they were still casually dressed and having coffee in the dining room when the President-elect said, "Okay, here's the drill for today. We start out just over an hour from now. We walk across the street to have brunch with the Bowers at the White House. We then leave in separate cars for the inauguration, which takes place at noon. The Secret Service wants us to arrive no more than ten minutes before that. You'll enter with President and Mrs. Bower and be seated in the front row. At precisely 11:59 the Chief Justice of the Supreme Court will step to the podium. I'll be waiting in the wings and when I see him arrive at the podium I'll walk to meet him. He will administer the oath of office and when I'm finished, in about thirty seconds, you'll be First Lady of the United States of America."

"Well," she said smiling, "that makes me important. What's to become of you?"

Mason chuckled and said, "Uh, I'll be married to the First Lady. I think that makes me President."

She broadened her smile and said, "Yes, yes it does. And no one deserves it more. Oh, sweetheart, you've had such grand dreams of how this country could move forward and what it could accomplish. It is such a thrill for me to see that you now have a chance to make those dreams a reality."

Mason turned serious. "Well, it won't necessarily be easy. We have a fairly well-balanced congress. Our party has a one vote majority in the Senate and a four vote minority in the House. I won't have a rubber stamp."

"You don't need a rubber stamp. Your ideas are so well thought out and they benefit all Americans. Even the other party can see the good in them. You'll win them over with just common sense."

Mason snorted. "Yeah, common sense. Unfortunately, sometimes politics overrules common sense. Sometimes, I think too many times, politics play so much a role in everything that achieving real progress is stymied. Each party feels they have to vote right down party lines to differentiate themselves to the voters. It seems to be more about getting re-elected than running an effective legislature." He shook his head. "What a waste. It'll take a lot to convince some of them that party politics and voting strictly along party lines regardless of the value of the proposition is harmful to the citizens that put us here. You know, sometimes it feels like an impossible task. But, I really think the time is right. The American public wants something different than politics as usual. I really think so," the President-elect said, almost pleadingly.

"Okay, Pollyanna, we have to get dressed," his wife laughed, then continued, "seriously, though, I do believe in the same things you do, and I do hope we can break down the barriers to change. I also believe that if anyone can do it, it's you." She smiled at him, not wanting to bring up her worries yet again.

As they stood up and went to get dressed, Mason thought, Yeah, great dreams, but I have to make it alive through today. Sure hope they catch that guy.

***

After a restless night, Grant was up by 5:00 a.m. Sam by 5:15. They met in the kitchen of their apartment where Grant had already started coffee. Both were still in PJ's.

Grant took in a deep breath and let it out slowly. "Well, today's the day," he said.

"Yes. And I pray it all goes well."

Grant nodded. "I know we've done all we can, but I still have an uneasy feeling. We've no clue what Vladimir is up to. We don't know what's gonna happen and, although we've tightened up security so that a gnat couldn't get through, I still don't know if it's enough."

"Yeah, we just don't know how clever Vladimir is." Sam brought her eyebrows together and pursed her lips before continuing, "You know, one thought. We've been concentrating so hard on the actual inauguration, have we overlooked anything regarding security for the rest of the day? As I recall, the note only had a date, not an event or a time," she said.

"You're right," Grant said. "We've gone over the whole day many times and have spent about as much time on it as we have on the event. Secret Service has taken the lead on the walk to the White House, the trip from the White House to the event site and the procession back to the White House. They, along with FBI security, have also focused on the parties the President and First Lady will attend. There'll be hoards of extra Secret Service men and women in and around each venue, but I'm still not happy and I don't know what to do about it. Guess I'll spend the rest of the morning going through all the security plans one more time." He paused a beat before continuing, "I sure would like to get a shot at this guy. I wouldn't miss."

Sam said, "Well, while you concentrate on protecting the President, I'm not going to let you out of my sight. You were on that list too, remember? So covering your back is my top priority for the day."

"Thanks. Look, if you see him, don't immediately just blow him away. We'd really like to question him to find out why he's doing this. We don't even know if he has a backup in case he gets caught or killed. We could waste him and there would be another one following through on what he started. We need to question him."

"Got it. I'll shoot him only if I have no other choice. But if I have him in my sights and I feel he is a direct threat to you or anyone else, he's dead," Sam said determinedly.

"Fair enough," Grant replied.

***

Barry called Grant at 6:30 a.m., just after arriving at his office and he immediately opened with, "Thurmond, where are we?"

"Sir, we already have our security folks deployed throughout the route and at the inauguration site. We have approximately a hundred fifty of our people in civilian clothes along the route and more than twice that around the bleachers and in the spectator area. We also have about three hundred more uniformed officers throughout the area. All are armed and have a photo of the suspect. We're as ready as we can possibly be. But, he's still out there."

"Damn, I'm nervous. Are you sure he can't possibly get through?" Barry barked.

Grant sounded calm when he replied, "No, sir, I'm not. There's no way we can be sure. I just know that we've done all we can."

"I'm sure you have . . . . I just hope it's enough," the DNI replied and then hung up without waiting for Grant to respond.

Yeah, me too, Grant thought.

Barry's driver arrived at 11:00 a.m. to transport him to the ceremony. He planned to get to the bleachers at least twenty minutes before the ceremony was scheduled to begin so he could look around. Because of the overhanging threat, he was one of the few that would be parking directly behind the bleachers. The others were the current President; the President-elect; the Vice President and the Vice President-elect and their wives, who would all be in the same car; the Chief Justice; and the Chairman of the Joint Chiefs of Staff. Six cars in total. He knew the Secret Service had set up an elaborate examination plan for every vehicle that would be within a hundred yards of the ceremony and, although he was on the cleared list, his car would have to be examined as well. That would take about ten minutes. He had plenty of time.

He said to his driver as he entered the car, "Good Morning, again. Looks like Matt isn't going to make it? I know you said earlier he was still going to try to relieve you by mid-morning."

Vladimir didn't miss a beat. Standing with the back door open he said,"Yes, sir. I talked to him again about an hour ago. He was at the doctor—diarrhea. I didn't want to hear the rest of it. Certainly was disappointed that he couldn't drive you to the ceremony today. Said he had really been looking forward to it, but there was no way he could make it. I promised to call him tonight and give him all the details." Vladimir smiled pleasantly.

Barry, wanting to make sure his driver knew the routine, looked up from his plush leather seat and said, "You know, we'll have to go through two checkpoints. The first one is about a hundred yards from the bleachers and the next one, which is a more intense examination of the vehicle, is at the entrance to the parking area. I'll get out when we get to the second security checkpoint and join you in the VIP parking area right after the ceremony."

"Yes, sir. All the drivers received a thorough briefing yesterday morning. Matt gave me a complete update." Vladimir continued smiling as he closed the door got into the driver's seat. This was going very well.

The rest of the drive was made in silence. The DNI spent the time looking out the window with a brooding look on his face. Vladimir was only a little bit nervous as they approached the first checkpoint. The first check was made with both the driver and the DNI in the car. It was a brief conversation with the DNI to make sure he wasn't under any duress and a visual check inside and outside the car. The Secret Service security agent asked the driver to pop the hood and then checked thoroughly in the engine compartment looking for anything out of the ordinary. Another agent had a mirror on a long pole she used to examine the undercarriage of the car. Yet another agent thoroughly checked the trunk. Less than five minutes later they were waved through.

At the second checkpoint, adjacent to the bleachers, the agents asked both the driver and the DNI to exit the car. The DNI walked over to the bleachers and started to look around. The search of the car was exhaustive. They combed over everything both inside and outside the car. Instead of a mirror on a pole, an agent was on his back on a mechanic's slide and actually went under the car for a close-up look. If anything was amiss he would have seen it. But thanks to Vladimir's careful work, it all looked normal and after fifteen minutes he was finally passed through to the parking area. Relief poured over Vladimir as he drove the car forward.

Vladimir realized he would have to spend some time mingling with the other drivers before he could slip away. He figured he only needed to get about seventy-five yards away to be safe. Then he'd just wait. Since the oath of office was to be broadcast on speakers all around the area, he could easily hear where he'd be waiting. He'd set it off right when the new President said the last word. He chuckled as he thought of the confusion in the aftermath. Who would be the new President? Nearly the whole immediate chain of succession would be wiped out—both the current and the newly elected. It would be months before the country settled down. In that time he would be well into his new identity and life. It would be good. In the old days, the Soviets might just have used the chaos to launch a pre-emptive nuclear strike. The temptation would probably have been overwhelming. But, not today. Today, Russia was weak, corrupt and nearly bankrupt. Today, America, his new home, was the world power.

As planned, his car was the first to arrive. The next was the Chairman of the Joint Chiefs, followed by the Chief Justice. He watched them as they exited their cars and moved to the front of the bleachers. There were already several dignitaries in the bleachers, maybe a hundred or so, but they had parked somewhere else. The Vice President's car arrived next and the four occupants moved to the front row of the bleachers. The President and President-elect arrived at exactly 11:55. They were each in a Presidential Limo which was completely armored, supposedly even protected from below. Fortunately, other cabinet member's cars were just regular cars without protective shielding. Nothing more than tinted glass. The DNI's included.

Vladimir figured that might change after today. He'd been hanging around the parked cars talking with the other five drivers for a while, then, just as the Presidential limo arrived, he said he needed a smoke and started walking away from the others. As he lit a cigarette, a Marlborough, a great American cigarette, no one paid him the least attention. All eyes were on the President as he approached the podium. Vladimir was standing, smoking his cigarette about twenty yards away. He started walking towards the capitol building at the same time President-elect Ted Mason stepped towards the podium.

In the meantime, Grant and Sam arrived at the bleachers at 10:30 and were watching everyone who approached within fifty yards. They especially watched everyone who was on, immediately in front of and immediately behind the bleachers. That included the drivers. He wasn't particularly worried about the drivers. They'd all been through metal detectors and the body scanners, and they all checked out.

Sam, always a stickler for details, knew there were six cars authorized behind the bleachers and that number jibed. However, when she looked at the cluster of drivers, there were only five.

"Grant," she whispered into her microphone, "There's a driver missing!"

Grant immediately looked and saw she was right. He swung around and looked in the area adjacent to the bleachers, trying to pick out anyone in the dark uniform all the drivers wore. He scanned the area for a few seconds and about sixty yards towards the capital building saw what looked like one of the drivers walking swiftly away from the ceremony.

The Chief Justice held out his hand, on which was a bible.

Grant started running towards the rapidly walking driver. At the speed with which the driver was walking, Grant figured he could make up the time in about ten or eleven seconds.

"I, Theodore Roosevelt Mason, do solemnly swear," the Chief Justice started.

"I, Theodore Roosevelt Mason, do solemnly swear," the President-elect repeated.

Grant was closing the distance, but now he was worried about being detected. If this driver was the assassin, he could trigger a remote device any time. That had to be it. It was too late for him to be looking for a rifle or something else. It had to be explosives, but where? They had looked everywhere. It was obviously not a suicide bomb—the guy was walking *away* from the bleachers. Where the hell was it?

". . . that I will faithfully execute," the Chief Justice continued.

". . . that I will faithfully execute," the President-elect said.

Sam was following Grant, struggling to keep up. She knew she wasn't going to be able to catch up with him, but she had to keep going. He might need her.

Grant was getting closer, but he wasn't closing the gap as

quickly as he'd like. Fortunately, the guy wasn't looking backwards. He was probably trying not to look suspicious by looking around. There were a lot of people all over the place. Grant knew that if he sounded an alarm, all hell would break loose and the people currently just sitting, listening to the ceremony would start moving around and he would lose his quarry. It had to be Vladimir. It just had to be.

". . . the Office of President of the United States," said the Chief Justice.

". . . the Office of President of the United States," repeated the President-elect.

He was within twenty feet now and closing fast. Just a few more seconds to go. If he could just catch him before he set off the explosives . . . .

" . . . and will, to the best of my ability," continued the Chief Justice.

" . . . and will, to the best of my ability," followed the President-elect.

As he was running, Grant had another thought. What if the explosives were on a timer? What if he caught this guy only to have the explosives go off and kill everybody? Shit! Why do there have to be so many options?

" . . . preserve, protect and defend . . ."

" . . . preserve, protect and defend . . ."

Vladimir was walking fast and thinking, with one more phrase, the President will complete the oath, and as soon as he says the last word, I will trigger the bomb. It will be perfect. He removed the triggering device from his pocket. It had a flip-top covering the actual plunger and to avoid accidently setting off the explosion, he left it in place. He would flip it up the last second before pushing the plunger with his thumb.

At that moment, Grant leaped out and tackled the uniformed driver from behind. He was bigger than Grant had thought and much more muscled. Although surprised at the blow from behind, Vladimir recovered quickly. They wrestled on the ground for a few seconds, until the man touched and then pulled Grant's new compact .45 out of his shoulder holster and held it under Grant's chin. Without a word they stopped wrestling. The man stood up. As Vladimir pulled back the hammer and started to apply pressure to the trigger, Grant heard two sharp reports in rapid succession. Looking up at the man he knew only as Vladimir, Grant saw that he had a surprised look on his face. He also saw a red stain begin to spread on the front of the guy's white shirt. The man, without changing expression, fell forward, landing partially on Grant.

Grant looked around and saw two people standing with guns drawn—Sam and just behind her to the right, Garcia. Not a double tap, then. Two individual shots. Somewhere off in the distance Grant heard,

"... the constitution of the United States."

"... the constitution of the United States."

And he knew the President was safe.

Chapter 55

I Plus 1

When they found the trigger clasped in the assassin's left hand it was clear that there were explosives somewhere close by, so they searched everything around the bleachers. The Secret Service eventually discovered the explosives in the gasoline tank of the DNI's car, but only after entirely dismantling all six automobiles parked behind the bleachers. It was the weight of the gas tank after it was drained that finally led them to find the explosives. It was an ingenious system which, had it not been for Grant and Sam, would have worked.

The shots that Garcia and Sam had fired were accurate and powerful. Garcia's jacketed hollow-point .40 caliber slug passed directly through Vladimir's skull and broke into pieces, scrambling his brain. Death was instantaneous and Vladimir was frozen the instant it hit. He never got a chance to flip open the latch covering the triggering button on top of the transmitter he was holding. An instant later and he would have successfully wiped out the entire present and future leadership of the most powerful nation in the world.

Grant finished up his time in Washington, saying goodbye to everyone. The last person he talked to was Sam. They were standing just outside his office in the Pentagon.

"Well, Grant, you got your man," Sam said smiling.

"*We* got our man," Grant replied, emphasizing the 'we'.

"Too bad you didn't get to question him, but I really didn't have a choice. I had to shoot. Apparently Garcia felt the same way."

Grant put his hand on Sam's shoulder and said, "I know you didn't. Don't worry about it; you did everything right. I don't know if he would have talked anyway. He was a pro, so we probably wouldn't have learned anything from him. We just have to hope he was acting alone and wasn't part of a larger network. Otherwise, they might try again. I had a chance to explain this to the new President, so at least he and his Secret Service detail are aware of the possibility."

Sam asked, "What's next for you, Grant?"

"Well, I've finished my debriefing and have been released from active duty, so I guess I'll go home," Grant said, his hand still on her shoulder.

"Grant, I want to tell you how great this has been. I've never had a scarier or more wonderful time in my life," she smiled at him.

Looking deeply into her eyes he said, "I'm going to miss you."

"I'm going to miss you terribly," she replied. "But, I still have some time on my enlistment, so I have to stick around here. Don't know what they'll have me do, but I'm sure they'll think of something. They told me I'll be staying with DIA."

"I'll call you, soon." He paused and then added, "You can call me, too, you know."

Looking up at him she smiled wistfully. "I know. And I will. Probably more often than you'd like. But it will really take some getting used to."

"What will?" Grant asked.

"Not being close to you," Sam replied.

Grant stepped forward and took her into his arms. She laid her head on his chest. After a moment he lifted her face to his and kissed her for a long, long time.

***

At the same time Grant was saying goodbye to Sam, Garcia was walking upstairs to a meeting with the Director of the CIA. He was shown into the inner office by the Director's assistant.

"Hi, Marty. Thanks for coming in. Have a seat," the Director said, motioning to the chair across his desk.

"No problem, sir. What's up?" Garcia replied as he sat down and crossed his legs.

The Director leaned forward and said quietly, "Just wanted to talk with you briefly to wrap up the mission you just completed. Have you told anyone about my instructions to you?"

"No, sir. At your request I've not spoken to anyone about it . . . and I won't. I don't know why this guy had to die, but if you tell me he had to, then that's good enough."

"Good. Thanks for keeping this confidential. In the interest of national security, I can't tell you the reasoning behind the kill instructions nor why this must remain secret forever. You'll just have to trust me on this one. You did a great job, by the way, and as of now you are one grade higher and will take on some new responsibilities. Nora will brief you on them within the week."

"Nora still doesn't know about your instructions to me?" Garcia asked.

"No. You and I are the only ones who know and, as I said, it has to stay that way . . . forever."

"You got it, sir." Garcia replied.

"Okay, Marty, thanks. I'll talk to you more after you assume your new role."

"Thanks for the promotion," Garcia said, rising to his feet.

"You earned it. See you."

After Garcia left his office, the Director leaned back in his comfortable leather chair and wondered if he could really trust him to keep quiet. People, including many in his own agency, would start asking too many questions if they discovered that he had given Garcia instructions to kill the assassin before he could be questioned. He could arrange for Garcia to be taken out, but he might want to use him again. Garcia was clever and could be very helpful in his new role as special assistant to the DDI. With that thought, the highest ranking Russian mole in US history turned back to the paperwork on his desk.

Garcia, meanwhile, sat at his own desk and mentally reviewed all the conversations he'd had with the Director about this. He'd keep it confidential, but he couldn't help wondering why. It just seemed, from a CIA perspective, that it would have been more useful to take Vladimir alive and find out why he was intent on killing the President. There may be other people involved. We still don't know if Russia was backing him, he thought. Oh, well, the Director must have his reasons. He was really pleased with the promotion, though. Special assistant to the DDI, even though it was Nora, was a big deal. He sighed and leaned forward over his desk. The paperwork had really piled up while he was on this mission and he might as well start wading through it.

Chapter 56

I Plus 20
West Texas

Damn, it was cold. Late January in western Texas was even colder than November. They said December was the coldest month, but having spent this past December in Eastern Europe and then in Washington, Grant couldn't verify that this winter. The stove, as usual, had died out by 3:00 a.m. and Grant could see his breath in the air.

At six, Grant had dragged his naked ass out of bed, grabbed a coffee cup, filled it up with yesterday's coffee that he heated for one minute in the mike, and then walked outside. Now he was standing, covered in chill bumps but still naked, sipping his hot, but stale coffee and going over the same thoughts he'd had a hundred times before. Why was he such a loner? Damn, he sure missed Sam. They talked frequently on the phone, but, well, it just wasn't the same as talking in person. It sure would be good to see her again, though he wasn't sure when that might happen. Maybe he'd have to go back to Washington.

Whup, whup, whup, whup—a helicopter lifted up over the bluff, backlit by the sun, and landed in his back yard. With the sun behind it, he couldn't immediately identify it and, although he didn't know who they were or why they were here, he was worried it wouldn't be good news.

"Aw, Damn! Again?" he said and turned around, heading into the cabin to put some clothes on. By the time he had reappeared, dressed, on the back porch, the rotors had stopped moving and two people were exiting the chopper. Like the chopper, they were backlit so Grant couldn't tell exactly who they were.

"Good morning Mr. President," Grant said, finally recognizing the chopper and the man approaching his porch. At that point, Sam stepped up next to the President. He noticed that she now wore an officer's uniform and had shiny new gold bars on her shoulders.

"Good morning, Colonel," the President said warmly.

"Uh, sir, may I ask why you're here? Oh, sorry, please come up

222

on the porch and have a seat. Would you like some day-old coffee? I could brew a new pot—won't take but a few minutes." For some reason that he couldn't pinpoint, Grant was a little nervous. He and Sam exchanged a quick glance but he couldn't read her expression.

The President smiled and said, "Don't worry about it. I've had plenty already." He held up a rolled up paper he'd been holding in his hand and said, "Grant, I'm here to officially thank you for the outstanding work you did to prevent the assassin from exploding the device. It would have killed all the leadership of the United States, me included. Your country owes you a debt and so do I. As of this minute you are promoted to Brigadier General. Also, although the details of what happened and your involvement will remain classified forever, I do want to present you with a Presidential Certificate of Merit."

The President handed the paper to Grant who unrolled it. It read:
Presented to
Brigadier General Grant Thurmond, USAF, For
OUTSTANDING MERITORIOUS SERVICE IN THE
PERFORMANCE OF INTELLIGENCE DUTIES IN SUPPORT OF
OPERATION I MINUS 72. YOUR GREAT ZEAL, DEVOTION,
INITIATIVE, EXUBERANCE AND PROFESSIONALISM WERE
INSTRUMENTAL AND CONTRIBUTED SIGNIFICANTLY TO
THE ACHIEVEMENT OF ALL OPERATIONAL OBJECTIVES.
YOUR OUTSTANDING ACHIEVEMENT REFLECTS GREAT
CREDIT UPON YOURSELF, THE DEFENSE INTELLIGENCE
ACENCY AND YOUR COUNTRY.
Signed by Theodore Roosevelt Mason
President of the United States

He couldn't help chuckling. No one could write superlatives like the government, particularly when it came to DOD awards.

"Mr. President, I'm honored. I'm just thankful it turned out as well as it did. I'm sorry it took until the last second to be resolved." Grant turned his head to look at Sam. "And congratulations on your well-deserved promotion, Sam."

"Thank you Col . . . , sorry, I mean General." She smiled and continued, "The President was kind enough to promote me, too. And congratulations on your promotion. You're going—"

The President interrupted, "Grant, there's something else I need to talk with you about. I'm creating a new position of special

223

intelligence assistant to the President. I want you in that job. It will involve extremely sensitive special assignments that you and I know are needed, but, because of their sensitivity, we don't want anyone else to know about. As a result of recent events, we've taken a close look at the internals of all our intelligence agencies and have identified several moles, both past and present. One of them was discovered in the department I worked in at DIA. We now think that's how your network was compromised. I just don't trust these old line agencies and, as President, I *need* someone I can trust."

"Will this position report directly to the DNI or be part of DIA?" Grant asked.

The President shook his head. "Neither. It's too sensitive. This position will report directly to me and be accountable to no one but me. I'm not exactly sure what the assignments will be, but they'll be somewhat like the one you just completed. Be honest, you didn't really need to be part of DIA for you to be successful, did you?"

Thurmond smiled. "No, Mr. President, I didn't. If anything, they got in the way," he paused. "But I'm retired now and I'm not sure I want to go back to Washington full time."

The President reached out to shake Grant's hand. "Grant, you don't have to make the decision right now. Take your time. The position was written for you and, until you let me know one way or another, I won't be looking for anyone else to fill it, even if that takes a couple of months. So take the time you need. Be sure of your answer. Remember Grant, your country needs you now more than ever. Well, I've got to get back to Washington." He turned to head back to the chopper. "Coming Lieutenant?" he said over his shoulder.

Sam glanced first at Grant, and then looked at the President. "Uh, Mr. President, I think I'll find my own way back. With the . . . General's permission, I'd like to hang around here for a while."

The President smiled and nodded. Without a word he turned and walked back to the helicopter. *Whup, whup, whup, whup* . . . and then it was silent.

Standing on the porch, they watched the helicopter until it disappeared. Then, finding each other's hands, they wordlessly turned and walked inside.

Don Tompkins grew up in central Illinois, graduating from Bloomington High School. He spent over ten years in the U.S. Navy, serving most of that time in various intelligence assignments at both the Headquarters of the Atlantic Forces and the Headquarters of the Pacific Forces. While in the Navy, Don earned, among others, the Vietnam Service Medal and the Joint Service Commendation Medal. He was also awarded a Certificate of Merit for Intelligence duties while at the Pacific Command. After leaving the Navy, Don had a successful career in the corporate world as a senior executive.

I minus 72 is Don's first novel. He is hard at work writing the sequel, which will feature the same team as his first, but in a more contemporary setting.

Don graduated from Chaminade University of Honolulu. He and his wife, Kelly, reside with their black pug, Cricket, in a suburb of Grand Rapids, Michigan.

www.ingramcontent.com/pod-product-compliance
Lightning Source LLC
Chambersburg PA
CBHW060429180626
46817CB00007B/2739